Praise for

Island Life

"...brooding, misty Scottish atmosphere... Many fears come into play—agoraphobia, claustrophobia, acrophobia...solid prose commands attention...through to the climax..." **Cemetery DanceMagazine.**

"...draws the reader in, weaving a tightly spun web of folklore, horror, and suspense from which there is no escape..." **Modoc Record**

"Hard to put down, difficult to forget, Meikle weaves a nightmarish story that leaves me wanting more." **Bookbrowser**

I picked it up and didn't put it down. Read it cover to cover and enjoyed one helluva monster story. **Reallyscary.com**

"It was gripping right from the beginning and held on until the end." –**Breakout Books**

" my first introduction to the work of William Meilkle and the one that fixed him firmly as one of my favourite authors." **The Reading Beast**

Books by William Meikle

Island Life

The Hole

The Invasion

The Valley

Watchers

Berserker

Eldren: The Book of Dark

The Midnight Eye Files: The Amulet

The Midnight Eye Files: The Sirens

The Midnight Eye Files: The Skin Game

Clockwork Dolls

Professor Challenger: The Island of Terror

Dark Melodies

Night of the Wendigo

Crustaceans

The Creeping Kelp

Carnacki: Heaven and Hell

The Concordances of the Red Serpent

Sherlock Holmes: Revenant

Sherlock Holmes: The Quality of Mercy and other
Stories

ISLAND LIFE

William Meikle

Gryphonwood

Island Life by William Meikle

Copyright 2013 by William Meikle

ISBN 13: 978-1-940095-03-5
ISBN 10: 1940095034

Published June, 2013 by Gryphonwood Press
PO Box 28910
Santa Fe, NM 87592
www.gryphonwoodpress.com

Dedication

For Tim Stevenson and the screeching demon in the lighthouse without which this book would never have existed.

Prologue

The sun had just come up as he crawled out of the tent, wincing at the chill in the air outside. He went back in to pick up a sweater

'Welcome to Scotland -- the Riviera of the West,' he muttered.

And to think I could have been in the South of France, sipping Pina Coladas and watching the nubiles bouncing on the beach.

But then he wouldn't have met Janice.

He looked back at the figure wrapped up in his sleeping bag and a small smile crossed his face as he remembered the frolics of the night before. He thought about crawling back in and wakening her -- getting it all going again -- but the pressure of last night's beer weighed heavily on his bladder.

He knew that if he didn't do something soon he would have what his mother used to call *a little accident.* It wouldn't do to blow his cool by stepping out with a damp crotch.

There was no movement from the other tents and, looking at his watch, he saw that it was only six-thirty… plenty of time to snuggle back inside for a couple of hours.

Whistling softly he made his way to the cliff edge, passing the site of the dig. Someone had placed a tarpaulin over the entrance and he felt a thrill just looking at it. They would finally go inside today, and all their work would be shown to be worthwhile. He hoped old misery guts would chose him to be in the first team, but didn't think he had a chance -- one of the girls would get it.

He wondered if one of them was sharing the old man's tent, and giggled to himself at the thought of the old man *on the job*. He probably lectured them on post-glacial settlements during his passion.

He thought about sneaking a look behind the tarpaulin, but he didn't have time to take a closer look at their find; the pressure in his bladder had become heavy and painful.

This had almost become a ritual. Every morning he rose early and urinated over the cliff edge, watching as it fell in a myriad of droplets, following it down till it was out of sight.

He felt the sun on his back, just starting to warm up as he strode over the damp grass. Ahead of him, in the distance, a bank of mist crept slowly southwards and down below him the sea was lightly ruffled by a soft wind.

He unzipped himself and, still whistling, looked down to find his direction.

He saw the hand first.

Grey and scaly, it came at his feet from beyond the cliff edge. He tried to jump back but it was too fast, catching him round the left ankle and bringing a shooting pain as thin talons entered his flesh. He didn't have time to dwell on it as his feet were pulled out from under him.

He tried to grab a hold as he was dragged toward the cliff edge but he came away with only a few stalks of grass. Looking down towards his feet he saw more of whatever it was that had him; a long arm, thick muscled, looking like a piece of iron.

The pull on his leg got stronger and his feet, then

his ankles, then his thighs were pulled over the edge. Then gravity took over.

1

Duncan

This is how it began.

Duncan McKenzie was trying to fight off the remnants of a nightmare as he stood on the viewing platform around the top of the lighthouse. He didn't remember a great deal of it -- only that it involved the bedroom in his flat back in Glasgow and a monster creeping up the stairs towards him while condensation dripped off the walls and his radio blared in a loud bass thump.

The chill of a sea breeze and the taste of his first cigarette of the day eventually drove it from his thoughts.

From his vantage point high on the south end of the island he saw the sun beginning to haul itself up over the horizon, washing the lower clouds in fluffy pink and banishing the darkness for another day.

Summer in the Outer Hebridean Islands of Scotland could be notoriously fickle, with rain and cloud scudding across the face of the sea with little warning, as often as not coming out of a bright blue sky. This morning he was due out in his dinghy to take water samples so he was pleased to note that most of the sky to the east had cleared, the pink clouds breaking ahead of the advancing sun.

He circumnavigated the top of the lighthouse, smoking his cigarette and trying to remember exactly what it was he had to do that day. As he walked round to the other side of the platform he saw that the situation was not as promising as he first thought.

Far to the north, the island beyond was just visible over the top of the second lighthouse, and the other islands in the chain were covered in a bank of dense fog, a bank which crept ever closer. He would just have to take his chances with the weather, as usual.

He stubbed out his cigarette against the railing and flicked the butt away, watching it falling out over the edge. As his gaze followed it down he caught sight of a movement in the grass at the foot of the lighthouse. He whistled loudly and was answered by the happy barking at Sam.

Sam was the only sheep-dog on the island, and he was getting too old for the job. Duncan guessed that at one time the dog had shown a clean pair of heels to anything else in his territory, but nowadays the best he could manage was to keep up with the farmer on his rounds, wheezing heavily as a result of a chronic chest complaint.

Duncan smiled as he went down the stairs. A slobbery wet tongue on his face was just what he needed to get the day started.

By the time he reached the door. Sam was scraping frantically to get in. When he'd first arrived Duncan had wondered where the marks on the paint had come from, but it hadn't taken Sam long to get acquainted -- Duncan was a soft touch.

Once the door was open the dog leapt at him, almost knocking him over, its tail wagging strongly enough to set up a small breeze.

Duncan had made great friends with the dog the summer before -- much to the disgust of its owner. John Jeffries, the local farmer.

John was not a believer in pets -- to him Sam was a working animal who had to earn his keep, Duncan had heard him going on about it in the bar -- how the dog was getting too old for the job and that he would take his shotgun to it one day soon.

How anyone could be so callous about such a friendly animal was beyond his comprehension. But then again, John Jeffries was well known on the island for his truculent attitude. If it wasn't about farming, John wanted nothing to do with it.

Sam started his usual attack on Duncan's groin region.

What was it with dogs and groins? Some hormonal thing probably.

Then again it had been a long time since Duncan's hormones had done anything.

It didn't seem to worry the dog though. The nuzzling got more frenzied and he half expected the dog to start mounting his leg.

Laughing he pushed the animal away and went back to the kitchen to fetch a biscuit.

'Just a second boy,' he shouted back over his shoulder, but when he turned towards the door, the dog had gone.

Looking over the field he saw it walking sedately towards a figure in the distance. Duncan could just make out that it was John Jeffries. He raised his hand to wave but the farmer turned his back and walked on, heading towards the cliffs on the western side of the island.

It was just possible to make out that he carried a shotgun. This was not unusual. The farmer often carried the gun around, although there were no large -- or even small -- predators on the island. Not even rabbits.

Occasionally Duncan would come across a dead crow, and once he found a kestrel, blown into three distinct parts by the farmer's gun. He'd confronted Jeffries about it in the pub, but had got exactly the answer he had expected.

'Vermin. That's all they are -- only fit for shooting.'

Since then there had been little love lost between the men and they could barely bring themselves to say hello when they met. Not that it bothered Duncan -- he pitied a man who couldn't see any wonder in the natural world.

He stood at the door and watched the farmer and the dog until they disappeared over the horizon. He smoked a second cigarette down to the filter before looking around.

The weather was closer in on the north side of the island, a fine mist beginning to descend over the craggy cliffs.

If he was to have a comfortable time doing his sampling he would have to leave pretty soon -- he knew how quickly a fair day could turn foul in this part of the world. He had been caught out before and he didn't intend subjecting himself to a drenching.

Turning, he headed indoors to finish his morning ablutions.

One look at his tongue confirmed what his stomach and head had already told him. Too much beer, too many cigarettes and not enough sleep.

Just the right preparation to face the rigours of a day at sea in the Scottish summer.

Turning away from the mirror he bent to pick up his rucksack. He'd packed it up last night. Now all that was needed was to pick up something for a snack to keep him going during the day. He smiled to himself. He now had an excuse to visit the shop.

As he walked along the gravel path away from the lighthouse he could already feel a light mist in the air, leaving tiny droplets clinging to his beard.

He always enjoyed this walk -- especially the stunning cliff views to the north and east as he headed up the small slope towards the shop. The sea birds squawked noisily overhead and he caught the sudden flash of black and orange as a puffin darted along the cliff-top ahead of him. As always, he kept well away from the cliff edge.

Heights made him dizzy.

If you stood him on a cliff edge and made him look down, his knees would threaten to give way and he would see the bottom of the cliff wavering from side to side, slipping in and out of focus.

Paradoxically he was perfectly all right if faced with a man-made height. He could stand atop the lighthouse with none of the life threatening feelings he associated with cliffs, as long as he knew the railings were there to hold him in.

One morning he forced himself to venture closer to the cliff edge and attempt to look over, but his knees betrayed him and he had been compelled to sit down and edge backwards until his eyes brought things back into focus.

This morning he kept to the path, contenting himself with the views out to sea. Out over the water the wind was picking up, whipping the surface into white horses and sending them scudding off into the distance. Closer to shore, in the area where his sampling would be taking place, the water looked a lot calmer and he was hopeful of a quiet day ahead -- he didn't feel like spending all his time wrestling with the currents and getting soaked by flying spray. He prayed to Mother Nature for good weather as he tramped along the path towards the shop.

The shop, post office and pub -- it fulfilled all these functions -- stood on the only crossroads on the island. The main path ran from the south lighthouse to the other lighthouse at the north end of the island. The segment that he walked was only five feet wide and had recently had gravel put down. From the shop the path ran both northwards to the far end of the island and eastwards down to the harbour.

On both these stretches the path widened, making it large enough to carry the island's only vehicle... a land-rover that was used by the lighthouse men to carry provisions and by the shop to bring the stock ashore from the supply boat.

The shop itself was a squat, ugly, sandstone building on two floors. The upstairs provided the living quarters for the McTaggart family with the downstairs split into two main rooms -- the shop and the post office to the front and the pub to the back.

The McTaggarts had run the pub for more than twenty summers but it was their daughter Meg who Duncan most wanted to see.

As he turned into the shops' small yard, he saw her, standing with her back to him washing the small square windows.

They were just too high for her and Duncan watched in admiration as she stood on tiptoe to reach the farthest corner, causing her T-shirt -- skimpy at the best of times -- to ride six inches up her back, exposing an area of well tanned skin.

'Hello Meg. And how are you this fine morning?'
She let out a small squeal before stumbling

backwards and knocking over the metal pail of soapy water at her feet. Her eyes flashed angrily as she turned, then softened when she realized that it was Duncan.

Her hair hung black and wavy over her face and Duncan longed to reach out for her, to move the hair aside and press a kiss on her lips.

But he could never bring himself to take that step, to force the initiative. He watched her mouth move as she spoke and felt the heat spread in his stomach, the old adolescent lurching that you never really lost.

'Oh. Now look what you've made me do, you big fool. Imagine creeping up on people like that,' she said, her mouth angry but her eyes smiling. 'You could have given me a heart attack.'

She spoke in the lilting, sing-song accent of the Highlands, making Duncan think, once again, that he must sound like a guttural lowlands drone compared to her.

'If you had a heart attack, would I get to loosen your clothing?' Duncan said. He saw a wicked gleam in her dark green eyes as she considered her reply.

'Only if you promise to take full advantage of the situation afterwards,' she finally replied, staring up at him from under her fringe, her eyelashes fluttering. He was never sure if she did that deliberately or not, but whatever the cause it brought a new burst of heat in his chest and he felt it spreading to his face.

The flirting had been going on for several days now, each time becoming a little more risqué, each time causing Duncan's heart to beat a little faster.

He found that he spent more and more time thinking of her -- how she would feel in her arms -- and less and less time concentrating on his work. More than once he had wondered if she was the reason he had come back this year -- the search for love taking over from the search for truth. He didn't like to continue that train of thought -- it brought into question his devotion to his work, and that was the only thing that kept him going.

This time, as before, he pulled back from continuing with the flirtation -- more in embarrassment then trepidation -- he wasn't used to being teased.

'Is the shop open yet? I need to get some chocolate to keep me going today,' he said, trying to get the conversation back to more mundane matters before he felt tempted to pounce on her.

Meg responded quickly. She wasn't yet ready to give up the chase. There was a gleam in her eyes, a teasing, dancing joy. Duncan realized that she was enjoying herself, and again he felt the heat rise inside him as she spoke.

'Chocolate? Is that what you need to keep you going?' Her tongue flicked out to lick the corners of her mouth. Duncan found that he couldn't take his eyes off it.

'I'm sure that I could keep you going better if you took me instead,' she said, and her tongue did a quick tour of her mouth. Duncan had to fight off an urge to nibble it.

He responded nervously, pulling at his beard. Although he didn't know it, he always did that whenever she got too close.

'Aye. I'm sure you could keep me going. But we'd probably ship so much water that we'd sink the dinghy. Can you imagine them calling out air-sea rescue, only to find us going at it like rabbits?'

He noticed, too late, that he had embarrassed her. He knew that he had brought sex into the play too early. He was definitely out of practice at this sort of verbal fencing.

He was about to speak, to try to repair the damage he had caused, when they were interrupted by a shotgun blast in the distance.

Meg was first to respond.

'I see John's playing with his weapon again.'

Duncan smiled to show that he appreciated the double entendre, then continued.

'Aye, but I wonder what he's shooting at.' He suddenly thought of Sam, and how old the dog had looked that morning. A cold shiver ran down his spine, and he almost missed Meg's next sentence. He had to force himself to concentrate on what she was saying, but his brain was furnishing him with pictures of the sheep-dog lying, bleeding on the grass.

'He was in a foul mood this morning when he came in for some cigarettes. Something has been at his sheep. He lost two last night and he muttered about a bloody eagle or something' Meg said, her eyes crinkling as she tried to remember what the farmer had said. 'He was ranting a bit -- you know what he can get like sometimes. He even tried to blame the students.'

Duncan smiled. 'Aye. I know what he can get like. If it wasn't born here then it doesn't belong here. Isn't that his motto? But what does he think the students have to do with him losing some sheep?'

Again he thought of Sam. Had the dog got so old that it turned against the sheep -- forgotten its training and reverted to its wild ancestry?

'Hey. Big boy?' Meg almost shouted. 'Is anybody in there?' she said, tugging at his left ear.

Duncan grinned sheepishly.

'Sorry. I was miles away. You were saying about

Jeffries?'

Meg sighed, an exaggerated shrug.

'Oh, he thinks that the students might have smuggled a dog onto the island,' she said, laughing. 'Can you imagine another dog on this place without any of us knowing about it? It was after I pointed that out to him that he started going on about the eagle.'

'I suppose that it's possible,' she continued, 'But I've lived here all my life and I've yet to see an eagle. I think he's going senile. The whisky has finally got to his brain.

'Anyway', she went on, drying her hands on her skirt, 'I think it's time for a cigarette. Have you got any?'

They moved round to the other side of the building to take a seat in the dim morning sunlight and watch the clouds scampering across the sky.

Duncan knew that it was time to get going if he was to avoid the afternoon rain, but he felt closer to Meg than he ever had previously and was not about to let the chance pass him by. They sat in silence while they smoked their cigarettes -- a silence that was broken by them both trying to speak at once.

'What did...'Duncan said.

'What were you...' said Meg, who was allowed to continue by a wave of Duncan's hand.

'What were you doing with that pretty blonde girl last night? You needn't try to deny it -- I saw you -- canoodling in the corner.'

'I was never canoodling,' Duncan said, but a blush spread over his cheeks. 'We were just having a chat about her work -- how things were going -- stuff like that.'

Meg took full advantage of the situation.

'And her work involves sticking her tongue in

your ear does it? What was she looking for? Ancient wax deposits? Iron-age hearing aids?'

Duncan went pink from his neck to his hairline and stuttered over his words as he replied.

'Honest Meg. I've never met a woman as brazen as her. One minute we were talking away about their work on the burial mound -- the next she's sitting in my lap and threatening to melt my eardrums.'

He looked sideways at her, a slow smile spreading across his features.

'You're jealous -- aren't you? A wee slip of a lassie takes a shine to me, and you get jealous. I'll tell you what -- I'll make it up to you. Come on over to the lighthouse tonight and I'll cook for you.'

Somewhere deep down he realized how big a step he was taking, but his mouth was running on, not giving him a chance to think.

'Afterwards, if you get lucky, I'll show you my zooplankton collection.'

He'd said it without thinking and now he could only wait and worry about her reply. He saw that she was thinking about it and, as he turned towards her, she slid along the bench and wrapped her arms around him.

'You took your time asking me, didn't you?' she said, laughing into his hair. 'I've been waiting a week for that. Why don't you come down to the pub first, then you can walk me back to your place.'

He hugged her, marvelling at the silky smoothness of her hair against his cheek. He was wondering whether she wanted to be kissed when they were interrupted by someone clearing his throat behind them.

Duncan turned his head, disentangling himself

from Meg's body and saw Jim, her father, smiling down at them. He almost knocked over the bench in his rush to stand up, but before he could begin to say anything, Meg started speaking.

'Aye, I know, I should be down in the cellar getting the stock sorted out -- I just stopped for a quick chat with Duncan -- there's no law against it is there?'

Before her father could reply she had turned back to Duncan. 'You had better not forget our date tonight. I'll see you in the bar around seven, OK?'

Without waiting for an answer she left, flouncing up the path towards the shop, Duncan watched her buttocks move inside her denims, then remembered her father was standing behind him. He cleared his throat noisily to cover his embarrassment.

He father laughed and then called after Meg.

'If you want to make that date, you'd better watch out that the smugglers down in the cellar don't get you.'

She glared back at her father and for a second Duncan thought he saw something in her eyes, something that looked like fear. She shook her head, and with a smile and a wave to Duncan, was gone.

'And to think I wanted to call her Galadriel Moonchild when she was born,' the man beside him said, still laughing. 'I'm glad Anne talked me out of it -- I can't imagine her as anything other than Meg.'

Jim McTaggart was a tall skinny man with rapidly receding shoulder length, wispy blond hair, and Duncan had never seen him dressed in anything other than denims. Jim was an aging hippy, fifty-plus and still clinging to his ideals of the Sixties.

He had arrived on the island at the hind end of the Seventies -- him and twelve others, ready to set up a commune and work the land, filled with peace and love and the urge to get back to nature. Duncan had heard the stories -- the initial resentment of the locals, the scandal over the sleeping arrangements, even the island's one and only drug bust when an eighth of an ounce of marijuana was confiscated and later, as rumour had it, shared around the police station back on the mainland.

The first winter had severely depleted the peace and love, leaving only Jim and his wife Anne behind. How they had survived that winter was a mystery to Duncan. They had lived in a tent through the wind and the sleet and the snow, with little food and only a fire built from driftwood for heat. But survive they had.

Jim's big break came when he was offered the chance to run the shop and pub. He jumped at the opportunity -- not only were they close to starving but Anne was pregnant with Meg.

During the summers he made enough money to keep them going for the year, supplementing their living with a small income from leading nature tours around the island. When the National Trust took over in the late 1980's, Jim had stayed.

To the best of Duncan's knowledge neither Jim nor Anne had left the island for any length of time since first stepping off the boat more than twenty years earlier.

Jim didn't seem to be flustered at finding his daughter in the arms of a man who was nearly old enough to be her father, but Duncan knew that he was rarely flustered by anything; his laid back approach to life provided a barrier sufficiently strong to hold against any adversity.

'What did you mean about the smugglers?' Duncan asked, trying to strike up a natural conversation but being betrayed by the tremor in his voice.

At first he thought the man wasn't going to respond -- he had a far away look in his eye, remembering a far off memory. But finally he spoke.

'Oh, that's just an old nightmare of Meg's. Did you know that we have a smugglers cave under the pub?'

Duncan shook his head, but Jim wasn't really expecting a reply, he was already continuing. 'Meg got into it from the harbour end one day -- she can't have been more than nine years old at the time. Seemingly she was looking for pirate's treasure.' He smiled at the recollection.

'The entrance is just round in the big bay north of the harbour -- you know the one? There's a concealed cave behind a huge clump of rhododendron. We never found out how she discovered it.'

Jim stopped and looked off into the distance, remembering the day, picturing the scenes before he spoke again.

'Thoughts too morbid for a summer's morning; they deserve to be related in the depths of the night, when the blood has slowed and the wind is howling and you're sitting in front of a roaring fire. For now, on this fine morning, all you get is the edited version. To cut a long story short, she turned up in the cellar, screaming and weeping, both knees badly cut and bruised, telling a story of how the smugglers had chased her through the cave and up to the cellar. Of course I went and had a look round, but there was nothing there. The poor kid had just got herself psyched up and nearly frightened herself to death. I shouldn't have ragged her about it... it gave her nightmares for months and we've had the hatch to the cave closed up ever since.

Duncan was intrigued. He'd spent many nights sitting in the bar, sipping whisky and listening to many stories about the island, but this was one he had never heard before.

'Do you think that any smugglers would use the cave now?' he asked, wondering whether he might have found a reason for John Jeffries disappearing sheep.

Jim looked amused, his eyes crinkling at the corners and betraying his real age. The only time he looked his age was when he smiled -- the rest of the time he could pass for a thirty-year old.

'No. I went down a couple of years ago and had a look round. The way in is completely overgrown. It would take a lot of effort to get through the bushes. Any of today's modern smugglers would just use a small powerboat; they don't need to store their goods away. It's not like in the old days when the excise men were a lot stricter.'

Jim nodded his head, affirming the facts to himself, before turning back to Duncan.

'I can't stand around here all day chatting. Things to do you know? Do you need anything from the shop before I shut up?'

Duncan had almost forgotten about his snack. Following Jim into the shop he bought a pint of milk -- produce of John Jeffries' one and only milk cow -- and a couple of bars of chocolate.

'I don't suppose you fancy a quick pint to get you going?' Jim asked.

Duncan laughed and refused, reluctantly.

'No thanks Jim. Do you remember the last time we started this early?'

The two men had got together on Duncan's birthday. By lunch-time they had been sozzled, and by six in the evening neither of them was capable of walking. Jim had been put to bed by his wife and was sent to Coventry for two whole days.

Duncan had tried to make it back to the lighthouse but had woken in the morning having slept under a rhododendron bush. He'd had a two-day hangover and couldn't move more than ten yards from a toilet in all that time.

It had been a great birthday.

Both men smiled at the memory. Duncan realised that he was considering it -- just forgetting everything else and letting drink wash him down into oblivion.

He heard the sounds of beer barrels being moved, the noise filtering up from the cellar, and that made him remember his promise to meet Meg later.

'Some other time, eh Jim? But let's make it sooner rather than later.'

As he left the shop, Jim followed him out, closing the door behind him.

'So, what's on your agenda for today? Anything exciting?' Duncan asked.

Jim laughed. 'Aye, riveting, I've got to clean out the toilets and pump out the septic tank. Luckily there are no visitors today, but tomorrow we've got twelve bird watchers from Denmark and probably a whole boatload of tourists, so I've got to get things ready. What about you? Are you taking your wee boat out again?'

'Yes. More samples of the Dead Sea I'm afraid. Do you want to come along?'

Jim had accompanied him on several occasions, always amazing Duncan with his in-depth knowledge of the local wildlife and where it was to be found. He was always glad of the man's company, but he saw Jim shaking his head.

'I'm afraid not. I've got too much to do really -- I don't know why I even considered having a drink -- Anne will kill me if the chores aren't done. I might take a walk up and see how the students are doing later on this afternoon, once I've got the work out of the way.'

The students -- one of who had caused such embarrassment for Duncan -- had arrived earlier in the summer to start work on digging out a recently discovered burial chamber.

To Duncan's eye they had not done much work so far, seemingly alternating their time between the bar and their tents.

'How are they getting on? They don't seem to do much.'

Jim smiled again. Duncan realised that the man smiled more than anyone else he had ever met.

'They're doing fine. I think they made some sort of discovery yesterday, but they were keeping very quiet about it last night. Your little blond didn't whisper anything to you did she?'

Before Duncan had a chance to protest, Jim had continued.

'No, I suppose she had other things on her mind. Anyway, I'll probably take a walk over there and sniff around a bit. In the meantime, I'd better be getting on. See you later -- if you don't take fright from Meg.'

Duncan waved to the other man as he headed off, wondering -- not for the first time -- what the tourists made of Jim when they arrived for their nature trips. There they would be, all done up in their oilskin jackets and sensible shoes and Jim would turn up in his denim cut-offs, thirty year old Deep Purple tee shirt and mirror shades. They probably thought that he was the strangest piece of wildlife on the island.

As he watched Jim walk away, he saw that the weather had closed in even further over the north end of the island. It was definitely time to get going.

He recovered his backpack from beside the door and, with one last wave to Jim, headed off down the track.

Before turning off on the path to the harbour, he turned back for a look up the length to check the weather. The far north end was now completely shrouded in mist and he saw, about two miles away, the tents in which the students were living, arranged symmetrically beside the ruins of the old Mansion house. As far as he could tell they had yet to get out of their sleeping bags -- which was hardly surprising given the amount of alcohol they had got through in the bar last night. As he watched, the mist rolled over the tents, obscuring them from his view.

Although the other end of the island lay in mist, the south side was bathed in watery sunshine as he made his way down to the harbour.

The first part of the walk -- several hundred yards through a deeply cut valley with a small river gurgling alongside, caused no problems for Duncan. The rhododendron bushes successfully concealed any dropping away of the ledge and he could walk along quite happily.

The second part was another matter.

His heart thumped faster in his chest, the roaring in his ears started and the strength in his legs ebbed away as he surveyed the path in front of him. No matter how many times he did this journey, he always had to stop at this point.

At the foot of the valley, the river fell away in a small waterfall, splashing down into an unseen gorge beneath him. Here the track narrowed and swerved around a rocky outcrop, leaving nothing but the thickness of the path between him and a forty foot drop onto the sharp rocks below.

When he was in company, he always made sure that he had the inside line at this point and the presence of other people coupled with the prospect of severe embarrassment always allowed him to make it along the twenty yard length of path. It was a different matter when he was alone.

He turned his back on the drop and, face pressed to the wall, palms clutching the rock, stood there for long seconds. He heard waves splash feebly on the rocks beneath him He heard loose pebbles rattling like gunfire as they were dragged down by the undertow. He felt the rough edges of the rock and, with his left hand he touched the small mosses that clung there for life. He smelled the salty tang of the fine sea vapour in the air.

What he couldn't do was move.

Using his left hand he grabbed the rock, pulling away a small amount of the moss before taking hold of the rock, feeling its edges graze his palm.

He pulled hard and the upper part of his body moved, finally compelling his legs to follow along.

Painfully, slowly, he edged sideways, his eyes firmly shut, squeezing tears from their corners, progressing slowly, inches at a time, as the minutes passed and his heart threatened to pound out through his rib cage.

Finally, after an age, the edge became less threatening, softened by some gorse bushes and, eventually, stopping only where the ground fell in a gently slope, a long grassy swathe down to the harbour. Only then was he able to turn himself around.

He leaned back against the rock face and lit a cigarette, waiting for his legs to tell him that they were now able to function, waiting for his heart to slow to a reasonable rate. He knew that he had been perfectly safe on the outcrop, the path being at least eight feet wide, but he was still helpless in the face of his fear of falling.

He had no idea why the phobia had become so strong in recent years. In his early childhood he had strolled along cliff edges with no fear, had climbed sheer rock faces as if it was no more dangerous than walking down a street.

But sometime in his twenties he had become more cautious and, over the years since then, it had taken hold of him until he had reached his present state.

One of the reasons he chose this island in the first place had been an attempt to force the problem to the front. He knew that he would have to face up to it, but it had not been getting any easier over the previous ten days.

At least it was better than last year. Then he had only managed to negotiate the ledge when in company, never when he was alone.

He resolved that he would be braver on the way back up, but in the back of his mind he knew that it was a resolution he would be unable to keep.

Sighing, he headed down the grassy slope to the small harbour, noticing that his black rubber dinghy had been left on the shore by the falling tide. The only other craft in the harbour was a small yacht belonging to the McTaggarts. Jim used it occasionally to take visitors around the smaller islands to the north.

As he pushed off from the shore and hauled himself into the dinghy, he saw that the mist was now covering most of the island and, looking back up the trail, he saw it rolling down the valley towards him.

He tried to spot the entrance to the smugglers cave as he passed the next bay to the north but, as Jim had said, the vegetation was too thick and no evidence of a cave could be seen.

The small dinghy bobbed over the dark green waves, handling the swells with ease. Further out the white horses whipped up and, far to his right, a small fishing boat bobbed alarmingly in and out of his sight. But the waters close to shore were calm, protected from the worst of the wind and current by the massive cliffs. Steering through the calm waters he headed for his sampling point.

During the previous year he had made an extensive sampling of the waters around the island, keeping track of the diversity of the marine life, recording the populations and generally monitoring the condition of the environment.

This year he was back to make comparisons, his studies given added significance by the fact that the local fishermen had reported an almost total failure of fishing stocks in this area. Many of them were on the point of going bust, and if that ever happened it would be a disaster for the local economy. He intended to provide them with some sort of explanation but he believed that the problem was of their own making -- there had simply been too much fishing going on for too long.

This part of his life was the most enjoyable, being out in the open, in touch with the very nature whose secrets he was trying to unlock. It was the work he had to do in the claustrophobic laboratories of the University that got him down.

He had graduated more than twenty years ago, a fresh faced youngster of twenty-one with large ideas for saving the environment and plans for integrating his zoological research into one vast new science, the study of the whole planet. That was before the realities of life set in. The pressure of keeping up intensive research and also holding down a steady relationship began to tell, first with his long time girl friend leaving him, and then with the ridiculing of his work by his peers.

After that he lowered his sights, now being content to monitor the marine environment and to try to spark some students with the remains of his vision. He settled into a routine of work, study, lecturing and field trips, and for the past ten years and more he had scarcely thought about the opposite sex. When he did, it was usually with a tough veneer of cynicism and defensiveness, a desire to keep them at arms length lest the hurt came back.

He rarely thought about Catherine nowadays, and when he did it was with no sense of sadness. He had no feeling now of an opportunity lost. Back then it had been different.

They had met in the Citizens Theatre in Glasgow. He had arrived late to find her sitting in his allocated seat. She shuffled up one and he sat next to her.

The performance was an all-male version of Macbeth, with a homosexual pairing in the lead roles. Duncan found it heavy handed and only occasionally diverting and found himself more and more glancing across at his neighbour. At the interval he asked her if she'd like a drink and they adjourned to the bar.

They never saw the rest of the performance, spending the remainder of the evening catching up on life histories. Back then he had still been living at home with his parents and travelling in to the University, but after meeting Catherine it was only a matter of weeks before he had found himself a flat, and only two weeks after that before she moved in with him.

In those early years he was almost blissfully happy. They had fitted together so well, both of them being science students, both keen to get a decent degree but equally keen to enjoy themselves while doing so.

Their studies dovetailed with their social life and they were delighted to find that their friends were not mutually exclusive. They both graduated with good degrees and life had never been rosier.

Things started to slide when their careers had taken different turns. Duncan continued his studies, moving in to a PhD in the Zoology Department. Catherine had gone into computers.

Back then the mass produced PC was just a twinkle in IBM's eyes. Computers were mainly huge bulky things that sat in massive machine rooms and could only be communicated with via punch cards. She found an aptitude in herself for programming and got a job with a bank in Glasgow. That's where the contention came.

She started working later and began socialising with the people from her new office, people with whom he couldn't feel comfortable. They all had a thrusting, go-getting air, totally at odds with his slower comfortable way of life.

To Duncan, the biggest change was in her dress. From being a free spirit in her dress code she began wearing a business suit, almost a uniform.

She worried about her appearance far more and took to wearing make-up. He felt them drifting apart. Worse, he felt used; merely as a comfort station…

someone for her to come home to and dump her problems on.

Over the next three years the rift got wider until Duncan made his mind up that it was do or die. They took a holiday, their first long break together since she started working. On the island of Orkney, sitting on a beach watching the sun go down, he had asked her to marry him.

She laughed at him.

That's when he knew that the rift had got too wide for repair. Two weeks after their return she was gone, taking up a highly paid post in the Stock Exchange in London.

He hadn't even known that she had been to an interview,

Just last year he had seen her on television, talking about the effects of new technology on Britain's banking system, but they had never met in person since she walked out of the door all those years ago.

At the time he had been devastated, turning increasingly to drink and neglecting his studies, but his love of nature had brought him back to work and had kept him going ever since.

He had paid little attention to the opposite sex until he met Meg.

He was brought out of his reverie by a splash nearby. He turned towards the noise but was unable to see its cause. As he turned back, he noticed that he had almost reached his first sampling point.

The next ten minutes were taken up with scientific measurements and collecting samples from various depths in the water around the small red buoy. By the time he finished, the fog had lifted slightly, moving away over the south end of the island.

He had an uninterrupted view across the sea to

the lighthouse in the north and could just make out the small figures of the lighthouse keepers in the doorway at its base, dark shadows against the clear blue sky to the west.

His second samples were to be taken from the small bay beside the promontory on which the light sat, so he decided that it would be a good time to stop for lunch and a chat. By the time he reached the lighthouse half an hour later, the early mist had been dispelled and the sun had come out. He felt its heat through his rain-proof, worming its way in to dispel the dampness. He pulled the dinghy ashore and divested himself of his wet clothing before heading up the stone steps to the quay where the keepers sat, waiting for him to join them.

'Morning Tom, morning Dick,' he called as he made his way towards them. A small tabby cat appeared as if from nowhere and began winding itself around his ankles. He smiled down at it.

'And good morning to you as well Harry.'

The cat's name was the closest Tom had ever come to making a joke. He had brought it ashore from his last trip to the mainland; ostensibly to keep down the mice; but Duncan had a feeling that Tom had a soft spot for small furry animals, despite his dour stony exterior.

'Good afternoon Duncan,' said Dick. Dick was new to the job and as garrulous as Tom was taciturn. He was a tall gangling chap, all knees and elbows, standing well over six feet tall -- a feature accentuated by the fact that he was the thinnest person Duncan had ever clapped eyes on.

'Come and sit down and tell us about your wee beasties,' Dick said, waving Duncan in the direction of a nearby fish crate. 'And don't mind old misery guts here. He's got the spooks this week and I can't shake him out of it.'

Tom didn't reply, merely grunted and returned to the piece of wood that he whittled. Dick seemed oblivious to the older man's rebuff, and kept going. Duncan knew from experience that it was best to let Dick ramble on for a while; let him get all the trivia and nonsense out of his system early in the conversation. Only then would things settle down into some semblance of a normal chat. He sat on the crate, noticing that his trousers were stuck to his thighs with damp, and dug out his cigarettes. Luckily they had avoided the worst of the wetness and he only had to straighten one out slightly before lighting it. After a few puffs he got it going to his satisfaction and sat, quietly looking out across the sea as Dick continued.

'I don't know what's got into the old chap,' he went on, as if Tom was not there. 'This morning he wouldn't let me go out while it was raining. And last night he locked all the doors and all the windows and refused to go to the pub. He even threatened me with violence if I opened any of them. Completely cuckoo if you ask me -- who's going to try to burgle us out here?'

He didn't wait for a reply and Duncan knew better than to try to give one.

'And do you know what he said when I confronted him?' Dick's voice dropped about an octave in a startling impersonation of the older man. 'I know wit I know.'

His voice resumed its normal register as he continued. 'Now what the hell is that supposed to mean? And another thing. He's been nervy as a whipped pup since last night and I can't get a thing out of him. Can you do anything Duncan?'

This time Duncan thought he might get a chance to reply, but before he did so, Tom spoke up, surprising the other two with his vehemence.

Tom's usual voice was a slow deep, thickly Scottish brogue. You sometimes had difficulty understanding him as he rumbled through his sentences. This time however, his voice raised in pitch and he almost shouted.

'There's some things best left unsaid. It wid be best if you jist heeded my warnings and left it at that. That's all I'm going to say on the matter.'

At that the older man got up to leave them, knocking over the fish crate on which he had been sitting. As he passed Duncan, he leaned over and spoke directly to him. Duncan saw fear in the weather-beaten face as he listened, noticing that Tom's voice was falling back to its normal level.

'If I were you Duncan, I'd get back to the pub as soon as possible and lock myself in wi' your wee lassie. You don't want her to be wandering around at times like these.'

With that he left, favouring his bad leg, the one which had been damaged in a navy accident in the Fifties. Duncan noticed that the limp was more pronounced than usual and Tom grimaced as he negotiated the stone steps, the small cat attacking his heels all the way to the lighthouse.

Duncan turned back to Dick to see his face creased in a huge grin. The younger man hunched his shoulders and screwed up his features before delivering a fair impression of Charles Laughton in the Hunchback of Notre Dame.

'Beware the moon and the rain. There are dark forces abroad. Heh heh heh.'

Duncan couldn't help it. Although he knew that the older man would still be able to hear him, he had to laugh. But at the same time, the memory of the look in the older man's eyes sent a cold shiver through him, a cold which refused to be melted in the heat of the sun.

Dick was still talking.

'Seriously. I'm worried about him. I've heard stories about lighthouse madness. All the solitude sometimes sends people a bit loopy -- they call it cabin fever I think.'

Duncan finally managed to get a word in.

'I'm sure it's not that. Tom seems stable to me. It's probably just another one of his Hebridean superstitions. You know what the folk out here are like when it comes to ghosts and ghoulies. If I were you I'd humour him for a while -- see if it gets any worse.'

'Aye, maybe you're right. But if he tries to lock me in again I might not stand for it. Last night we were all ready to set off for the pub -- just standing around outside the door, when he went quiet. He looked out to sea, and a fog was coming in. He was listening to something. But I couldn't hear a thing, just a few seals barking away at each other. You know the sound?'

Again, the younger man didn't wait for a reply.

'The next thing I knew I got bundled back inside, the doors were all locked and he told me that nobody was allowed out. I was angry with him, I'll admit that, but he was adamant. By this time we were both shouting at each other, but I couldn't get the keys off him. I threatened to hit him, but he just laughed and said he had taken bigger and better men than me and invited me to try.' Dick looked sheepish while he remembered.

'I gave in to him in the end -- it was impossible trying to get him to see sense. I'm still pissed off though. I don't like being treated like a naughty schoolboy.'

Duncan smiled. A naughty schoolboy was exactly the impression he had of Dick, even accounting for the fact that he must have been at least twenty-four years old and a couple of feet taller than most schoolboys.

'I don't think you should make a big thing of it,' he said when he was given a chance to speak 'He most likely got a bit spooked, that's all. Now he's probably embarrassed about the whole thing. Anyway, changing the subject, I had that little blonde that you've been eyeing up sitting on my knee last night.'

He enjoyed seeing the pained expression on Dick's face.

'Come on Duncan. You said that you had no interest in her. You promised.'

Duncan couldn't resist winding him up further. Two nights ago he had been alone in the bar with Dick, and Dick had confided that he was in love -- well, in lust anyway, with the young blonde student. This was too good an opportunity to miss.

'She said that she'd got tired waiting for you last night,' he said, and before Dick had a chance to reply, went on. 'She's got a very small waist you know. And very big up front, if you get my meaning,' motioning in the air with his hands to illustrate the point.

The younger man was furious but laughing at the same time. He knew he had no need to be jealous of Duncan. Meg would have stopped him if he had got close to any indiscretions.

'That's does it. I'm going down the pub tonight. I don't care what the old buffer says. It'll take more than a couple of spooks to keep me away.'

Turning to Duncan, he prodded him in the chest

with a long forefinger, 'And don't you go getting in my way.'

Duncan laughed. 'That's OK Dick; I've got no intention of stealing your wee lassie. Besides, I've got a date with Meg tonight.'

Dick's grin turned into a leer.

'Ah ha. You've finally seen sense then. That might cheer Tom up. He says he's seen it coming since you were here last year.'

Duncan was surprised. He'd paid little attention to Meg the year before, being preoccupied with his work. He didn't have time to argue, Dick was already running on.

'She's a fine looking woman, that's for sure. A wee bit flighty for me though. I don't like them too independent or too intelligent. Barefoot, pregnant and in the kitchen, that's where they should be.'

Both men laughed. Duncan knew that the other man didn't mean it; it was just that the old jokes always provoked a reaction and this was one of the ones it was necessary to laugh at in these times of woman's liberation.

'Do you want to come in for a cup of coffee?' Dick asked, motioning towards the lighthouse. 'I made a pot ten minutes ago.'

He refused gracefully. The coffee brewed in the lighthouse was legendary across the island. It was said to be useful as paint stripper, but not for much else.

'No, I think I'll sit here and eat my chocolate in peace. I've got to get moving in ten minutes anyway.'

The leer was back on Dick's face. 'Hurrying back to preen yourself for the big night eh? Well be careful. A man of your age has to watch what he's doing with young women... you don't want to do yourself an injury.'

Laughing, Dick walked away towards the lighthouse, leaving Duncan alone on the small quay, with only two squawking seagulls for company.

He looked around, enjoying the play of light on the sea and the stillness in the protection afforded by the little harbour. At one time this had been a proper quay, but a heavy rock-fall from the cliffs had filled it in substantially.

It was too far away from any shipping lines to be considered important. In time, all the boats which came to the island began using the harbour at the south end of the island, leaving this one to fall further into disrepair until only small dinghies were able to navigate its waters safely.

The lighthouse sat on a rocky promontory jutting up from the sea just offshore from the island and was joined to it by a metal bridge some twenty feet off the ground.

At high tide the bridge was the only link with the island, but at low water it was possible to scramble round the rocks and make your way up the cliff. That is, it would be possible if you didn't have Duncan's fear of heights.

He sat there for several minutes, looking out to the islands to the north and noticing that a new bank of fog was making its way down the chain, slowly engulfing the golden beaches.

Even at this time of year, when you would expect at least some tourists, the beaches were empty, the only sign of life being the ever present flocks of gulls and the occasional oyster-catcher.

It was almost time to get going. He took out a cigarette and lit up. As he stood to leave, smoothing out the drying creases in his trousers, Tom made his way down the steps towards him.

'Can I jist have a wee word wi' ye Duncan. It'll only take a minute.'

Duncan nodded, noticing that Tom now had his voice under control. He saw that something was troubling the older man. He only hoped that Dick hadn't been right about the "cabin fever".

'Get back to the pub as soon as ye can', Tom said, 'Stay oot of the mist and away from any rain. That way ye should be all right.'

Duncan was confused. Looking into those deep blue eyes, he saw that Tom was completely sincere. But more that that, he was very frightened. Now that he was close to the man he noticed the unshaven bristle on his chin and the heavy black smudges under his eyes. This more than anything else convinced him of Tom's sincerity -- the man had never before looked anything other than clean-shaven and healthy -- the old navy routine as he had told Duncan only a few days ago.

'What do you mean? What could go wrong?'

'It's the bad time again,' Tom replied, his voice dropping to a whisper. 'I can feel it coming. You might think that I'm jist a stupid auld man, but there's something bad on its way, and I'm worried that I know what it is. Jist keep out of the mist, that's all I ask.'

The older man shuffled off without another word.

Duncan resolved to let the rest of the islanders know of Tom's strange state of mind, but again he failed to shake off the cold shiver that ran through him. He stubbed out his cigarette, flicking the end into a rock pool as he headed for the dinghy.

Five minutes later he was on his way again, turning around to wave at the keepers as he made his way out of the bay and around to the western side of the island.

The sea was rougher on this side, with the wind sweeping down across the North Atlantic, and he had to pay more attention to steering the dinghy. However, he still could not get Tom's words out of his mind.

He had told Dick that the Hebridean people were still known for their feyness -- which was true enough. There were as many tales of the faerie folk in this area as there were islands.

Duncan himself was a confirmed sceptic. The wonders of nature were enough for him without having to invent more. He'd had several experiences at University that his friends were convinced were paranormal, but Duncan preferred to believe that they were merely his mind playing tricks.

He didn't need the emotional crutch of superstition. Since childhood he had eschewed the trappings of religion and the alternative pseudo-mysticism of most of his friends, preferring instead to put his trust in science. He realised that science had brought many terrors into the world, but he firmly believed that the best way to progress and get the planet out of the mess that was coming was through the efforts of scientists. He saw no future in the laissez-faire attitude of his New Age friends. By doing nothing they were merely postponing the inevitable. He at least was examining the causes, even although he had yet come up with no answer to his particular problem.

The next hours passed quickly for him as he busied himself with collecting samples from around the third and fourth buoys. He was surprised to discover that it was three o'clock in the afternoon when he next looked at his watch.

The sun had moved round to bathe this part of the island in its watery afternoon rays. He stopped his engine and drifted, taking in the sight of the light on the rock face, the interplay of light and shadow. He was somewhere around two hundred yards from shore and the slight wind was pushing him closer.

High on the cliffs above the sun bathed the massive ruin of the Mansion on the cliffs.

He knew very little of the building's history -- only what he had picked up from the locals in the pub. It had been built by a Victorian gentleman in the mid-1860's, a summer residence at the time when the Queen had made popular all things Scottish.

The gentlemen had been a notorious eccentric and bon-vivant and had thrown several wild parties at the house, parties that were still talked about around the islands over a hundred years later.

There had been a fire -- or so Duncan had been led to believe, and the gentleman and his servants had perished. Since then the building had remained empty and was shunned by the locals, except when some of its stone might be needed for building work.

He saw no sign of the students, but knew that they would be there, on the other side of the house, on their hands and knees trowelling through layers of sodden mud. Mentally he wished them luck, although he much preferred his own area of interest.

As he lowered his gaze, he saw the narrow staircase that led from the house down to a small sandy bay. The staircase was no more than five feet wide and Duncan had been told that many of the steps were dangerous.

He didn't know from personal experience and he had no desire to find out.

The small bay was barely twenty yards long but

he had often spotted as many as thirty seals laid out on the golden sands, basking in the sun. Today the beach was empty.

Absentmindedly he lit a cigarette and was forced to cough as he inhaled through the wrong end. He had just flipped the smouldering stub overboard when his cough was answered, not once but in a chorus.

He looked up to see that he was being watched by a large group of grey seals, only their heads visible as they bobbed, twenty yards from him. In unison, they barked, an amazing hoarse cacophonous sound that rang in his ears long after they had stopped. As one, they lifted their heads slightly, seeming to nod in his direction, then they submerged, like a troupe of synchronised swimmers.

Duncan was stunned. He had never come across behaviour like this before. Seals had shown as interest in him on previous trips, but never en-masse, and never acting as if with a single will. He lit another cigarette, properly this time and waited to see if there was going to be a repeat performance, unwilling to start his dinghy's motor in case he should frighten them off.

Towards the north end of the island the mist was beginning to creep in again. From his position he couldn't see the lighthouse, but he wondered if Tom was battening down the hatches again. He smiled to himself as he thought of poor Dick trying to talk his way out, desperate not to miss another opportunity for a chat with the blonde student.

A scratching on the underside of the dinghy interrupted his thoughts. At first he thought that he had run against a rock but on checking his position he realised that the water here was too deep. He must be snagged on a piece of flotsam. He looked over the rim of the dinghy, but couldn't see anything.

The scratching got louder, then, without warning the dinghy gave a lurch and he felt, underfoot, some of the rigidity of its structure give way. The craft dipped on its left-hand side, shipping a small amount of water that quickly soaked through his boots.

It started to sink.

He tugged at the cord for the outboard motor, four times before the engine caught. His only hope was to head for the shore and try to beach the craft before it went under. It swung alarmingly, heavy in the water, as he turned it towards the cliffs, more water spilling in as he struggled for control.

He wasn't going to make it.

Half way to the beach he was caught side-on by a large swell and was dismayed to see his sample jars float off as the dinghy stopped rocking.

Water poured in all around him, only the forward motion stopping him from going under completely.

He waited until the last possible moment. Grabbing hold of his rucksack in his left hand, he launched himself in the seas, gasping at the sudden lash of the cold water, before managing to get himself facing in the right direction. He kicked off from the dinghy, using it to give him some momentum, and set off, swimming one handed towards the shore.

Ten yards out he was caught on a rising wave and propelled through the surf, landing, gasping at the water's edge, face down in the wet sand. Wearily he pulled himself up the beach, out of range of the waves and turned back to search for his dinghy. There was no sign of the craft, not even a ripple to indicate where it might have been. In the distance he saw two of his sample jars bobbing along and glistening in the sun's rays.

He was at a loss to explain what had happened. He must have caught on a piece of floating wood which had somehow managed to puncture the thick rubber of the dinghy. But he had a feeling that the appearance of the seals must have had something to do with it.

Putting it to the back of his mind -- a puzzle to be pondered later, he turned to survey his next obstacle.

His heart beat faster and a heavy weight settled in the pit of his stomach as he looked up, and up, at the steps hewn into the rock in front of him.

At one time there had been a wooden railing protecting the steps, but that had long since fallen into disrepair. Now almost the whole length was open to the elements and at some points the cliff fell sheer away in drops in excess of thirty feet.

He wasn't sure that he would make it.

2

Anne

Anne looked out over the cliff-tops as she washed the dishes, but she wasn't seeing the view. She was seeing the letter -- the one that arrived that morning, the one from which she could only remember one word, a word which she could almost see, its giant red letters dancing across the internal screen of her mind -- POSITIVE.

How was she going to tell Jim? Only two days ago he had been saying how much he looked forward to Meg getting old enough to fly the coop, how much he looked forward to them having some time on their own. How could she tell him that, at the age of forty-four, she was going to be a mother again?

She wondered when it could have happened. Taking the pill was one of the things she was scrupulous about. Every night before bed -- the packet placed in a prominent place in the bathroom to remind her.

Anti-babies Jim called them. 'Have you had the anti-baby?' he would ask at bed-time, every night without fail.

Well, almost every night.

It must have been her birthday -- that was the last time she had forgotten to take her pill. Both of them had been drunk.

Too drunk to take precautions, not drunk enough for the

dreaded brewer's droop to have occurred.

It was ironic really -- at his last visit the doctor had told her that her chances of fertility were so low as to be negligible. At the time it had seemed a liberation, a chance to escape the heavy-bodied curse of the pill. But her body betrayed her, much in the same way that it had done with Meg all those years before.

She could still remember Jim's reaction then: 'What do you mean -- pregnant? How did that happen?' At that moment he had looked like a confused schoolboy, his lip stuck out in petulance. She had almost walked away from him then, left the island and scurried back to her mum's cosy suburbia.

Instead she had tried to be flippant.

'Well -- you put your dick inside me, waggled it about a bit, and there it was, a baby. Didn't they teach you anything at school?'

And then she had burst into tears, unable to contain it any longer. There had been a long moment when they were apart -- only by a foot, but it was like a gaping chasm between them. Jim was the first to move. He had held her tight, and everything had been all right again. She hoped he would take it as well this time.

The main thing she worried about was having to leave the island. She loved this place, loved the peace and tranquillity of it, but it was no place to bring up a youngster. The nearest school was 100 miles away, the nearest family was twenty miles away, and it sometimes took six hours for the doctor to answer an emergency call -- six hours too long in the event of a real emergency.

They had got away with it in Meg's case -- their youthful exuberance and zest for life had blinded them to the dangers. It had been difficult, but they had coped, taking turns with the nightly floor walking. But now they were older -- a bit wiser and a lot more careful.

Except when it came to taking precautions.

Heavy tears ran down her face, falling to mingle with the washing up water, and she wasn't sure whether they were tears of joy or tears of sadness.

She noticed she had finished the washing up, but she didn't remember doing it, and was surprised to look down and see an empty bowl -- she had been lost in a world of diapers, sleepless nights and hectic days. Was she up to it?

She realised that she had come to a decision while washing up. Jim need never know. All she needed was an excuse to get to the mainland for a bit, find the right clinic, and then it would be heigh-ho back to the island, back to sanity. Again tears threatened to push themselves out, but she forced them back. Strength was what was needed here, and she had found over the years that she had it in abundance.

The house was quiet, only the occasional rattle from the cellar breaking the silence.

At least Meg was helping out with the chores now. It hadn't been that long ago that the girl was going through the usual teenage trauma -- the tantrums and arguments made worse by the fact that there was no one of her own age around, no-one to back her up in the endless rows against stubborn parents.

Nowadays she had settled down, and Meg hoped that the blossoming relationship with Duncan would come to fruition. Even though he was almost old enough to be Meg's father he seemed to have his head screwed on the right way.

She stood for a while, just drinking in the peace and quiet of the house. This was how she liked it -- no tourists, no customers, just her and her house.

She couldn't remember when it had become "her" house rather than "their house", but that was how she now thought of it -- her small place of sanity in a mad world. When she watched the nightly news she was increasingly glad that they had chosen to stay here.

It had been like a dream come true all those years ago when they had got the job.

'It's only for a six month trial period,' the man had said, and she had seen the look in his eyes. He didn't believe that two hippies, however cleaned up they might be, had the necessary strength for the job.

But they had proved him wrong. Oh, it had been hard at first, but not as hard as the winter they spent in the tent.

She smiled to herself as she remembered *the old days*. That's how both she and Jim thought of them. Not *the good old days*. No, there had been little good about them.

If they hadn't genuinely loved each other they would never have survived. But there had been something comical about Jim sneaking off in the middle of the night to milk John Jeffries' cow. Old John had been on short milk rations all winter, and he never twigged.

Sometimes, in the bar, when she had to put up with the farmer's boorish behaviour, she was tempted to tell him. But it remained their little secret, something to giggle over in the depths of the night.

A further rattle of bottles from the cellar brought her back to the present.

She glanced at the clock and was surprised to find that the morning had almost gone -- she might not remember doing the washing up, but she had certainly taken long enough about it.

Jim would be back soon, stinking from cleaning out the septic tank and demanding *munchies*. Well he was just going to have to make do with what came to hand -- she was in no mood for slaving over a hot stove.

She went to the cupboard, and discovered that she had some work to do anyway -- the vegetable rack was empty. She was sure that she'd had some carrots the night before. And then she remembered Jim's midnight snack.

Her husband was an inveterate carrot eater; so much so that Meg had nicknamed him Bugs. That had been years ago, but the name had stuck. Sometimes she thought Jim played up to it a bit too much, but even she had to admit to fits of laughter when he cuddled up to her in bed and whispered "What's up Doc?" in her ear.

She signed as she picked up her wicker basket from beside the sink. It wasn't that she minded her little visits to the vegetable plot -- just that some days, like today, she wished she had someone else to do it for her.

That feeling passed as she made her way down the garden. The sun glinted off the sea and white clouds scudded playfully across the sky. Down here in the garden there was only a gentle breeze, just enough to rustle the rhododendron bushes. The grass on their small lawn was getting long again. Jim would have to be bullied into getting the lawn mower out.

She passed through the arch of rambling roses and into the vegetable plot, a small walled garden some thirty feet square, open at the far end with a stunning view over a small strip of greenery to the cliffs falling down to the sea.

When they'd first arrived this had been a proper garden, all dwarf conifers and fancy heather, slightly gone to seed, complete with a stagnant pool and a heavily mildewed bench.

It hadn't taken them long to realise that the practicalities of life didn't allow for such luxuries, and together they had dug it into a vegetable patch. Nothing fancy... just the basics; potatoes, carrots, onions, cabbage and sprouts.

Jim made several attempts to build a greenhouse but they all ended in failure, sometimes due to inclement weather, but often due to Jim's ineptitude with any kind of tool -- except, apparently, for the one he kept inside his trousers.

Tears threatened to spring at the corners of her eyes.

She shook her head, hard, and anyone watching would have thought she was having a mild fit.

'That's it,' she whispered. 'No more reminiscing.' She felt hot and heavy, like she usually did on the day before her period started. This time the feeling wasn't going to go away the next day. Sometimes she wished that there were no such things as hormones -- they only got in the way.

She spent the next ten minutes trying to find some vegetables that were edible. It was getting near the end of the season, and a lot of their produce was beginning to rot in the ground which was always wet no matter how dry the summer had been. Luckily she had stocked the freezer during the good months, so she wasn't too perturbed.

Jim wasn't going to like it though -- they were definitely short of carrots. Old Bugs was just going to have to find something else to nibble on during the long winter months.

She giggled at her own double entendre, then stopped suddenly as a sudden noise rasped nearby.

Yes. There it was again -- a harsh scraping, as if someone climbed on the outside of the wall.

She wasn't frightened.

Not yet anyway.

'Is that you Jim?'

The noise stopped, and the garden fell silent, the air suddenly heavy and oppressive.

'Come on Jim. Stop playing silly buggers. There'll be no carrots for Bugs tonight.'

Jim was always playing jokes, creeping up on her when least expected and frightening the living daylights out of her. It was something she had got used to a long time ago, and something she didn't think he'd ever grow out of, no matter how often she scolded him.

The noise started again, louder this time, and Anne started to back away, moving for the entrance, not noticing that she was trampling on the last decent patch of cabbages.

'Right. That's it,' she shouted. 'Sod you and your stupid games.'

The noise became frantic, as if something scrambled for purchase, and there was a deep cough -- a noise which really terrified her and caused the hair to stand stiff at the nape of her neck. She didn't recognise it as a noise Jim was capable of making.

And then the smell hit her, a rancid rotting odour.

She backed off further... and screamed when she hit a warm body.

She was still screaming when she turned into the arms of her husband.

'What's all the shouting?' Jim said. She screamed into his face.

'You bastard. You complete bastard.'

She pummelled her fists against his chest before falling, weeping, against him. She only stayed there for a second though, forced away from him by the smell rising from his clothes.

'God. You stink. You could at least have had a wash.'

Jim grinned, that slow sheepish grin which always made her stomach tumble and left her feeling like the giddy schoolgirl she had been when they first met.

'Yeah,' he replied. 'The tank was a bit ripe this time. I think John Jeffries must have been farting in it again.'

That was all it took -- the tears turned to giggles, and soon they were both holding each other as their shoulders heaved in time. It wasn't long before she had to push herself away.

'You really do stink you know. Get back to the house and get changed. That smell will linger in the bar all night if you're not careful.'

Jim grinned again. 'I don't suppose old John will notice any difference.'

Old John was renowned for the killing power of his eruptions, and he made a point of noting them. Jim reminded her of the fact by scrunching up his features and impersonating the old farmer.

'Hello arse -- I thought you were dead.'

That brought another fit of giggles, but when Jim moved to hug her she pushed him away -- the smell was just too strong.

'Get away with you,' she said, landing a hard pat on his backside as he turned to go. As she left the garden she had one last look at the wall, but there was no recurrence of the noise.

Maybe it had been Jim after all. She'd forgive him, this time.

By the time she got back to the house Jim was already in the shower. She heard the old plumbing rumble and creak, but she wasn't complaining -- at least it drowned out Jim's singing. Her husband had one of the worst singing voices she had ever heard -- he was lucky if he ever hit one right note in the course of any one song.

She was at the sink, washing the vegetables, when she felt Jim press against her back.

'I'm nice and clean now,' he whispered in his best sex maniac voice. 'How do you fancy coming upstairs and making me dirty again?'

She turned into his arms, then just as quickly pushed him away again.

'You might have washed -- but you're still wearing the same Tee-shirt.'

He gave her the sheepish grin and looked over the top of his sunglasses at her. That was another thing she had never managed to wean him off. A Deep Purple Tee-shirt and mirror shades were so much a part of what he was that she couldn't imagine him without them.

What was he going to be like when he was seventy years old, sitting in his rocking chair, still with the shades, still screaming along to the old albums? She hoped she was around to see it.

She pushed him further away.

'Go now. Go and sort out the till or something. We'll be opening up soon.'

He grinned.

'And who are you expecting? There'll only be old

John -- and we're still giving him 'tic remember?'

She remembered well enough. It was one of Jim's weaknesses -- he allowed John Jeffries almost free access to the bar. Maybe he was guilty about the milk all those years ago. The thought brought back her earlier musings.

'Jim,' she called, and was amazed to hear the trembling in her voice.

He must have caught it as well, for there was concern on his face as he turned back to her. She studied his face closely, seeing the fine lines at the corners of his eyes, the greying hair at his temples. Suddenly it wasn't so difficult to imagine him as an old man.

And what would another child do to him, to both of them.

She had been about to tell him, she would have told him just a second ago, but now she steeled herself again.

'What's up Doc?' he said, but she didn't reply, merely waved him away with her hand and turned back to the sink. She heard his sigh of exasperation as he went into the other room, and immediately felt sorry for him.

God she was a mess this morning. She quickly went to him and hugged him hard.

'I'm sorry darling,' she murmured in his ear. 'It's the bloody hormones again.'

She hugged him harder before continuing.

'Get me a stiff vodka. I've got something to tell you.'

This time she didn't get the sheepish grin -- she got the raised eyebrow before he spoke.

'And about bloody time too. I've been tip-toeing

round you all week. What is it? A bad case of the monthlies?'

She sat down hard on a chair.

'Just get me a drink. And make it a big one.'

She hated to see him worried, but she was afraid it was going to get worse. When the drink arrived she took a large gulp. There was no easy way out now.

'I'm pregnant,' she said, watching his eyes closely.

If there was any real joy there she didn't see it. What she saw was shock, at first, followed quickly by despair, and then a huge, false smile which didn't quite reach his eyes.

'That's wonderful,' he said, and if she hadn't been watching him closely, she might have believed that he meant it.

'Is it Jim? Is it really wonderful?' She took a large gulp of vodka. If she was to steer this conversation in the right direction she would need all the Dutch courage she could get.

He got out of his chair to come round the table but she waved him back.

'Sit down would you. We need to talk about this.'

This time it was him who took a shot of vodka.

'Come on Anne. What is there to talk about? You're going to have a baby -- I'm going to be a daddy again.'

He tried to be flippant, and almost, but not quite succeeded. She knew him too well to be put off by his act.

'Yep. You're going to be a daddy again. No more restful nights. No more keeping the bar open till all hours for the regulars, months and months of changing nappies...'

He butted in.

'It can't be any worse than draining the septic

tank.'

But she wasn't going to let it go that lightly.

'No, probably not. But how do you fancy draining the tank every night for a year? How do you fancy spending every night walking the floors with a baby in your arms than having to do the chores the next day?'

She saw that she had confused him.

'We did it before, didn't we? He said. 'It wasn't so hard.'

That made her angry.

'Oh yes it was -- it was bloody near impossible. And you know it. And we're twenty-odd years older. How do you think we'll cope?'

It was several seconds before he replied, and when he did his voice was low, almost a whisper.

'So what are you saying?'

And suddenly the moment had come -- the one she'd been dreading, the one she'd hoped to avoid. She had to have two attempts before her mouth would form the words.

'I'm saying that I think I want an abortion.'

She watched his eyes again, and this time it was anger she saw there, anger and hurt.

'Oh no,' he said, barely audible. 'No, no. We can't kill a child -- not for any reason.'

He shook his head, and it was as if he had forgotten Anne was there while he mumbled to himself.

'We can't, we just can't.'

She knew it was going to come to this, but what she hadn't prepared for was the anger that flared in her.

'What's with all this <u>we</u> crap? I'm the one who's carrying the damned thing -- it's my decision,' she said, fighting to keep her voice under control, trying not to shout, aware that Meg was still in the cellar.

He mumbled something that she didn't quite catch, and she had to ask him to repeat it.

'I said, it's not just yours. It's mine as well.'

That made her even angrier. She stood suddenly, almost overbalancing her drink.

'If you want the fucking thing so much, you have it.'

She left him sitting there with his drink and headed for the toilet. She only just made it in time before she lost her breakfast in one hot, heaving bundle.

Strangely she felt better than she had all day. The worst was over now. Either her and Jim came to an accommodation on the matter or they didn't. Either way she had told him. And she was going to have an abortion -- of that she was now certain.

She was cleaning herself up when she heard the knock on the door. That in itself was a new thing. Neither her nor Jim had ever been bothered by the presence of the other in the bathroom. For him to knock now was an act of contrition, a request for forgiveness.

'Come on in,' she said. 'It's not locked.'

As the door opened she tried to steel her heart for the confrontation, but when she saw his face her insides melted.

Jim had been crying and his eyes were red and puffy. He held his hands out to her, and she saw that his fingers were trembling.

'I'm sorry darling,' he said. 'I've been doing some thinking, and I guess you're right. We'll do whatever is best for you.'

She went into his arms and soon they were both

crying again.

'I hate it when we argue,' she said, looking up at him through blurred eyes.

'Yeah,' he replied. 'But making up is fun isn't it.'

She hooked a finger in the top of his jeans and, in a fair imitation of his sex-maniac voice, said 'Come with me big-boy. I'll show you the meaning of the word fun.'

Their lovemaking was as sweet as any had been over the past twenty years, and when they were spent they lay in bed, cradled in each other's arms.

She was on the verge of sleep when Jim nudged her.

'Honest darling. I meant it. We'll do whatever you want.'

She turned so that she could see his face, cupping his chin in her hands.

'You're damned right we will,' she said, and they both giggled. Suddenly Anne knew that everything was going to be OK or, if not OK, as good as could be expected in the circumstances.

She pushed him out of bed.

'I suppose you'll want something to eat now?' she said. 'That's the trouble with men -- slake one of their desires and another one rears its ugly head.'

'Talking of desires,' he said, pulling back the sheets and climbing back into bed. 'I don't think this one's slaked yet.'

'Oh no you don't,' She pushed him away. 'You need a wash. It's not the tank you smell of now.'

She got out of bed before he could grab her again.

'You go and wash. I'll make us something to eat.'

She waited until Jim had finished in the bathroom

before cleaning herself up. She heard him singing as he made his way downstairs -- discordant and off-key as usual, but a sure sign that he was happy. Anne smiled as she finally made her way to the kitchen.

As she passed the trapdoor she heard the clink of bottles from below.

'Meg.' She shouted, then louder when there was no response. 'Dinner in half an hour.'

There was a muffled "OK" from far back in the cellar that Anne took as a sign of assent.

She gave Jim a pat on the bum as she passed, but he was already engrossed in adding up the takings in the till. She wiggled her bottom and got a low wolf whistle, which was enough to be getting on with for now.

She started by peeling an onion that was so strong that she was forced over to the sink to escape its pungency. She had just started on the carrots when she heard a commotion in the bar.

Jim was shouting -- nonsense words in a high pitched voice, and then there was the slam of the cellar trapdoor closing.

Turning around was like turning into a nightmare -- something stood between her and the doorway, something that was man-shaped but not a man, something black that filled the space with its bulk. A scream built inside her and she wasn't sure if she could contain it. The thing began to move towards her, and at the same time she heard Jim screaming, a terrible sound but mercifully one she didn't have to endure long before the blackness of a dead faint took her away for a long time.

3
John Jeffries

It was early afternoon before John Jeffries got back to the farm, and by that time he was almost incandescent with rage.

His rounds hadn't gone well. First of all the old dog was even slower than recently, and then, just as he thought everything was going to be OK, he found the first carcass.

Three more sheep gone… throats torn out and guts spread across the field. And it wasn't as if it was the old and weak ones. These had been some of his best animals.

'Bloody students,' he said to the empty room. 'If they've brought a dog here I'll kill the mutt then I'll throw the lot of them off the bloody cliff.'

He hated students with a venom he usually reserved for the extremes of weather on this God forsaken rock.

'Bloody waste of taxpayer's money.'

This was his standard phrase, one which failed to mention the fact that it was at least six years since he had made a tax return, and six years before that since he had legally declared all of his income.

But students were different… everybody knew that, what with their posh voices and their diet lagers, and that Nancy-boy way they had of throwing darts. All of that, and the fact that they thought they knew all there is to know, before they'd had time to really learn anything.

And they probably spent all their time screwing in those tents.

Thinking of the tents made him remember the sheep. He'd never seen anything like it. To be honest it didn't look like an animal attack.

They had all been done the same way -- their entrails spread out on a fan around their bodies. But what had made it worse had been the red seeping holes where the eyes had been -- he'd almost lost his breakfast when he'd seen that.

One had been bad enough -- but three? Three was a disaster. He would have to get to the bottom of it; otherwise he could kiss the farm goodbye.

'And where the hell were you when all of this was going on?'

The old dog was a quivering ball of nerves in the corner, trembles running over its whole body. It averted its eyes, knowing from long experience to keep out of Jeffries' way when he was in one of his moods.

The old man let out a snort.

'Too old and too decrepit. What would you do if you caught those bastards at my sheep -- gum them to death? They probably gave you biscuits.'

The dog's ears perked up at the mention of one of the magic words and its tail thumped, just once, on the cold wooden floor. It soon realised that it was a forlorn hope as the farmer stomped into the kitchen, his heavy footsteps echoing around the room, the cleats on his boots gouging small splinters from the floorboards.

He put his shotgun down on the table, having to move several days worth of washing up aside to make space.

'What a fucking mess,' he growled. He didn't think he'd ever get the hang of housework -- that was his wife's job. Thirty years he'd fed and kept her. And what thanks did he get -- what thanks had he ever got?

'Bugger all,' he muttered. 'I hope she's fucking happy.'

The maddening thing was she was probably as happy as a sandboy -- shacked up with that cackling old witch of a mother, holding genteel tea parties with the vicar -- that was just her scene.

'Well fuck her then.' As he moved to the kitchen sink his gaze was caught by the view out the window.

'Fog. That's all we bloody need,' he muttered as he filled the kettle. It was when he was on the way back to the stove that he heard the lowing of the cow in the barn.

'Oh shit,' he said. He'd forgotten to milk the damned thing that morning. Well, not so much forgotten as ignored. As he put the kettle down it lowed again, louder and more plaintive this time.

'OK. OK, I'm coming,' he shouted. 'Christ. Some days it's just one long grind.'

Over the past year he'd come to hate having to milk the cow, to detest the cold slimy feel of its udders as he coaxed and teased the small quantities of milk it deigned to produce.

'Carve you up and have a few steaks,' he muttered as he made his way to the barn. He called for Sam to follow him, but the dog stayed cowering in its corner.

'Just stay here and whimper then. That's all you're bloody good for anyway. It's about time I got a new dog as well. Fuck this for a carry on.'

He thought about going back and locking the

door while he was out, but decided, for the first time ever, to leave it.

'Just let one of those long-haired students try to come in. I'll blow their fucking heads off.'

As he made his way to the barn he noticed that the fog was getting thicker, causing him to curse the weather for only the fifth time that day.

As he approached the barn he noticed, not the first time, that it was in dire need of repair. The left-hand door hung on one hinge, there was a three-foot hole in the roof, courtesy of a particularly high wind last winter, and the cow lived in a stinking pile of its own excrement. But somehow he just couldn't be bothered to do any work these days.

The cow raised its head as he approached and gave him a sad-eyed stare as he lifted the three-legged stool and the iron bucket.

'Bloody women's work,' Jeffries muttered.

His wife had been the one for milking, and it had been her who had bought a cow in the first place. 'Thirty years of sodding cows and not one of them a decent milker.'

'Should have made her take the bloody thing with her when she left,' he said, and laughed at the thought of his mother-in-law having to deal with a cow in her oh-so-perfect little house.

'Cow shit on the carpet would really give her something to moan about,' he said aloud, and laughed again at the mental picture of the steaming pile on the carpet in front of the unnaturally clean fireplace.

He didn't even bother warming his hands before he went to work. 'If it was good enough for the wife it's good enough for you,' he said as the cow gave out a long, pained low.

He slapped the animal hard on its side.

'Just you be quiet there lass. It'll be over soon.'

The cow put up with the indignity as Jeffries began teasing her udders. 'I wish the missus had managed to stay as quiet,' he muttered, and laughed again, a cold, hard thing. He bent forward once more, just as the cow gave a sudden lurch backwards, knocking him off the stool and onto the muck-strewn floor.

'Bastard,' he shouted. 'Ungrateful bastard.'

The cow started to low again, a frightened cry of sheer terror. Jeffries rose to his feet, brandishing the stool as a weapon.

'Knock me over would you,' he shouted, and raised the stool to strike the animal.

He never saw what hit him.

Something large and black came out of the shadows, pushing the cow aside as if it were no more than a rag doll. Jeffries felt a sudden sharp pain at his chest. 'Heart attack,' he thought, a sudden cold chill in his spine.

Then the barn was falling away from him and he felt the bounce as his head hit the floor. His left hand groped for his chest, then there was a tearing, flaring pain as it was torn roughly away.

The last thing he saw before darkness took him away was the taloned hand reaching for his eyes.

Some time later Sam padded into the barn. The old dog whimpered as it smelled blood, then crept slowly over to the still form of his master, tail dragging along the floor and forelegs ready to spring at any sudden movement.

It nuzzled the body until it was sure that no movement was likely, then whimpered again as it caught the smell of something strange. Lifting the master's detached arm it scuttled back to the shelter of the farmhouse where it curled itself around the arm, protecting it from any harm.

4
5,215 Years Before

The sun threw its first rays onto the great pyramid of the Sky Father, and the vast crowd moaned, a communal sigh which spoke to Am-Rho of loss and of bereavement.

'They don't know what they're doing,' he whispered to his companion, but was prevented from continuing by the hot cut of the lash across his back.

The crowd hissed. He saw the compassion in their eyes, but more than that, he saw the fear.

The lash hit again, and hot blood slid across his back. He muttered an oath, a plea to the Sky Father, but there was no power there, no joy -- the priest of the Mother had seen to that.

The crowd suddenly fell silent, and parted as a figure strode through the throng. Am-Rho recognised him immediately -- the source of his downfall -- Dron, priest of the Mother, suckler of the teats of the great whore. He tried to spit but found that his mouth was suddenly dry.

Dron stood in front of him, and Am-Rho saw the victory in his opponent's face.

It could have been so different -- Am-Rho could have been the victor. There they had stood, face to face in the chamber in the pyramid... the realm of the Father which this usurper would tear down and consecrate to his own ends.

Am-Rho had been confident -- the Father had

been with him for many years, feeding his power through his seed -- the great stone he had sent from the sky many eons before.

He had called on the Sky Father, called on him to strike down his enemies in the old way, to send them crawling on the ground. But the Father had stayed silent and Am-Rho's confidence had deserted him.

In the end it had been Dron who had struck the stone from its pedestal, Dron who had smashed the seed of the Father into lifeless pebbles, Dron who had Am-Rho bound and stripped and humiliated.

And now he was helpless in the face of his people, helpless to stop Dron from renouncing the Father.

That was when he swore his great oath -- the oath that was to mould his destiny. He felt the last remnants of the Father's power surge in him as he swore revenge on these people who had renounced their true creator. He swore it in the name of the Father, and as he called his rage to the sky he saw Dron tremble before him, shrinking back as if ready to flee.

But the sky stayed clear, and the sun still shone as Am-Rho and his companion were strapped to the trunk of the great tree and cast into the sea, given to the mercy of the Mother. The last thing he ever saw of his homeland was the great pyramid sinking over the horizon, the rays of the sun bathing it in a soft, golden glow.

They drifted, carried by the current and lashed by the sea and the wind.

The first day was the worst -- the sun threatened to boil their brains, and after a while his companion refused to speak to him. He felt the hunger gnawing inside, but there was no way they could eat -- they were bound too tightly to the tree.

He tried to ignore the hunger, to ignore the growing cramps in his stomach, but his rage didn't allow him the calm he needed for distraction, and the blazing sun threatened to sear his eyeballs. The day seemed endless as he tried to will the sun away across the sky, but when night began to creep in he almost wished the sun back.

A wind whipped the sea into small frothy waves, splashing cold spray over their bodies, and the cold began to settle in his bones.

But all thoughts of cold were forgotten when the figure of the Sky Father strode over the horizon to take his place in the heavens. Am-Rho said the old litany, but was dismayed at how little power surged into him. The Father was weak -- that in itself was a mystery -- but Am-Rho vowed to bring him back to his proper place.

A wispy cloud passed over the Father, momentarily obscuring his great belt, sending a fresh chill through Am-Rho, but then it moved on and the Father blazed his glory across the sky. Am-Rho almost felt the old, orgasmic rush, and at that moment he knew that he wasn't going to die, but still he couldn't call up his full power.

The waves and the current carried them on through mountainous seas, northwards and westwards. By day they were burned by the sun and tortured by its glare on the water, but by night they were healed, soothed under the gaze of the Father.

Strangely he had stopped feeling the hunger after the first couple of days. In the heat of the sun he slept, and at night he soared amongst the stars, at one with the Father. And still they drifted as the days turned into weeks and they grew ever weaker.

And then, one day amongst the countless others, they heard a new noise -- the surging of waves against rocks. He didn't have time to tense his muscles before they were buffeted and battered by heavy surf.

The tree to which they were strapped overturned and he breathed in a gulp of salt water, choking and spluttering before it once more righted itself. They were dashed, again and again, against hard, unyielding, rocks before being finally thrown onto a gravelly shore.

Even then their ordeal wasn't over -- a large wave broke over them, threatening to pull them back into the raging sea, back into the hungry rocks.

Suddenly there was a counter pull, pulling against the waves. Am-Rho looked up into the wide, staring eyes of his rescuers.

There were four of them -- four scantily clad savages, their fur coverings reminding Am-Rho of the slaves who had worked around them in the great palace.

They were small, seemingly frail creatures, but their strength was evident as they pulled the trunk up the beach, away from the sucking tide.

One of them spoke to Am-Rho, a soft lilting sound that was almost a song, but it was a language he had never heard. He tried to focus on the pictures in the man's mind, but he didn't have the energy for the old ways.

He was untied, and helped to his feet.

It was only then that he looked at his companion -- the woman who had stood beside him, who had refused to follow the soft, seductive call of the Mother. He felt a tugging in his heart at the sight -- her limbs chafed and red from the bonds, her skin burnt almost black by the sun. He took a step towards her and his legs gave way beneath him. Blackness came and took him as he fell to the ground.

When he came round he was lying on his back, staring through a patchy roof of dried leaves at the stars beyond. He felt stronger, and said a silent prayer to the Father, then gasped as the power flooded through him.

'You feel it too?' a voice to his left said, and he turned into the arms of his companion. Her eyes blazed blue in the dim light in the hut.

'The Father's seed is here. He has sent us a sign.'

He felt exultant. They had survived the sea, and the Father was still with them. He tried to sit up, but even that simple action was too much for him, and his heart thudded wildly against his ribs. He lay back, gasping.

'We must grow strong,' he gasped, and his companion nodded assent. 'The time of the great rite is growing near. If we are strong then the Father will reward us.'

He heard a noise at the entrance to the hut, and went quiet. A female came in and placed two overcooked fish at his side before leaving, without saying a word.

His companion spoke first.

'They have no Gods -- can you feel it -- there is no power among them.'

He nodded, just once, but didn't reply -- the smell of the cooked fish was making him salivate. They fell on the food, tearing at it like animals, and when there were only bones left they slept once more, wrapped tight in each other's arms, just like in the old days.

He dreamed, of fiery revenge.

It was two months before they fully regained their strength -- two months in which they lived the simple lives of the natives. There was little to do except fish, eat and sleep.

They found that they were on an island, an island which they could easily walk round in a day. The only people were the small tribe of natives who had saved them, but there was other life. At least one great bear roamed the woods on top of the cliffs -- a fearsome creature some eight feet tall whose roar split the night -- and there were several smaller but equally fearsome cat like creatures, whose ferocity even frightened Am-Rho.

And amongst all this sat the Father's seed, the stone from the heavens. Am-Rho had pinpointed its position, but he hadn't approached it yet -- he still didn't have the necessary strength, and the stars were not yet right.

Then one night as the stars wheeled into position and he readied himself for the rite, the Father sent him another sign -- the cry of a new born child in a native's hut. It was the work of seconds to take the baby from its mother, and they reached the top of the cliff before they heard the screams of discovery from the village below them.

He carried the baby in the crook of one arm, sending calm pictures into its confused, kaleidoscope mind, and it didn't cry, didn't give them away. It was too late for that anyway -- the villagers would never attempt to follow them in the dark.

The Father blazed in the sky as they approached the stone, which was already flaring blue in the moonlight, a blue brilliance which almost scorched their eyes as they approached.

Am-Rho felt the old power course through him, heating his very bones until he too felt as if he glowed like a star. He held the child above his head as he began the great rite -- the calling of the Father.

A wind came, as if from nowhere, sending his hair flying in a sheet behind him, and the stars grew in his eyes until all he saw was the blue coldness of the Father.

The child began to burn, a harsh cold fire which consumed it in seconds, its life taken in one searing burst. And as it went Am-Rho called on the power to help him, to fulfil his oath.

And the Father sent him the old strength. It ran through him, and he felt the burning as his old body was renewed in the strength of the Father, felt something shift inside him as the Father entered him and he almost cried out in the ecstasy of the moment.

Something came into the clearing, something old beyond time, something which felt like the very essence of the wind itself. Am-Rho focused it, welding it to his desire, sending it gleefully out over the sea.

As it went the sea rose to go with it in a towering column of water that rose, and rose again into a great wall, a wall of death that sped away to the horizon.

Am-Rho saw the pictures in his head -- the people, softened and bewitched by the Mother, cowering as the water broke over their city, crashing into the great pyramid, sending it down into the sea, crushing the people into bloody pulp as the water washed over the remains of his once proud city. He stood by the stone and cried his joy to the skies as Atlantii sunk forever beneath the waves.

5
Dick

Dick stood at the door and watched Duncan's dinghy until it rounded the headland and passed out of sight.

'Lucky bastard,' he muttered to no one in particular.

He always envied the scientist for his seeming freedom, his boyish good looks and his unassuming ease with women. Duncan always seemed happy in mixed company, capable of making small talk on a wide variety of topics. He even had the knack of not allowing his eyes to glaze over at the wrong moment.

When it came to the female of the species Dick was turned into a blithering idiot -- a stammering, red-faced buffoon who was all elbows and knees, capable only of giggling inanely and asking stupid questions.

'Poise -- that's what I need,' he whispered to himself. He hoped the new correspondence course would help.

"Self belief and how to achieve it. A series of twenty cassettes which will change your life forever." That's what the blurb said anyway. It arrived yesterday, in a plain brown envelope, making Dick feel slightly furtive, as if he'd been caught taking a glossy man's magazine from the top shelf in a newsagents.

Of course Old Tom laughed.

'If you dinnae believe in yourself at your age then you never will,' he had said through his chuckles. 'Best to put it away and forget about it -- you don't need all this nonsense -- be yourself man -- you cannae be anybody else.'

But he knew the old man was wrong -- he had spent the best part of his life being someone else. Inside he felt shy and awkward, but by treating life as an act he could get the necessary distance which allowed him to survive. But it was a struggle, which was why he hoped that the tapes would work. Especially now, with the students on the island.

A smile came to his face as he thought of Sandra. She had taken to him right from the first.

'You're got an innocence and naivety that I like' she had said after spending a couple of hours drinking with him. 'Plus the fact that you're as cute as hell.'

He had reddened at that, a blush which started at his neck and quickly spread all over his face.

She had laughed loudly, showing a perfect set of teeth, before giving him a quick kiss on the cheek.

Since then they had sought each other out every time they were in the bar. They couldn't really be said to be "going steady", but things were moving along very nicely and he looked forward to the weeks ahead with mounting anticipation.

He came back to reality with a start when Tom hit him on the shoulder and waved a coarse hand in front of his eyes.

'Hello. Is there anybody in?'

When Dick didn't reply the older man went into his usual tirade. Dick was getting used to it -- the old man liked to get the chores out of the way early on in the day, and today was going to be no exception.

'Are you going to stand there all day?' Tom said, 'There's the generator to check and the mirrors to clean. And that lobster pot needs to be brought in sometime. And...'

Dick smiled at the old man but only got a scowl in reply. He tried to break the ice but even as he spoke he knew that the old man was too keyed up.

'OK. I get the message. Christ, you're worse than an old woman sometimes.'

As he'd thought, Tom wasn't taking the bait. He merely grunted and pushed past Dick, heading for the kitchen again. Dick made a face behind the old man's back, wiggling his fingers at his ears, and sighed loudly and theatrically.

'I'll do the lobster pot first,' he shouted, but got no reply. 'Talking to myself again,' he muttered. 'I always knew that's what it would come to.'

He hoped the old man wasn't going to be difficult again. Last night he had given in, having seen that Tom was becoming more and more agitated, but he didn't intend for it to happen a second time. He didn't want to have an argument -- not with someone he had to live with day in, day out.

As he headed for the harbour a fine mist was creeping down the island chain, shrouding the cliffs in a thick grey sheet. He groaned -- it had been the onset of the mist which set Tom off last night -- that and the noises.

Dick hadn't heard anything other than the barking of seals, but Tom had thought otherwise.

'Seals dinnae talk to each other,' was all the older man would say before locking everything up tight for the night. Tom had made a big point of closing all the shutters, even though there had been no storm warnings and the night was as still as it had ever been. He had even locked the door at the top of the light, the one which only led out on to the walkway.

After that they'd sat facing each other across the table drinking terrible coffee and trying hard to ignore each other. Neither had spoken until they made their way to bed. And all the time Dick had the impression that Tom was listening for something.

And this morning hadn't been much better. Old Tom was definitely scared of something, but he wasn't giving anything away.

'Jist stay away frae the mist, and everything will be hunky dory.'

That was all the old man would say on the matter. Christ, it was like living in one of those crap horror movies -- the ones where the old guy goes round spouting doom and gloom, just before the badly animated monsters came and got him.

There was nothing else to do. Dick was just going to wait it out -- after all, where else was there to go?

He shook himself out of his reverie.

'Places to go and people to see,' he muttered to himself.

Fetching in the lobster pots was one of the highlights of Dick's day -- it got him away from the lighthouse for a bit and gave him a chance for some time alone.

And then there was the wildlife. Wildlife was not something you saw a lot of in Glasgow -- not if you didn't count the drunks on Saturday nights anyway. No, the wildlife was definitely one of the big bonuses of the job.

He'd even taken to sharing Old Tom's interest in bird watching, something he'd previously associated with strange nervous chaps in anoraks and sensible shoes. He could identify over thirty different species of sea birds, and took great delight at watching the different feeding habits of the birds.

And it wasn't just the birds. Most days he saw seals, and on one famous occasion he'd almost been frightened out of his wits when the sleek black fin of a killer whale surfaced only ten yards from his dinghy. He'd been a nervous wreck as he headed back to the lighthouse, hands shaking like an old man's, and without the lobster pot.

Tom had laughed when Dick got back to the harbour.

'That's just Old Blackie -- he's been coming around here for years. You don't have anything to worry about from him -- it's only the salmon that he's after.

Since that day he'd seen the Orca six times, each time marvelling at its sleek power and its easy grace as it slid through the water, imperious and supremely confident in its power. Dick envied it. Maybe today he'd get lucky and see it again.

The sun still shone on the harbour and Dick said a silent prayer for good weather as he untied the rubber dinghy -- there was nothing worse than trying to manhandle a lobster pot when there was a heavy swell on and the rain crept down the back of your neck.

He was about to jump into the dinghy when he noticed that it was lying too low in the water. When he lightly put a foot on its surface it sent out a froth of air before slowly sinking to the bottom, still farting out bubbles. As it sank tatters of rubber streamed out from the side as if a knife had been taken to it.

'Now who the hell would do a stupid thing like that?' he said out loud. He turned back to shout for Tom then realised that the old man had gone inside. Sighing, he went down the steps, having to put both feet in the water before he could reach the tattered remnants of the dinghy.

When he pulled the heavy black rubber out of the water he saw the outboard motor lying on its side in four feet of water.

'Bugger that for a lark,' he muttered. 'If the old man wants it he can get it himself.'

It was only when he dragged the torn rubber out of the water that he noticed that the cuts weren't clean. The edges were serrated, as if someone had taken a blunt saw to them. Or teeth. A sudden chill ran through him and he turned away from the sea towards the sun.

That's when he saw her.

She stood on the cliff above the lighthouse, swaying from side to side, dangerously close to the edge. Even from a distance he saw the red splash across her white shirt. For a split second he thought it might be Sandra, come to brighten up his day, but this girl was bigger -- taller and stockier.

He knew it had to be of the students, but he had no idea which one -- it was impossible to tell from this distance.

He shouted -- nonsense words, but she didn't hear, seemingly lost in a daydream.

'Drugs,' was Dick's first thought. 'I should have known. Bloody students -- all those brains and still not an ounce of common sense between them'

He didn't have time to think further. She moved closer to the cliff edge, looking ready to jump, and that's when Dick started to run.

He almost didn't make it.

She was within a foot of the edge and starting to fall when Dick reached the top of the steps. Somehow he managed to get his body between her and the drop.

He had a bad moment when he thought that they were both going over and then she fainted, a dead weight in his arms. The sudden weight forced his knees to buckle and he staggered precariously before regaining his balance.

His vision swam and he almost overbalanced again before he forced himself to his feet, being careful to edge himself away from the edge -- he'd seen enough pieces of this cliff tumble into the sea to know how precarious his position was. He managed to get her upright, trying not to notice the weight of her breasts against his hand and cradled her upper body in his arms.

The coppery smell of blood was thick and cloying and it seeped into his jumper as he lifted her across his shoulder in a firearm's lift. Luckily she wasn't as heavy as she looked -- he didn't think he would be able to carry a heavier body down the flight of steps.

He shouted for Tom, a loud shout, but the body over his shoulder didn't move. He wondered if she was dead, but didn't have time to stop and check. He had to be careful on the steps and his knees were close to buckling before Tom finally emerged from the lighthouse. The old man's mouth fell open in an astonished gape.

'Come on then you old bugger,' Dick shouted. 'Are you going to give me a hand or are you just trying to catch flies?'

Tom met him halfway and together they managed to get her into the kitchen, laying her down gently onto a chair.

Tom took over -- he was the one with the first aid certificate. Dick was happy to leave him to it -- the sight of blood always made him queasy. He fetched and carried -- hot water, sponge, brandy. Blood had soaked into the back of Tom's favourite chair and he guessed that the old man would be fussing about it later, but for now he was all efficiency. Dick marvelled at the gentleness of his actions as he cleaned the girl up.

All the time Tom muttered to himself.

'Damn fools. Meddling where they shouldnae. These people can never leave things alone -- always poking their noses into places where they've no business. Ghouls and grave robbers the lot o' them. I said there would be trouble. And here it is.'

He kept on in this vein while he cleaned the girl up. The wound wasn't too deep; most of the blood had come from a cut on her scalp, a jagged line across the front of the hairline. She would have a bald patch where a clump of hair had been torn away, but otherwise she seemed whole.

She began to wake up when Tom started stitching up the scalp wound -- Dick was surprised she hadn't done so earlier -- there must have been quite a bit of pain. Her eyelids fluttered, at first showing only the whites of her eyes, and Dick had a quick mental image of the eyes opening and there being nothing there, just empty, milky whiteness, but then he saw a hint of blue pupil and he felt able to breathe again. It was only when she opened her eyes that Dick recognised her.

She was one of the newer ones, only having been on the island a couple of days -- they'd turned up on the boat, fifteen fresh faced youngsters on an adventure. He thought her name was Alison -- or was it Anne? Something beginning with A anyway.

He wasn't given a chance to ask her.

As soon as her eyes were fully open she screamed -- a piercing shriek which sent Harry the cat scuttling for shelter under the stove and caused old Tom to stand back, momentarily in shock.

Her head thrashed from side to side, hair whipping wildly across her face, threatening to pull out the new stitch-work. She flailed around with her arms, catching Tom on the side of the head and knocking him off balance.

Dick grabbed her, tight, and held her to his chest, just missing getting a hooked finger in his left eye as he hugged her tighter, forcing her arms to her sides. He murmured soft nonsense words in her ear, trying for calm which he didn't feel, hearing her heart thud wildly against his chest. He hugged tighter still.

The fight went out of her as suddenly as it had come and she slumped against him, sobbing loudly. She looked up into his face and he saw sudden heavy tears gather. Dick had to fight down an urge to smother her face in warm kisses and, reluctantly, released his grip on her.

'There there lassie,' Tom said, in the same tone as he used for the cat. 'You're all right now. Drink this -- it'll make you feel better,' he said, handing her a glass containing a very large measure of brandy. 'And maybe you'd better have one as well Dick' he said. 'I've got a feeling this lassie's got a story to tell.

Dick watched as she took a large slug of the liquor. Her pupils zoomed up to great black orbs as the spirit hit her stomach, and she spluttered, but she managed to keep it down.

Dick pushed her into a chair and went to pour himself a drink, and while he did it, she began to talk, hesitant at first, then with more power as the memory came back.

The men sat silent while her story unfolded.

'It started this morning,' she said, and had to take

a large gulp of her drink. Dick saw her eyes open wide again as it burned its way through her system. She gagged, twice, and he thought she was about to vomit. He started moving forward but she started to talk again.

'I woke up about seven o'clock. I had too much to drink in the pub last night, and I had a terrible hangover. The rest were already making breakfast but I couldn't face it -- not the burnt bacon and runny eggs, not in my fragile condition. Someone asked where John was, but no-one had seen him. That wasn't too unusual -- he often took himself off on rambles, and nobody was too worried. Maybe if we had been we would have been more prepared.'

She was rambling, but neither of the men interrupted her. She would get to the point in her own good time, and if that took a lot of wandering about the subject, then so be it.

'We were all eager to get going,' she continued. 'We breached the mound yesterday and we all wanted to be the first into the tunnel.'

Tom sucked air through his teeth and shook his head, but she didn't seem to notice.

'Old Evans the Professor had to be the first of course -- we all knew that, there was no way he'd relinquish the honour, even although it had been us who had done all the spadework, but each of us hoped that they would be next after him. That early in the morning he was still in his tent though -- he rarely surfaced before eight o'clock, and we were passing the time by wondering who he would pick.'

'We thought about sneaking a look -- of course we did, but we were all afraid of the old buffer -- he had a terrible temper.'

She stopped talking and began to cry -- huge heaving sobs accompanied by large tears which glistened and sparkled as they ran down her cheeks. Dick wanted to lift her up and hug her, but he couldn't bring himself to move.

'Just take your time lassie. We're listening,' Tom said in a soft voice. It was several minutes and two large gulps of brandy before she was ready to continue.

Dick realised that something serious must have happened -- that he should already be on his way to help, but he couldn't drag himself away.

'The mist was already coming down when the Prof got out of his tent,' she said, and there was still a tremor in her voice. Dick noticed that her eyes had taken on a far away stare, and he suspected that she was in shock, but the story had gripped and he had to see it out to the end.

'He didn't have any breakfast -- he was too keen to get going. He chose me to be the one to go with him -- I was so proud, and the rest of them were so jealous. I thought it might be me -- I'd seen the way the old letch looked at me and, I'll admit it, I wasn't beyond a bit of flirting if it led to a better grade at the end of it.'

She started crying again, agonised, heart-wrenching sobs. Dick moved towards her, but stopped by Tom's restraining hand.

'Let her tell her story laddie -- there's time enough for comfort later.'

She wiped her nose on the sleeve of her T-shirt before going on.

'It was eight-thirty when we went in -- I know because I looked at my watch so that I could write some notes.'

'To start with it looked just like any other old burial mound -- you know the scene, all damp sandstone walls and Viking graffiti. But it was at the back, right at the end of the largest chamber, that we found the tunnel.'

'That's what had excited the Prof so much. It had been dug down into the ground and it echoed loudly when you spoke near it. The Prof thought that it might lead to a whole cave system, and he was very excited -- I think that he hoped he would be able to prove a theory he had about the survival of pockets of old civilisations in caves, places where they had been forced into exile by an incoming stronger population.'

She looked up at Dick.

'I'm rambling, aren't I.' Her mouth rose at the corners, a semblance of a smile, but it never reached her eyes as she went on.

'Bones were strewn across the chamber, as if many people had died violent deaths there. I asked the Prof about it but he said that the disturbance took place long after death. He didn't have time to answer questions -- he was very abrupt with me -- but I didn't really mind, I knew he was excited.'

Dick realised that she was still rambling, trying to explain to herself what had happened to her -- he had seen it before when Tom had rescued a man from an overturned yacht. That time the man had talked over the story three times before he could cope with it. This girl was going the same way. He forced himself to pay attention -- he had missed a bit.

'...but there were no steps. It was steep and quite difficult -- our torches weren't that strong. The Prof was getting farther ahead of me all the time -- he didn't seem to bother with slippery rocks, just strode over them, daring them to make him fall.'

'I called after him, but he didn't pay any attention

-- either he couldn't hear me, or his enthusiasm was getting the better of him. I saw the light from his torch as it sprayed against the walls, and I followed it downwards.'

'We went down for a long, long time and we must have been nearly at sea level before I noticed that he had stopped moving. The floor was even slippier underfoot -- the rocks were covered in a thin green slime, and I could taste the salt in the air.'

Dick had never heard anything about caves at the centre of the island. He knew there were several along the coast, and he'd even been inside one with Jim McTaggart during one of their fishing trips, but it hadn't been very big, and it didn't stretch into the centre of the island.

He supposed that the girl and her Professor had managed to get down into one of the sea caves, but who could have built the tunnel? Even old Tom had never mentioned anything like this in any of his stories.

He looked over at Tom, but the old man was as impassive as a rock, one fist cupped underneath his chin, the other curled around a large glass of whisky. His eyes were troubled, and Dick saw the whitening of the knuckles around the glass. He hoped the glass would hold -- one bout of stitch-work was enough for one day.

The room fell deathly quiet as she started talking again.

'The noise I made as I moved echoed around me, like a large crowd of people whispering in the distance and it felt that we were coming out into a larger chamber. I felt a light breeze blow in my hair, and again I tasted the salt in the air.'

'The Prof shouted something to me -- something about hurrying up, and something else about it being the find of the century. I heard from his voice that he was very excited. I was getting closer to him -- probably no more than ten yards away I think. And that's when his light went out. There was no noise, no sound of a scuffle, just sudden darkness.'

Dick saw her pupils dilate as she relived the story. The more he heard, the more he realised that he should be on his way to the dig. *Just one more minute*, he thought, before turning his attention back to the story.

'I was in two minds. A big part of me wanted to run, back up the corridor, back to the light, but I had to make sure that the Prof was all right -- he might have taken a tumble and be lying injured. I've never been too keen of the dark though, and I could image all sorts of things crawling around down there. I really didn't want to, but I moved closer to where the Prof had been, trying to catch sight of him in my torch beam. Then I heard the noise.'

She shuddered, a trembling which passed from her shoulders to her head, and Dick thought she might start crying again. He moved towards her, but was beaten by Harry. The cat jumped into her lap and forced her to stroke its back. The action seemed to calm her and she could continue.

'I only heard it for a short time, but it sounded like something breathing, a deep gurgling breathing. It reminded me of the noise our old dog used to make when she had pneumonia. Whatever it was, it was something big. I called for the Prof, but there was no reply.

'Then it happened again -- the breathing, and this time it was closer. I think I even may have felt the cold breath on my face. I certainly smelled it -- it had the sharp rotting smell of old fish, and it was definitely getting closer -- much closer. I felt like screaming, felt it build inside me, but somehow the silence kept me quiet.

'I didn't stop to think -- I turned and ran. I don't know how I managed to avoid falling on the rocks, but somehow I stayed upright. I think I hit a few walls on my way up, but I'm not really sure -- it's as if it was all a dream.

'I didn't stop until I saw sunlight in front of me -- the entrance to the chamber. I slowed down enough to draw breath and try and compose myself-- I didn't want the others to see me in that state. Even then, it all felt like a dream. I kept expecting to wake up -- either that or to have the Prof appearing like a jack-in-the-box shouting "Fooled you". Now that I was almost outside I felt foolish -- foolish and cowardly. I wasn't brave enough to go back and look for the Prof though -- I couldn't do that alone.'

She stopped and looked over at Tom.

'I don't know if I expect you to believe any of this -- I'm not sure if I believe it myself. But at that point I'd made up my mind to tell the others exactly what happened, and then to get some of them to go down and look for the Prof. I stepped out of the tunnel... and that's when it got me.

'Something grabbed me from behind, by the hair. I felt the roots tear. That's where I got this,' she said, running her hand across her head and wincing as she tugged lightly at the tender patches.

'I was pulled backwards and my head hit a rock. I think I screamed, but then something hit me hard in the back and I fell to the ground. I heard movement at the mouth of the mound -- my fellow students coming to investigate the noise. I tried to scream, tried to warn them, but I was hit again, harder this time. I don't know whether I fainted or whether I was knocked out, but it all went black for a while.

'When I came to I didn't know where I was and it took a while to get myself sorted out. At first I thought I'd gone blind, but when I wiped my hands over my eyes they came away bloody and I could see. I soon wished I was really blind.

'I staggered out into the sunlight, and into a slaughterhouse.'

She stopped talking and began to sob again -- first quietly, then louder, and all the time her hands were frantically stroking the cat which, although it was trying to escape, was held tight in her grasp.

It was Tom who spoke first.

'And what then lass? What happened then?'

She stopped crying long enough to finally let go of the cat which gratefully took itself back under the stove. She looked at Tom for a long time before replying, and terror danced in her eyes. It didn't look like it would be too long before it took hold completely.

'I don't want to talk about it,' she finally said. 'Just take my word for it -- they're all dead. I think I went a little mad then, and I wandered around for what seemed like ages. And then you found me.'

The story had ended too abruptly, leaving too many questions unanswered. Dick was about to confront her when he felt Tom's strong hand in his arm.

'Don't worry lassie,' Tom said. 'We'll get the doctor for you and call the police on the mainland -- we'll let them sort it out.'

She nodded her head, then let it droop forward. Her shoulders shook again and Dick wasn't sure if she was crying or laughing hysterically.

Tom led him out of the kitchen, out into the sunshine which suddenly seemed welcoming. The old man was very disturbed, and there was something else in his eyes, something that looked very much like fear. It was that more than anything else which convinced Dick of the seriousness of their situation. He forced himself to pay attention as the old man addressed him.

'I don't want you bothering her until we can get the lads form the mainland out. Do you understand?'

Dick knew better than to argue with the older man, so he just nodded.

'Good' Tom said. 'And dinnae think about leaving the lighthouse -- I need you here.'

Tom went back into the kitchen, and Dick stood in the sun for a while, letting its warmth drive away the chill in his bones. He knew he should stay -- that the old man was worried -- that the girl needed looking after -- but he couldn't just leave all those people

The girl's story was just too weird, too off-kilter. He had to see for himself. She had obviously been through some trauma, but some of the others might still be alive. He had to find out.

He made sure that Tom was busy, waiting until the old man moved to the radio room before taking the shotgun and some cartridges from the cupboard by the door.

The girl didn't raise her head as Dick moved around the kitchen, and Tom was still on the radio when he left.

When he reached the cliff top above the lighthouse he turned for a last look. The mist had crept closer down the neighbouring islands but didn't seem to be moving very fast.

He hoped that Tom would be all right, but he

didn't plan to be gone for long. He turned his back on the lighthouse and headed for the land-rover which was parked at the top of the path.

He had the keys in his pocket -- he always did. Tom had never learned to drive, and before the land-rover had arrived he used to carry all his provisions across the island on his back. Even now the old man preferred to walk -- something Dick found hard to understand.

'You get to see the whole picture when you walk,' Tom had said, but Dick was none the wiser

Dick did all the driving, but he couldn't really say he enjoyed it. The road was almost straight across the island and was mostly flat until the steep hill down to the harbour. It didn't lend itself to any speed and there was never anyone else to overtake. The vehicle was usually only ever used to pick up provisions or, in extreme emergencies like heavy rain, to take them to the pub. Even that practice had been called to a halt when Dick put the land-rover in a ditch after a particularly heavy session with Jim, the landlord.

He got it started on the second attempt and negotiated the rutted parking area. As he turned to face the road over the island he looked for any sign of movement. The bright orange tents stood out on the skyline almost two miles away but there was no sign of life.

Not for the first time he wondered if he'd done the right thing in coming to the island.

He'd left the city with no regrets. He'd been a barman in a busy city--centre pub, a smoke filled, noisy barn of a place which turned into a steaming hell of bodies, beer and vomit on Saturday nights. He had been looking for a job in the country for several months when he saw the advert for Assistant Keeper.

One short interview later he was on his way.

He'd been given three months by his friends.

'There's no women out there you know -- and no parties. And you'd better watch out for that old man -- solitary confinement does strange things to people.'

That was the general gist of their comments. His mother had been even harsher.

'What do you want to be going away out there for? Some god forsaken lump of rock in the middle of nowhere. What's wrong with Glasgow anyway?'

Answering that question would have taken too long. Not that Glasgow was a bad place -- it was just like any other big city. And that was the problem -- Dick was bored with it.

That had all been over a year ago, and he had mostly enjoyed his time here, especially after the arrival of the students.

That thought brought back his worry about the group, and one young blonde in particular. He pushed the land-rover to the fastest safe speed, and two minutes later pulled to a halt in the middle of the campsite.

At first glance there was no sign of anything untoward, and he gave out a deep sigh -- the girl had been hallucinating, that was all. What harm could have happened here, in broad daylight?

Then he saw the blood.

It looked like someone had splashed buckets of the stuff around the campsite, great red swathes across the grass. He got out of the car, his feet almost sliding away from under him as he stepped in a pool of gore.

He screamed, twice, but there was only the answering cry of a gull as it sped by overhead.

'Fulmar,' he told himself, his mind wandering,

trying to force his attention away from the stinking mess on the ground in front of him. He felt blackness trying to eat its way into his mind, and his legs threatened to give out beneath him.

He closed his eyes, tight, and began to mutter to himself.

'Lapwing, shag, gannet, redshank, eider, puffin, oyster-catcher…'

He went through his whole list, twice, before he felt able to open his eyes again.

There was no sign of any bodies.

He didn't want to look any further, but forced himself to approach the nearest tent, loading the shotgun as he went, wincing at the sudden noise as he shut the gun. He realised that he was creeping, trying hard not to make any noise, bent over into a crouch as he shuffled forward.

'Stupid. Stupid. Stupid' he muttered to himself as he pulled the tent-flap aside, poking the shotgun through in front of him as if it would shield him.

The tent was empty except for a scrunched up sleeping bag and the odour of stale sweat. The sunlight glowed orange through the tent's walls, lending a warm light to the interior. With the barrel of the gun Dick moved the sleeping bag to one side and snorted with disgust when he uncovered a used condom. He let the flap fall back into place as he left the tent.

The rest of the tents were as empty as the first. The only item of note he discovered was a bright red jumper which he remembered as belonging to Sandra.

The thought that the blond student might be in trouble lent urgency to his actions. Reluctantly he realised that he would have to enter the mound.

It dominated the campsite, like a giant upturned

salad bowl. The entrance was on the far side from him and somehow he wasn't keen on a frontal assault. He decided to climb over the top.

He remembered that Tom had pointed the mound out to him on their first journey across the island.

'It's an ancient burial place,' he had said. 'And people should respect the dead -- even the bad ones, and not go digging them up for their own personal gratification. Damn ghouls and grave-robbers. No good will come of it.

That was when he'd first heard about the dig, back in a winter of gales, and it had taken until early summer for anything to happen. That's when the students started to arrive. John Jeffries had been railing against them in the pub, and several of them had almost got into a knock down fight with the old farmer, but there had never been any real trouble.

Until now. Dick didn't believe in ancient curses, but he started to wonder if Tom hadn't been on the right track all along.

The mound proved tougher to conquer than he'd imagined and he had to push himself hard to reach the crest. At the top he stopped to look around.

There was no movement anywhere on the island. To the north he could see the top of the lighthouse peering over the cliff, but Tom wasn't out on the walkway. To the south the pub and outbuildings looked as normal as ever.

The only sign of life was out to sea. Duncan's boat bobbed on the swell. He waved his arms, trying to make himself seen, but he wasn't sure if he'd been noticed.

After a while he stopped -- waving a shotgun at arms length got tiring very quickly. He stood still, listening for any sign of movement but his heart thudded so hard in his chest that it was impossible for him to hear anything apart from the cawing of gulls overhead. He made his way down the slope.

From his vantage point it looked like the blood was concentrated around the entrance, streaked and spread as if something heavy had been dragged through it, and as he got closer the smell hit him, in the sinuses and at the back of his throat. He almost gagged but forced the bile down. If there was a chance that any of them were still alive he had to look.

It was hard to imagine any terror on this island on a bright sunny day, and he had to keep reminding himself that this was real, that something terrible had happened. He thought of pinching himself, but he knew that this was real, more real than any dream he'd ever had.

He found it easier to believe when he reached the entrance. It wasn't just blood which pooled there -- there were larger pieces, looking like slabs of raw steak, already covered by thick black swarms of flies. He gagged again and his legs threatened to take him backwards. Then he remembered Sandra and got himself going forward again. His movement disturbed the flies which rose lazily from their feast. He tried not to look too closely as he threaded his way past them.

The entrance was black and uninviting and he cursed himself for not bringing a torch, but the sun was at the right angle to light his way into the chamber.

The smell got worse, then worse still. Dick realised that he was shaking, and despite the heat of the day a cold chill had settled in his bones. He double checked that the gun was loaded as he peered through the gloom.

The first chamber of the mound was not quite empty. At first he didn't want to look too closely at the bones strewn there, but then he realised that these were the old bones the girl had mentioned. He ignored them as he made his way across the chamber.

There was a noise, a slight rustling, just at the edge of his hearing, and he stopped, trying not to breathe, but the noise wasn't repeated.

He thought about calling out, but something about the stir of the echoes as he moved stopped him. The place reeked of age and the sandstone blocks ran damp and sweaty -- his palms felt cold and greasy where he had ran them across the walls.

The entrance to the second chamber was in shadow. He tried to peer through the blackness, but soon realised that he would have to move closer. He had to force his legs to move -- his brain sent the signals but his limbs were not receiving. Finally he managed to shuffle closer.

Dick didn't think himself as brave, but on the other hand he never knowingly backed away from any confrontation when he felt he was in the right. But now he was being tested. All of his instincts told him to flee, and only the thought of saving someone from further harm kept him moving forward.

He held the shotgun out in front as he approached the entrance, trying to ignore the strain on his arm muscles.

His eyes were getting accustomed to the gloom and he could make out some details of the chamber beyond. At first he didn't believe what he saw, then, when he did, he couldn't stop the gorge rising.

He backed out, fast, heading for the sunlight and sanity, and only just made it before the nausea hit him and he lost his breakfast in one expulsion. Several flies found this new delicacy too hard to resist, and this served to bring on another bout of retching which forced Dick to his knees with its ferocity.

He stayed there a long time, his entire body in spasm until he felt he was bringing up the lining of his stomach. Then, mercifully, he began to calm, began to get it under control. Shakily, he pushed himself to his feet.

It hadn't been the smell that did it, although God knows that had been bad enough -- it had been the stares. Ten bodies, arranged in formation around the walls, gazing at him, all with the same blank, eyeless stares and all with the same raw and bloody holes in their chests.

It looked like their hearts had been torn out.

When he recovered he turned and looked back into the mound. Only blackness faced him and he couldn't bring himself to return. He stood looking at it for long seconds -- the cold shiver was back again. There was a noise -- a shuffling in the blackness.

He lifted the shotgun to his shoulder and sighted along its length.

'OK you bastard,' he muttered, with more bravery than he actually felt. 'Come on out. I'm ready for you.'

The noise got louder, and Dick heard the watery gurgle of something breathing heavily. He still couldn't see anything and he had the feeling that it was hiding just out of sight.

'I can hear you. I've got a gun, so just come out slowly.' His hands trembled... the sight shook in front of him. He wasn't going to be able to hold the gun upright for much longer.

The noise stopped, and almost at the same time

the wind dropped. Suddenly Dick was in a pocket of stillness; time had stopped, waiting for something to kick-start it into action again. His hand tightened on the trigger, then tightened some more. His hands began to shake violently. He made his decision -- he pulled the trigger.

The shot rang loud in his ears as he turned and ran for the car, throwing himself into the driver's seat and dropping the gun beside him. He had a bad moment when he couldn't find the keys, but then his fingers touched metal and he had them. The wheels spun on the grass as he gunned the engine, and he was off and away. He didn't look in the rear view mirror -- he was afraid at what he might see.

Later he didn't remember anything about that drive, just the cold empty stares of the bodies around the wall of the chamber and the hot heavy stench of congealing blood.

Tom was waiting for him at the top of the cliffs as he pulled up in the parking bay.

'You stupid wee bastard -- you could have got yourself killed,' he said as Dick got out of the car. And then, in a quieter voice, 'Did you see anything?'

Dick told his story, including his flight from the sound. Tom didn't seem surprised by any of it.

'We're going to need more than just the polis to sort this one out,' he said, speaking more to himself than to Dick. 'But I suppose we'd better wait for them to get here -- nobody will believe this if they don't see it for themselves.'

As they headed for the steps Dick noticed that the mist was creeping across the sea towards the island. He pointed it out to Tom, and the older man immediately became agitated, grabbing Dick by the arm and almost frog-marching him down to the lighthouse.

'They'll be here before dark -- there's some sort of panic with a lost yacht down Islay way and the helicopter wont be back till later. They're going to bring the doctor with them -- I think we should hole up till then.'

Dick wasn't so sure.

'What about the pub -- shouldn't we make sure that they're OK?'

Tom shook his head, marching the younger man into the kitchen.

'They're just going to have to look after themselves -- we cannae risk it. You can always radio them if you're that worried.'

The old man double locked the door and went through the same ritual as the previous night, battening down the shutters, as if preparing for a heavy storm although the sun was still beating down outside.

Tom turned to Dick, and this time the fear showed fully in his face.

'The lassie's sleeping in your bed -- it'll be best if we leave her there -- she's had enough shocks for one day. Just let me see to the upstairs windows, then I'd better tell you the story.'

While the old man was away Dick tried to reach the pub on the radio, but all he got was the hiss and crackle of static on the line. He didn't know whether to be worried or not -- Jim and his family were often out and about during the day. They might just be busy, not answering. Somehow it didn't make him feel a lot better.

When he got back to the kitchen Dick headed for the whisky bottle. He had already drunk more than he was used to with the brandy earlier, but he had a feeling that he would need it.

When Tom returned he also helped himself to a large whisky before he sat in the chair. Dick settled back and readied himself for a long stint. Tom didn't talk much, but when he told a story he always took the long way round.

The older man took a deep sip of whisky before starting. 'I heard this from old Jim, the keeper here before me. He said he'd had it from his father, and his father before him.'

Tom stopped, his head cocked to one side, his face pale.

'Did you hear anything?' he whispered.

Dick shook his head, but it was a long moment before Tom continued.

'The mound has been a source of legends for many years, back as far as memory goes, and it has always been regarded as cursed. The Romans left this part of the country alone -- too cold for them probably -- and there is no other record of any activity until the time of Columba.

'You probably know that there are lots of stories about him -- he was a great smiter of heathens. Popular legend has painted him as a saint, but around these parts you'll get a different story.'

'The stories say that he was a sorcerer -- a very powerful one, who saw which way the wind was blowing and converted to Christianity. The church realised that he had the potential to persuade many simple people over to their side, so they sent him over here to convert the pagans.'

'He first landed on Iona, but it wasn't long before he heard about the cursed island. He came here with about twenty of his followers, and as soon as he saw the mound he knew that there was great power there, and decided to set up a demonstration. He broke open the mound and called out the creatures.'

Tom stopped talking, and seemed to be listening for something.

'Is that it?' Dick asked, but Tom motioned for him to be quiet before continuing.

'No, that's not it -- but it'll have to wait -- the chopper's coming.'

It was only then that Dick heard the throbbing of the approaching engine.

It took Dick's eyes several seconds to adjust to the light when Tom opened the door, and even then he thought that there was still something wrong before he realised that the mist was coming in, fast.

He followed Tom up the steps to the open space beside the land-rover and waited for the chopper to land. They had to turn their backs against the down-draught, and when they turned back two people were getting out running towards them, bent over to avoid the blades. Dick recognised them both -- the policeman, Angus McLean and the doctor, Richard Franks. They were closely followed by the pilot, Derek Brown. A minute later they were crowded into the small kitchen.

Tom seemed more at ease now that more people were around, but he still locked the door behind them and the shutters stayed shut. The doctor went to see to the girl while Tom dispensed more whisky and Dick re-told his story.

The policeman took notes. He made Dick stop several times to go over points of detail and by the end Dick felt that he had told the story three times over.

The doctor returned just as Dick was finishing.

'She's got concussion -- we'd better get her to the hospital. Are you ready to go back up again Derek?

You haven't been drinking too much whisky?'

Derek laughed. 'It'll take more than a wee drop of the cratur to stop me,' he said. 'But I think Angus needs to stick around for a bit longer.'

The policeman looked thoughtful. 'That's all right Derek. You take the Doc back, then come back for me. I need to take a look at the mound.'

The pilot shrugged and moved to help the doctor with the girl. A few minutes later they heard the throbbing of the engine and the three of them stood silent until the sound faded in the distance

Dick's blood ran cold as the policeman turned to him. 'Will you take me over there Dick?'

He turned to Tom, waiting for the old man to talk the policeman out of it, but the old man shook his head.

'I told you Dick -- he won't believe it till he's seen it himself. You'd better take him. But remember to shout when you come back -- I'm keeping the door locked and I won't be opening it to just anybody.'

The policeman's eyebrows rose at that, and rose even further when Dick picked up the shotgun from beside the door.

'You won't need that laddie,' he said, but Dick wasn't to be denied.

'I think I will. And I think you'll be convinced when we get there. Are we going to get moving, or are you going to stand there all day drinking the old man's whisky.'

At the last moment before they left Dick remembered how dark the chamber had been. He collected two flashlights from the equipment cupboard and handed one to the policeman.

Tom closed the door behind them as they left and Dick heard the iron bolt being drawn across on the other side.

The policeman didn't say a word as they made their way to the land-rover and Dick noticed that the older man had difficulty climbing the stairs. By the time they reached the car he was wheezing badly.

'Bloody fog' Angus muttered. 'It always goes straight to my chest.' Dick thought it might be something more than that -- something to do with the very obvious excess weight the other man was carrying. He kept his mouth shut -- he had learned as a teenager that contradicting policeman was never a good idea.

They drove across the island in silence.

'Do you believe the old man's stories?' Angus asked, just before they pulled up at the campsite.

Dick must have looked shocked, and said nothing as the policeman continued.

'Oh aye -- I've heard them before -- it's one of old Tom's favourites when he's in his cups. Everybody hereabouts must have heard it at one time or the other. I never expected to come out here to investigate it though.'

Dick thought that Angus looked haggard, and then he recognised what it was -- it was fear. Small beads of sweat had formed on his brow and his eyes had a wild, harried look. As they left the car he offered the shotgun to the policeman.

'Not for me laddie,' Angus said. 'I've been on the force for nineteen years and never needed anything more than my fists. Now show me where you found the bodies.'

It was only then that Dick understood -- the policeman didn't believe his story. His experience was of rounding up drunks on a Saturday night and keeping an eye on the holiday homes -- he just wasn't prepared for anything of this magnitude.

He followed the policeman to the mound, and got a small satisfaction from seeing the shock on the man's face when he spotted the blood, and another at the opening in the mound when the smell hit them.

'It gets worse inside,' Dick cried, bringing a nauseous expression to his companion's face.

'I suppose that I'd better go first,' the policeman said.

'Aye. I suppose you'd better,' Dick replied. He had no desire to re-enter the mound, but he followed the older man inside after checking that the gun was loaded.

The smell was worse than he remembered and as they approached the chamber where the bodies lay he heard the deep droning buzz of flies.

He stepped aside and motioned the policeman forward.

'They're in there. I don't think I can look at them again.'

He heard the gasp as Angus found the bodies, then the retching as the policeman's whisky made a reappearance . There was a sudden silence, then he heard a hoarse whisper from the chamber.

'Get in here laddie,' the voice said, and it had a tone that brooked no argument. Dick made his way into the chamber trying to keep his torch beam away from the bodies, but not quite able to avert his gaze altogether. The policeman was at the far wall, and as Dick got closer he saw the opening in the wall behind him.

'Look here,' Angus said, pointing his torch to the floor. A trail of gore led into the opening and off into the blackness beyond.

'Are you game for it?'

It took Dick several seconds to realise what was meant, and by then it was too late -- the policeman had already gone through. Dick thought he wasn't going to be able to follow, but his legs surprised him by taking him forward.

He tried not to think of the girl's story as he followed the light downwards.

It wasn't too steep at first, and the wetness was confined to the walls, but by the time they had gone ten yards the floor became slippery underfoot and Dick had to slow down to avoid losing his balance.

He was being so careful that he almost didn't notice that Angus had stopped.

'Hush up now laddie,' the policeman whispered. 'I think I heard something up ahead -- and I don't think it's friendly.'

They switched off their torches and stood, silent in the dark. Dick heard the laboured breathing of the policeman beside him, but gradually he became fully aware of something he had been hearing for some time -- the far off sound of chanting.

'So what now?' he whispered, and immediately regretted it as his voice echoed around the corridor.

'We go on,' the policeman replied, switching on his torch, taking care to keep it pointed to the floor. Dick had one last look backwards, at the dim, far off gloom of the entrance before he followed.

The chanting got louder, then louder still. Dick had a feeling that they were getting to the place where the girl said it opened out. His hands started to shake again and he had to grip the shotgun tightly to stop it falling.

And then it happened.

He looked up to see how far the policeman had

got ahead and he forgot to watch his footing. He slipped, his left foot sliding from under him, forcing him to throw his hands out for balance, forgetting that he carried the shotgun.

The metal barrel hit rock and the ringing crack sounded too loud in his ears. The chanting stopped, cut off as quickly as a needle lifted off vinyl. The only sound was the shuffling of his feet as he tried to regain balance.

He looked up to see the policeman coming towards him.

'Are you all right laddie?' the policeman asked. And Dick nodded, blinking at the sudden light as the torch was shone in his face. There was a new sound, a wet slap on rock, and the men froze into silence but it wasn't repeated.

'I vote that we get out of here,' Dick said, and this time it was Angus who nodded.

'Aye,' he replied. 'I don't think we're properly equipped for this.'

The policeman took Dick by the arm. 'Come on,' he said. 'Let's go.'

He had only taken one step when their worst nightmares came out of the darkness... dark shadows that were quick and silent. It was only when they got close that Dick heard the gurgling of their breathing.

He swung round, the shotgun pointing along the torch beam, and was almost unable to pull the trigger -- transfixed by the sight.

There were two of them -- side by side in the corridor. Time seemed to slow for Dick and he saw everything as clearly as if he had stopped the picture with a remote control.

They were huge -- seemingly filling all available space in the corridor. Their eyes glowed silver in the torchlight, almost all pupil with only the smallest, faintest sign of an iris.

Dick raised the gun, feeling as if he fought through a wall of treacle. The nearer of the creatures reached for him and he saw the talons, black and curved as they came closer. His finger tightened on the trigger.

The creature smiled, showing a mouthful of stained, pointed teeth and bringing with it the foul odour of rotting fish. A taloned hand reached out towards the shotgun barrel, just as Dick pulled the trigger.

Its head burst in an explosion of brain and bone and hot spots of blood peppered on Dick's face and arms. The force of the blast knocked him backwards, stumbling into Angus and almost taking them both to the ground. His ears rang and he could only dimly hear that Angus was screaming.

Frantically he swung his torch around, trying to find the second creature, but there was only the steaming body on the floor and the spreading smell of death.

Angus grabbed him hard by the arm and started dragging him away, up towards sanity. It took some time -- Dick went backwards the whole way, keeping his torch trained on the corridor, his finger tight on the trigger, ready to fire at the slightest provocation.

He almost fell twice, but Angus steadied him. The older man's breathing had become very strained but he couldn't afford to turn around to check on him.

Eventually he realised that there was more light around them. He was grabbed from behind and pulled into the outer chamber. He never thought that he could be pleased to see those bodies again, but his body lost some of its tenseness as he backed out of the mound.

It was a surprise to find that the sun was still shining. He guessed from its position that they'd been in the mound for less than an hour -- it had felt like days. It was only when they had backed away as far as the car that he felt able to look at Angus.

The policeman was in trouble. His face was pale. No -- not just pale, it was white. His right hand grasped the top of his left arm and he doubled over in pain.

He moved to help, but the policeman waved him away towards the car.

'I'll be all right -- dinnae worry about me laddie. Just get me back to the radio -- we need to get some help out here.'

Dick got into the car, then had to get out again to help the policeman. He managed to manhandle him into the passenger seat and he handed him the shotgun before closing the door.

He had one last look at the mound before getting into the car, but it merely sat, silent and calm as it had been on every day before.

He started the car and it was only when he turned north that he noticed the fog. It sat in a thick grey blanket across the whole north end of the island.

6

Sam

He lay on the cold farmhouse floor, guarding the arm, while the room got slowly darker and colder. He knew there was something wrong. Something bad had happened to the master.

He whimpered softly -- when bad things happened to the master then Sam was usually the one to suffer. He looked over to the wall and the leather belt which hung there.

The belt always hurt, was always used for "Stupid Fucking Dog". That's what Sam was when the master hit him, that's what the master called him. Sometimes Sam knew why he was being hurt -- like the time when he'd been left in the house too long and had made the smelling stuff all over the floor -- and not on the hard floor at that, but on the soft floor -- the one which was made out of the same stuff as the master's clothes.

But other times, especially when the master had been "down the pub", then he was hit for no reason, and at those times he didn't like the master at all. He looked over at the belt on the wall and whimpered again.

He was all right for a while -- the hurting thing was still on its hook. He wondered when the master would come back -- he was getting hungry. The smell of the meat he guarded made him salivate but he knew he couldn't eat it -- it would be bad. He didn't know why, but he knew. He'd already licked the blood from the torn end, and that hadn't tasted right at all -- it had tasted too much of the master.

The door through to the kitchen was open, and that made Sam whimper again. The master never left the door open -- not when it got dark. The master didn't like the wind which came under the door.

Maybe the master was with the sheep. Sam never knew why the man cared so much for the creatures -- they were stupid. They didn't know how to play and they didn't run. Even Sam, who knew he was getting old, even Sam was faster than those dumb things.

He was about to leave to find the master when he smelt it again, the bad smell he had noticed in the barn.

The old dog cowered lower to the ground, dragging itself backwards under the table. The smell got stronger, then he heard it, the noise in the barn.

Something heavy was being dragged along the floor of the barn, but the dog didn't move. He was being quiet, he was good at that, the man had made sure of it. But he couldn't prevent a small whimper escaping as a huge dark shape passed in front of the kitchen door.

Sam couldn't wait any longer. He bounded to his feet and sped out of the door. A big thing, smelling of fish, made a lunge at him, but Sam felt like a young dog again as he ran over the fields to fetch his master.

7

3,700 Years Before

For centuries Am-Rho and his people lived on the island, secure in the power of the Father. They had been fruitful years, and the clan grew and prospered.

It had been easy to sway the villagers in his favour -- the power was visible in him, and he was treated as a demigod, an emissary of the Great One. The Father had worshippers once more, and his power grew with the growth of the clan.

He knew that there were tribes on the other islands, for Am-Rho's people occasionally captured some of the unwary, but he had no desire to leave this place -- the Father was strong here, and the food was plentiful. For a while he was content, and the Father gave them longevity.

And so it went until the coming of the new people -- the farmers, the stone builders, with their axes and their cattle and their fire. And they brought the Mother with them.

Am-Rho had seen them coming, their small boats cleaving easily through the water. And although the sun was high in the sky he felt a cold chill run through him -- he recognised the power of the Mother, even at this distance.

He rallied his people on the island's beach, waiting for the invaders, but already he felt their strength. They sang as they rowed, and their voices carried clear and strong across the water.

They met them in the surf, and the battle was fierce and bloody. The newcomers sang, even as they died, and they washed off the boats in a surging mass, hurling themselves into the waiting ranks of Am-Rho's people.

He tried to call up the old power, but now, at the height of the day, the Father was weakened, and the horde from the boasts kept coming on, driving Am-Rho and his people back, out of the surf, and back onto the beach.

The sand soon ran red with blood, and Am-Rho had to fight for his life as his people were overrun. They were driven even further back, back against the cliffs until they had no option but to climb.

He regrouped his people around the sky stone, dismayed at how few of them were left. He looked over at his companion, and felt a surge of pride at her haughty grandeur; her back straight and her head high despite a gaping wound in her side.

And still the invaders came on, their song ringing through the forest.

Am-Rho put his hands on the stone, searching for its power, but there was only the barest flicker of blue through his fingers.

He sent his people down into the ground, down into a network of caverns where they could hide and protect themselves better.

Go now,' he said to his companion, trying to guide her to the entrance to the caves, but she refused.

'For all this time we have been together. If this is

to be the end, we will go there as one.'

Again he felt the sudden burst of pride, but he had no time to dwell on it, for just then the invaders burst out of the forest, and in the space of ten seconds had surrounded them, forming a tight ring around the stone.

Am-Rho noticed with some surprise that the sun was going down -- the fighting had lasted longer than he had thought -- but there was not going to be enough time for the Father to lend him strength. He had to try anyway.

He placed both hands on the stone and screamed, a cry of pure rage. Blue light spluttered between his fingers, and the invaders stepped back, one or two of them making a stabbing motion at him with their fingers.

The stone flared briefly, and he thought that his pleas had been answered, but at that moment the circle of invaders parted and a figure strode towards Am-Rho.

At first he thought he faced an animal -- the great shaggy head of a wolf stared back at him from atop a man's body. But then he saw it for what it was -- no more than an elaborate mask.

He almost laughed. If they believed that this thing would frighten him then they had underestimated him -- even without the power of the Father.

Then the shaman took something out of the folds of his clothing, and Am-Rho had to step back as the stone flared under his hands.

The object in the shaman's hand looked at first sight to be a small, circular rock, but as the man got closer he saw it more clearly and he had to step further back. It was the Mother -- the great whore. A crude representation, but the great, pendulous breasts were visible, as was the swollen, distended belly, the symbol of the fecundity of her spawn.

The sky stone flared -- one last burst, before falling quiet, and Am-Rho was forced to cower beneath the invader's idol.

He tried to look into the shaman's mind, but all he saw was the Mother, and he recoiled before the image.

His companion was made of sterner stuff.

The shaman chanted -- something in a harsh, guttural language, and she laughed at him. Again Am-Rho felt hope. Somehow she had always been able to show more resistance to the Mother than he. But his hope was short lived.

The shaman brought the idol up, and brought it down, and a second later his companion lay at his feet, her blood staining the grass as the life went out of her eyes. A great rage took Am-Rho, and he launched himself at the shaman, screaming.

The man didn't flinch, merely held the idol out before him, and Am-Rho was forced to stop, brought up short in front of him.

The man chanted again, and Am-Rho felt a lassitude in his bones. His legs gave way under him, and he was made to crawl, trying to pull himself away from his tormentor.

The man followed him, chanting all the time, and Am-Rho squealed in pain as the idol was brought down onto his back -- a hot, searing, pain as if a red hot iron had been thrust between his shoulders.

He rolled over, staring into the eyes of the shaman, and he saw no compassion there as the idol was brought up once more. He closed his eyes, waiting for death, waited for long seconds.

There was a wild howl from beside him, and a following one from the shaman. He opened his eyes to see his companion and the invader rolling together in the grass. He made to get up but before he could move the circle of men had moved in. An axe flashed in the red glow of sunset, and the back of his companion's head caved in with a soft, broken sound. Her eyes looked at him one last time, and her lips formed one word before her head fell.

'Go' she said.

He forced himself to move, his rage driving him as he dove for the cave entrance. He almost didn't make it -- the shaman was right behind him. He felt a burning at his left heel as he grazed the idol, and then he fell through blackness.

His landing was hard, knocking the wind out of him, and he expected at any second to be killed under the axes of the invaders, but no one came through the hole after him.

He reached out with his mind, trying to find his companion, but there was only blackness, and a low moan escaped his lips.

Even as the invaders built over the cave entrance, sealing them in with stone and spells, even then he was forming his curse.

Later, among his people, he called on the Father to bear witness -- he would have his revenge on the Mother. No matter how long it took, he would have his revenge.

And from that day on he was known as Calent, which, in the language of his old race, meant "The one whose time will come again."

8

Anne

Anne woke in darkness, her mind playing through a series of scenes.

The first was in the kitchen, in the split second between turning around and her fainting. That scene was etched in her mind like a photograph.

The creature blocks the door, but that is not what catches her attention -- not immediately. Under the creature's left arm, between it and the door jamb, she can see that the trapdoor is open and Meg's head is just visible, just beginning to emerge. Meg's eyes are wide open in terror and Anne follows her line of sight.

Jim is on the floor, and another of the creatures is bent over him, a long taloned hand reaching for his throat. Jim's eyes are open and pleading. He looks straight at her, his left hand outstretched towards the kitchen door.

She shifts her gaze to the creature in the doorway, all this taking place in an instant of time which seems to have stretched forever, allowing her time to memorise every aspect of the creature's face.

It is old. She doesn't know how she knows it, but there is something about its eyes which speaks of age, and strangely, of wisdom. It is the eyes which draw her first, great white saucers of eyes which glow almost silver, the pupils only pinpoints of black in the milky whiteness. But almost as stunning as the eyes is the hair, a huge shimmering halo of blackness surrounding the creature's head, reminding her of a giant imperial lion as the hair writhes like snakes around the massive head.

The creature's mouth is half open and she can see a hint of teeth there, but not quite yet, and she doesn't want that mouth to open fully.

The creature has its right arm extended towards her, and the last thing her mind takes in before the picture is taken away is the talons stretching towards her stomach, stretching towards her baby.

Anne cried in the blackness, cried for a long time, but her mind hadn't finished with her yet -- it chose to furnish her with other pictures, these ones moving, but still feeling as remote as photographs.

The first time she comes up out if the blackness she doesn't know where she is. She is being bounced along in a strange fluid motion, and at first she thinks she may be on a horse, a sensation she can only dimly remember from early childhood, but then she opens her eyes.

She hangs upside down over the back of one of the creatures and she can see the ground moving, impossibly fast, beneath her. Her mouth brushes against thick black hair, and for an instant she flashes back to the smell on Jim after his work on the cesspit. But this smell is even stronger, sharp and pungent, stinging her nostrils. It is the smell of rotting fish and seaweed, a smell of death and corruption.

Suddenly the movement stops, and she is able to move her head. At first she is only trying to put some distance between herself and the smell, but a movement seen from the corner of her eyes distracts her attention and she turns to see that they are beside one of the many small pools on the marshy land in the middle of the island.

Two more of the creatures are only five yards from her, moving away towards the pool and, as she watches, they wade into the water, first to their knees, then to their thighs. They wave to the creature holding Anne, an action which looks more like a salute, before sinking slowly into the black water. The last thing she sees is their hair streaming out behind them as their heads go under, and then it too is gone. The surface of the water has barely been disturbed, and there are no bubbles to mark the creatures' passing.

The creature carrying her begins to move again and Anne's head is bounced, hard against the creature's back. It is only a slight bump, but it brings blackness at the corners of her vision, and she accepts the chance it allows her to fall away once more into a faint.

In the blackness, Anne tried to calm herself, tried to stop her mind from showing her the pictures, but it wasn't quite finished yet -- the worst was still to come.

When next she wakens she is still on the creature's back, but it is moving more slowly. She manages to raise her head, and just avoids catching her jaw on stone as the creature ducks to enter the burial mound. She catches a quick glimpse of orange, one of the student's tents, and begins to shout for help, but her breath is stopped in her throat as she sees the blood.

It lies in great reeking puddles around the entrance to the mound, some of it streaked on the stone around her head. She has to move her head out of the way again as the creature swings around into a second, smaller chamber.

She almost wishes that she was still in the blackness as she sees the bodies. They are ranked against the wall, and all she is able to look at before she shuts her eyes on the scene is the gaping holes in their chests, red holes, some of them pumping slow rivers of blood down across the torsos.

They begin to go down, down into the earth, but she refuses to open her eyes, refuses to countenance any more horrors. There is only the slap of feet on rock and the whisper of echoes. Then, absurdly, the creature carrying her starts to sing, a high tenor, amazingly clear and almost beautiful.

She half recognises the tune, something old and melodic from her past, but she recognises the intent -- it is a lullaby.

Unable to fight the tune's power she feels her eyes go heavy and, rocked by the rolling motion and almost soothed by the echoes she falls into blackness one more time.

She abruptly came back to the present as a blast echoed around her. There was a scurrying in the darkness, as if a crowd had suddenly moved, then it all went quiet again.

Anne tensed herself to shout. Someone was here, someone who might help her, but she had just opened her mouth when a hand was clamped over it, a hand that smelled of rotting fish.

She began to struggle, flailing her arms, but she was grabbed tight around the waist, so tight that she found difficulty drawing breath.

Soon there were voices all around, voices which spoke in a harsh, guttural language, full of hissing and glottal stops, and not a word of it recognisable. The voices were halted by a command, just one word. There was more movement, and the hands that held her fell away.

She started to get her bearings. It was still pitch dark, but from the echoes around her she guessed she was in a chamber no more than ten feet square, and, judging by the thick breathing sounds, she shared it with one of the creatures. She had to fight hard to hold down the screams, but she knew that there would be no help. She was in hell, and there was no going back if she succumbed to its terrors.

She stretched out her arms in the dark, feeling around her, moving gingerly at first, then more confidently when nothing stopped her explorations. She found that she was lying on a thick bed of something soft and wet, something that felt like a rough moss.

A foot from her body her left hand met only air, while her right hit a rock face and came away wet. She licked her fingers and was surprised when she couldn't taste any salt, only the faint, metallic taste of minerals.

She started to explore further with her left hand... when the creature moved, coming closer to her. She stiffened, expecting an attack, and almost screamed when a rough hand caressed her stomach.

The creature barked at her, a rough dissonant noise, but even she could recognise a question when she heard one. She lay still, to scared to move, and when she didn't reply the creature barked the question again, more insistent this time, its hand still caressing her stomach.

'Leave me alone,' she screamed, causing the creature to move backwards, but two seconds later its hand was back, rubbing soft circles on her belly.

She strained to see, but the darkness was impenetrable, and all she felt was the hand.

'What do you want with me?' she asked, this time her voice reduced to a hoarse whisper.

The creature barked the question again, the hand moving up her body. She felt the bile rise as the hand stroked her breasts then moved up towards her throat.

She tried to squirm away, but her body betrayed her, refusing to move as the hand moved over her face, resting on her brow.

The creature spoke again, almost soothing this time, and the hand pressed tighter on her forehead.

Pictures rose up in her mind, pictures which she tried to force back but which bubbled up as if forced out of her memory.

They started with her and Jim, in bed, making love. As the pictures ran their course she felt her body responding, felt the orgasm rising once more, then felt the hot surge of Jim's semen as it surged inside her and her head lit up in blue sparkling flame.

And then the picture changed. She was still on her back, still with her legs open, but this time the pleasure had been replaced by pain, white hot pain as she gave birth to Meg. She felt the tearing as the head appeared, then the hot burst of the birth and the deep sad feeling of emptiness as the baby left her.

The picture changed again, and again she saw the letter is her hand, again she saw the red letters, the word 'POSITIVE'.

The creature's hand moved away and it let out a long sigh, sounding almost human.

Anne was left gasping, feeling dirty, as if she had been assaulted.

'Get out of my head, you bastard.'

And then it did the thing which chilled her blood more than anything else that had happened that day -- it laughed, a deep melodious laugh that echoed long after the creature had stopped.

The hand went back to her forehead and more pictures bubbled up from the depths -- her first day at school, her first illicit puff of a cigarette, her dad's funeral, her first taste of alcohol, the early, wild days with Jim, making love in a tent in the middle of winter, serving behind the bar in the pub, her whole life paraded before her like a Pathe newsreel.

She lost all track of time as the pictures came faster, and faster still, random images, like a badly shot rock video, and all the time in the pictures she talked, holding conversations, replying to questions, and the pictures came faster still.

She broke into a cold sweat as the hand tightened on her head, feeling the pinpricks as its talons threatened to break her skin. The creature plundered her mind.

Finally, after what seemed like an age, the hand was withdrawn, and the creature gave a sigh, deeper than before, one which sounded tired, as if the process had drained it.

It stood above her, and for a time all she heard was its deep, gurgling breathing. It cleared its throat, a remarkably human sound, and then it began to speak, haltingly at first, then with more strength, as if becoming more confident.

There was definitely cadence to the language, and it sounded like the creature expected to be understood.

Anne felt the cold shiver run up her spine again. The fact that the thing could speak made it less of an animal, more human, and a thousand times more frightening. She began to push herself away, scrambling on her bottom until her back was brought up short against the rock wall.

'What are you?' she whispered. 'What do you want with me?'

The creature laughed again, and Anne felt like joining in, just letting the laughter take her away.

And then it laughed, almost a screech, louder and more manic this time, and Anne realised that it was mad. A cold terror settled in her, and something gave in her resolve as she prepared for death.

It stood over her, and she felt its presence, getting ever closer. She shrank away, as far as she could get, almost as if trying to weld her body tightly to the rock at her back. It made a noise, a soft thing, and Anne thought it was talking to her again, but then she realised the sound for what it was -- the creature was giggling.

The creature stood upright -- Anne could sense it

drawing away from her, and, still giggling, stroked a hand down Anne's right leg. She screamed again, which only brought another giggle from the creature, a giggle which continued as the creature backed away from her.

There was another shuffling in the dark, and another voice spoke to her, a softer, more feminine voice this time, its tones those of a worried mother trying to calm a troubled child. But she knew this was no ordinary mother -- above the shuffling she heard the deep liquid gurgling as it breathed. Something was placed in her hands, something that was cold and wet, and the shuffling told her that she was once more alone.

She ran her hand over the thing she had been given. It was a fish, a small thin fish. By the feel of it, it had not been cleaned, it was still whole.

What was she expected to do? Eat it raw? Strangely the idea didn't disgust her -- food was going to be necessary if she was to survive this ordeal.

And she had to survive. Meg might still be alive somewhere out there, out there in a world which she had difficulty remembering, a world which seemed to have been taken from her in the time it took to faint.

She held the fish loosely in her hand. She knew she should eat it.

But not just yet. She wasn't that hungry, and didn't think she would be for quite a while. She laid the fish down beside her, making sure that it would not be underneath her if she rolled over.

She considered her position. Part of her wanted to run, get out, but where could she go in this pitch blackness? The creatures would find her in no time. Maybe later she would attempt the dark, but for now the events of the day had caught up with her, and she couldn't get a vision of Meg out of her mind, Meg being stalked through the beer cellar by the creatures.

And then she thought of Jim. He was surely dead -- those creatures would have been just too strong for him, and she couldn't see Jim letting them take her, not while he was still alive anyway. Hot wet tears ran down her cheeks and she hugged herself tight into a ball, huddled there against the wall, in the dark.

Some time later she had cried herself to sleep.

Her sleep was troubled, first by dreams, red fiery visions of rape and pillage, and then by the steadily rising cold which crept into her bones. She was finally brought completely awake by the feel of cold rough hands on her flesh.

She screamed, so harsh that she felt her throat tear. She knew that she would be hoarse in a few hours, but at that point she didn't think she had a few hours. Her arms thrashed wildly, but they were soon pinned to her sides. She was lifted off the bed and carried out of the chamber, into somewhere that was much bigger, much airier.

There was a rumbling in the distance, a deep sound which seemed to vibrate the air around her, a noise which got louder, first a growl, then a roar then a throbbing, raging thunder.

She started to be able to see. At first she wasn't sure, but then she realised that she could see the grey shapes which milled around her. She was in the middle of a throng, and she seemed to be carried in some sort of procession, the creatures walking in a slow, steady gait, like pall bearers at a funeral.

The rumbling got even louder and she was carried into a huge high cavern, a cavern which shone in pale green luminescence. In the centre of the cavern lay a wide pool, some forty yards across, a pool which was being filled by a waterfall. Her gaze rose up and then up further, finally finding the top of the waterfall some fifty yards above. It fell in one long sweep, three yards wide where it hit the water, sending the pool into a frenzy of foaming white.

She felt the spray on her face and licked at her lips. There was no trace of salt, or of minerals. This was clear, fresh water.

The creatures were everywhere -- she lost count somewhere around sixty, and they seemed to come in all sizes, from some four feet tall to over eight.

They were not all perfect physical specimens either -- some of them seemed deformed, with short, almost non-existent arms. Others were hunchbacked and twisted, and she had to look away when one individual stared at her, an individual who only had one great milky eye set in the middle of his forehead.

She couldn't see any sign of tools, and there was no hint that fire had ever been used here. There was a large net hung over a set of poles, and Anne was taken close enough to it to see that it was entirely woven out of the creatures' long thick hair.

The walls were a warren of caves, small rectangular caves, and again Anne had to look away as she realised that each cave had an inhabitant, a dead ,almost mummified creature, row upon row of them, all staring sightlessly out into the cavern.

There was a sudden shout, an order, loud even above the noise of the water, and the creatures raised her higher in the air, turning her round to face the owner of the voice.

As she got closer she saw that she was being carried towards some kind of throne -- no two thrones -- one large, one small. The thrones were white, almost ivory in colour, and seemed to be composed entirely of bone. As she got even closer she could see the individual bones -- tiny, needle thin bones -- like the bones from fish.

The large throne was occupied by a huge, aged specimen of the creatures, and although it looked older than time itself, she could still sense the strength in it.

Its muscles bunched under the skin, like small rocks, and the skin itself was stretched tight, so tight that it looked as if it might split as any moment. A huge mane of jet black hair streaked in silver surrounded the head like a halo and when it beckoned her closer she saw the long talons on the even longer fingers. Around the thing's neck hung a necklace of white bone, and it wore a crown fashioned from bone and pebbles; small stones which gleamed green and sickly in the dim light.

The smile was the worst -- a humourless, dead thing which did little except reveal twin rows of razor sharp teeth and the grey-black tongue which poked disgustingly between them.

The smaller throne was empty, and Anne was getting a sinking feeling in her stomach, even before the creature in the throne let out its manic, booming laugh.

She realised that this was the same creature which had violated her mind earlier.

The feeling grew as she was carried closer and the huge creature smiled at her once more. The throng began a chant, one word, over and over, a word she had heard the creature use earlier. She now knew its name -- Calent.

The creatures carried her to the foot of the larger throne and laid her at the feet of Calent. She began to squirm but was stopped as a heavy foot was placed on her stomach, pressing down on her, not heard enough to do her any harm, but more than hard enough to keep her from going anywhere.

The foot was almost as broad as it was long, and the toes were strange, flattened things. There was no sign of any toenails, and the feet looked tough enough to withstand any amount of wear and tear from the rocky habitat the creatures inhabited.

The crowd went quiet, and there was only the roaring of the water for several long seconds before Calent began to talk. The language was still incomprehensible, but pictures were again being forced into her mind, nightmarish pictures which she tried to block, but which forced their way through her defences.

She saw herself on the second throne as the crowd paid her tribute, saw herself giving birth, saw herself as an older woman, still sitting impassive on the throne while her child, a male of course, took its place as the prince of the people, mating with them, purifying the bloodline. And finally she saw herself in her old age, being laid in one of the small caves as she neared death and her child, a man now, took his place as leader of the tribe.

She hoped it was just her mind playing tricks on her, but she became more and more afraid that the pictures showed her future, that the creatures meant to make her their queen, meant to keep her here forever.

9

Duncan

The first, long step proved to be exactly as bad as he had first expected.

Nine inches up and nine inches across -- that meant a forty five degree angle. The cliffs were around two hundred feet high, four steps made three feet, that meant two hundred and sixty seven steps. So far he had been looking at the first one for ten minutes. At that rate he had over forty hours of climbing to do.

He knew that his brain was just making busy-work, anything to keep him from truly coming to terms with the climb in front of him.

He laughed to himself at the ridiculous spectacle he must be making, and looked round as if to confirm that there was no one watching him, no one lying in hiding just waiting to pounce, waiting to laugh. Mentally he steeled himself and ordered his leg to lift. But still he couldn't move.

His brain kept giving him busy work -- this time from his childhood.

Him, Gerry and John -- the three musketeers, running gleefully into the blackness, one torch between them, shouting and screaming and laughing as they got deeper into the dark.

Three ten year old boys, on their school holidays, escaped from their parents and in search of adventure and excitement and maybe just a little bit of terror -- not much though, just enough to keep the stories going for a while to relieve the tedium of school.

They had ran far into the cave, far enough that the light from outside was no longer visible, and then they had stopped and listened to their breathing, hot and heavy at first but dying down to three light whispers as their breath came more easily.

The cave had always been the focus of rumours in the town, thought anything from pirates to witches to sea monsters. It was an irresistible draw for young children and the boys were no exception.

It was the first time any of them had been inside and he couldn't remember what had brought them there, so far from the town.

Gerry had the chocolate -- that much he did remember vividly. Red hair, freckles and at least two stones of excess fat brought about by a compulsion to eat anything that was offered to him, that was Gerry.

The three of them had sat in the torchlight and eaten two bars of chocolate, just before John started playing silly buggers -- just before the screaming started.

'Bet you can't find me,' John had said, just as they finished the last of the chocolate. Thirty years later he could still hear the small click as the torch was switched off and the shuffle as John moved away in the darkness.

A small hand had grabbed his upper arm causing him to give out a shriek of surprise.

Gerry had been very frightened and his sobbing had been loud and echoing in the confines of the cave.

'John. Come back,' he had said. 'Gerry is scared. We're going back out.'

There had been no reply and he had taken Gerry by the hand, hoping that they were going in the right direction as they shuffled along, keeping their free hands brushing the walls. They had just noticed that they could see their hands in front of them, that they were nearly out, when they heard the shouts behind them.

'Help,' John was shouting. 'I'm stuck. Don't leave me here.'

Gerry hadn't wanted to, but they had gone back in.

'Watch out,' the voice had said, and a sudden light had lit up the darkness, seemingly coming from the floor of the corridor. 'There's a big hole and I can't get back up.'

The two boys had shuffled towards the light and stood over the hole, looking down to see John's pale face looking up at them from more than ten feet below.

'Are you hurt?' Gerry had shouted, but it was obvious that John was all right. The sides of the wall looked smooth and there didn't seem to be any handholds.

'Can you see any other way out?' he had called, and the light had disappeared as John swung the torch around.

'There's another entrance down here, and there's a big pool of water,' John called back. 'Just stay there and I'll go and have a look round.'

He had held tightly onto Gerry's hand as the light disappeared again and John moved away and they were left once more in the darkness.

They had sat for several minutes in the dark and the quiet before they heard the shout.

'Hey, you guys. Get down here. This is amazing.' The light from the torch reappeared but there was something different about it, a rippling and shifting as it glowed through all the colours of the rainbow and the walls seemed to melt in its glow. Gerry edged away backwards but another shout from John drew them closer to the hole. John was there and he was excited. Words spewed out of him in a breathless rush.

'It leads out into a huge cave and there's bats and skeletons and stuff -- and there's lots of little caves -- and there's a hole, a deep one. There's bound to be a way out and I want to explore. Come on.'

Gerry looked at him and he looked at Gerry, neither of them wanting to make the decision, then John did it for them --

he took the light away.

'Just let yourself drop down,' he said as he moved away. 'It's not too far.'

Gerry and Duncan were left in the dark. They took the decision together and together they dropped down into the darkness, landing hard but managing to stay upright.

It was still dark and there was no sign of John.

Standing there at the foot of the stairs, in the cold light of day, it all came back to him, like a scene from a film, playing over and over in his head.

They are standing in the dark, hand in hand, straining to hear, eager for the slightest noise to tell them where John has gone. All they can hear is the drip of water into a pool to their left. It sounds like a long way down. There is only the dripping, their breathing, and the occasional skittering of a bat overhead.

'I'm scared,' Gerry says, and Duncan nods his head in agreement before he realises that Gerry can't see him.

'Me too,' he says, squeezing Gerry's hand tighter to reassure him.

'John. Stop messing about,' he shouts and the echoes whisper back at him and more bats are frightened into flight around their head, their tinny cries echoing around the chamber.

Gerry cries out, hands striking out at the air above them and screaming as a bat lands in his hair.

And then there is a scream and a heavy body comes out of nowhere with a loud giggle and knocks Duncan to his knees.

He is disoriented and doesn't know which way he is facing as he pushes himself to his feet.

Gerry is still screaming and then there is a sudden burst of light as John switches the torch on. He can see Gerry's face, screwed up tight with tears streaming down his cheeks. John is talking, trying to calm Gerry down.

'Hey! Come on Gerry. It was only a joke.'

He reaches out to touch Gerry's shoulder and the red-

*haired boy jumps as if prodded with a sharp stick. He lashes out
a hand, catching John on the jaw and knocking him into
Duncan. Duncan staggers, trying to keep his footing but his left
foot meets only air and his body tumbles over.*

*He feels the other two boys hit him as they struggle, and
then one of them trips -- he's not sure which one. A heavy body
strikes him on the back, knocking the air from him in one
whoosh, but he has no time to breathe as a second body hits him.
The other two are still screaming at each other, and a flailing arm
hits Duncan in the face. He tries to sit up, pushing himself
upright, shifting the weight above him.*

*There are twin screams which fall into the dark, and it
seems like forever before he hears the splashes.*

He came back to the present with a start.

He had been found a whole two days later by a
search party, but the bodies of the other two were
never recovered. He spent the whole summer in
hospital, but when school time came round he was
back home. Kids heal fast.

Or so he had always thought. Maybe he hadn't
healed all that much.

He looked at the steps again. Shit -- Meg could
get up and down there in no time.

It was the thought of Meg that finally did it. That
and the cold.

The chill from the soaking he had received was
beginning to settle deep in his bones and his teeth had
begun an involuntary chatter as he put his left foot on
the first step and tried to get his right foot to follow.

After another ten minutes he still stood there, still
looking upwards at the task ahead of him. His heart
beat was up -- he now didn't feel the cold, only a deep
heavy sensation, a lump of concrete settling in his
bowels which threatened at any moment to fall
earthwards.

His palms were slick with perspiration, feeling greasy as he rubbed them against his trousers. The only way he would do this was to take it a step at a time.

He fell to his knees, feeling the cold of the stone creep stealthily through his trousers. Laying his hands flat on the fourth step he started to crawl, slowly, almost pulling his useless legs behind him, his heavy rucksack swaying perilously across his back, threatening to unbalance him and toss him screaming into the sea.

Twenty long steps to the first turn, the first checkpoint, then there was a wider place where he could stop and rest. Surely a grown man could manage that? He wouldn't be much more than twenty feet off the ground. Christ, a kid of five could run up and down these stairs all day and never be worried.

'OK', he thought, his mind slipping into a Groucho impression. 'Someone send for a child of five.'

As his knees were pulled roughly across the ragged edge of the first step he felt the harsh coarseness of the stone through the thin weave of his trousers and felt the small pieces of razor-sharp gravel under his soft hands as he inched slowly upwards.

The gravel scraped harshly against his skin bringing a flare of pain closely followed by a sudden rush of heat as his skin broke and hot blood flowed. That made things worse -- his hands slid on the rock and he had to wipe them dry every few seconds, leaving red, bloody streaks across the front of his waterproof.

Every time he put his hands down again they left a red-bloody palm print in place, a palm print which was just as quickly smudged out as his hands shook and slid their way towards the next step. 'Wiping out the evidence,' he thought to himself, and giggled.

The sound was so out of place that he stopped immediately and, like a guilty schoolboy, checked that he hadn't been overheard. He felt the giggles building in his mind and had to force them down -- he knew how close he was to giving in to them.

Somewhere overhead there was a gunshot, and Duncan thought again of John Jeffries. He wasn't about to cry for help with that man about. He gritted his teeth and pushed onwards.

It took fifteen minutes to cover the twenty steps, slowly pulling himself up with his arms, his legs being pulled along like two slabs of dead meat, still refusing to respond to his commands. He turned thankfully onto his back, shuffling over to rest against the one foot restraining wall at the first corner, trying not to look down at where he had been.

Fifteen minutes for twenty steps, that meant over three hours for the climb. Much better than forty anyway. He burst out laughing. He was accelerating.

He turned to look at the second stretch. It rose away from him in one long portion, and he saw that so far he'd done the easy bit.

There was somewhere between eighty and one hundred stairs to navigate and, near the top of the stretch, the cliff fell sheer away into the sea which, after a quick mental calculation, he realised must be nearly thirty yards below.

His hands and his knees would never make it. The heels of his hands were already rubbed raw, shining red in places and pocked in others by the small pieces of grey gravel embedded in them. His knees were faring even worse. Both legs had tears in the trousers and, through these, a small amount of blood oozed thick and red from numerous cuts.

He prised some of the material away from his left

knee, wincing as the pain hit, and saw more small pieces of gravel embedded in the soft flesh over the kneecaps.

He sat and thought. Slowly reality filled in around him.

He faced south. The sky down that way was a pale blue, tinged with weak yellow from the sun which had started its long drop into the sea on his right. A slight wind blew across his right shoulder, bringing with it the salt tang of the sea and the waves sucked noisily at the sand on the small beach below.

He reached into his breast pocket and took out his cigarettes but the packet broke up in his hands, leaving only a mess of paper and wet tobacco.

He saw that he would have to take the next stretch in a different way. When he was a child he was always getting told off for shuffling up stairs on his bottom. He could still remember the pleasure it gave him, seeing the foot of the stairs recede away from him as he ascended. Reverting to childhood. It seemed somewhat apt, conquering a child-like fear in a child-like manner.

Turning onto his back, he noticed the dark sky to the north, the first hints of mist signalled by the moisture which flopped against his face. Dimly, somewhere at the back of his mind, he remembered Old Tom telling him something about the fog, but he was too busy to think of that now.

Shuffling over, he came to the first step.

Keeping his gaze on the small restraining wall in front of him, he began pulling himself upwards. It went fine as long as all he could see beyond the wall was sky, but after the fourth step the sea came into view and, by the sixth step, he could see the cliffs falling into the foam at sea level and could imagine the increasing drop on his left hand side.

He closed his eyes, forcing himself slowly up the incline, his bottom getting numb from the cold and the seeping damp, his hands green with the algal slime from the stones and red from the seepage of blood from numerous small cuts. He counted as he went.

At twenty he stopped for a rest, keeping his eyes tightly closed, massaging his thighs to try to get some life back into them. He heard the waves beneath and to his left, their soft lapping having changed to a harsher slapping as they hit rock instead of sand. In his mind he did calculations.

Forty steps is thirty feet is just less than a sixth of the way up, is ten yards from sea level.

He could survive a fall of ten yards. Easy.

It's not that far, only five body lengths.

If he dropped his body over the edge it would only be four body lengths. Find a nice patch of sand to land on, he could do that with no bother. He still couldn't bring himself to open his eyes and look.

He pushed himself upwards. Twenty-one and the steps were more slippery, his hands grasping for purchase. Twenty-five and he was back on a drier patch, moving more confidently. Thirty-one and his right hand hit what felt like a seagull dropping, sliding six inches and causing his breath to stop and his heart to leap wildly before he found purchase.

Thirty-nine and he thought of what Hitchcock would make of this. Forty-eight and he stopped for another rest.

Sixty-eight steps was fifty-one feet, just over a quarter of the way up. He wondered what time it was, but knew better than to open his eyes to check.

If felt like he had been doing this for ever. His

bottom was completely numb and gave him pain with every movement. The gravel ground in his knee joints with each small move upwards and his hands felt like slabs of frozen meat on the ends of his arms.

But he was getting there. He was doing it.

Starting again was the hardest part. His body told him to stay where he was -- he was safe, secure, unlikely to fall if he didn't move. His mind told him to get going, otherwise it would be midnight before he got to the top. Besides, Meg would be waiting for him.

He continued upwards, inches at a time. Step eighty and he felt secure. Surely he was nearing the second corner by now. He opened his eyes to have a look round.

And found that his left hand was barely an inch from the edge of the path, barely an inch from a fall straight to the sea below.

His vision swam, falling in and out of focus -- the sea sliding first left and then right across his vision, as if on a giant swing.

Only the counterbalance of his rucksack prevented him swaying over, plunging headlong to the sharp rocks again.

Inching sideways to his right he closed his eyes again, breathing heavily and waiting, waiting for a long time, until his heart stilled and he could carry on.

At step ninety-two he was brought short, his rucksack banging against the restraining wall at the second corner. One hundred and twelve steps meant eighty-four feet, much more than a third of the way up. He leant back and opened his eyes, ignoring the screaming pain in his arms and his lower back.

The worst seemed to be over. The third flight of steps stretched ahead of him, but only a few yards up it became a gully, protected on the seaward side by at least six feet of solid rock.

Behind him he heard the sea, still sucking hungrily at the rocks in its reach, but it had missed him again. He leaned against the wall and took a deep, renewing breath, taking stock of his condition.

His back hurt, his knees were on fire, his arms felt like they were dropping off, he was cold, he was damp and he was out of cigarettes. But he had made it. He was alive.

Five minutes later he had reached the top of the stairs, never once looking back until he had moved inland, at least five yards from the cliff edge.

When seen from here, the steps looked innocuous enough -- a gentle slope down a steep-walled gully, but he now knew that he would never be able to go that way again. He turned his back on them and headed inland.

The ruins of the Mansion house loomed up in front of him, the low sun turning its stone golden, thrusting his shadow far ahead across the grass ahead of him.

There was no noise from the direction of the dig, which was fine by Duncan. He had no wish for anyone to see him in his current state. His trousers were torn to shreds at both knees and gleamed darkly where the blood had soaked in.

His hands were filthy -- a mixture of slime, blood and grit. He tried to clean them off on his trousers, but that only seemed to spread the muck around more evenly.

By feeling around he could tell that the seat of his trousers was caked in slime, a thick oily slime which came off darkly green in his hands.

He could only guess as to the overall impression

he would give if he happened to meet someone, but he realised that it probably wouldn't do his reputation any good.

As he walked the realities of life crept back. He'd have to report the loss of the dinghy to the University. Loss of equipment was taken as a serious matter.

He groaned as he realised the amount of paperwork, not to mention the recriminations, which lay ahead. The University liked everything done just so -- and in triplicate. It didn't look kindly on field researchers playing fast and loose with the equipment.

Ah well -- there was nothing he could do about that now. He'd just have to appear suitably contrite and hope that was enough.

He'd also have to explain his loss to the people in the pub. Jim was going to crease himself laughing at this one. He prepared his excuses as he strode over the long grass.

He'd tell them about the dinghy. There was a good little story in that, although he would have to steel himself against the inevitable leg pulling that would follow. But no way would he mention his scramble up the steps. That much was going to stay private for a long time. In fact he doubted if he would ever be able to talk about it to anyone.

Passing if off as a piece of good fortune that he came ashore at the right place seemed like the best option. He could even see how he could play it for the sympathy vote. That would come in useful with Meg at least. Inwardly he scolded himself for such mercenary thoughts, but now that he had it straight in his head all he had to do was get back and get cleaned up without being seen. Judging by the silence, he stood a good chance.

He stopped at the graveyard, the highest point on this end of the island, and had a long look round. To the north, the weather had closed in yet again, obliterating the Mansion house and its surroundings. Far to his left the sun hung, large and red, just above the horizon, painting the sea in shades of pink and orange. 'Red sky at night, shepherd's delight', he whispered to himself, then remembered that old John was the nearest thing the island had to a shepherd, and it was hard to imagine that man being delighted with anything.

He checked his watch and noticed, surprised, that he could hardly see the hands in the gloom. After some peering he could make out that it was after seven o'clock.

His dinghy had sunk just after three, or sometime around then, so he had spent the best part of four hours negotiating less than one hundred and forty steps.

Over to his right was the cluster of buildings which made up the shop and its outhouse, but from this distance he couldn't make out any signs of life.

He wondered if Meg was watching the clock, wondering where he was, wondering whether he had taken fright, and found he cared about the answer. He had butterflies in his stomach and his head felt light and airy. In fact he felt better than he had done for years. He laughed out loud, then had to stop, suddenly guilty at his intrusion on the silence.

After confirming that there was no one around to notice him, he set off at a fast walk for the lighthouse. By the time he reached it the sun had hit the horizon, dyeing the water around it in blood red ripples as it sank. Although already late for his rendezvous with Meg, he stood there for long minutes until the last thin crescent of red disappeared from view and the first stars winked into life overhead.

There was a moment of panic when he thought that he had lost his keys, but then he found them, deep in his jacket pocket, wrapped in a mess of soggy tissues.

First things first. He got one of his spare cigarettes and went back outdoors to smoke it and look at the appearing constellations. Once, when he was ten or eleven years old, he could have given the names of them all, and plotted their positions for any given month. Now he was content to merely look and wonder at their stark, cold beauty.

He smoked right down to the butt before stubbing it out and going indoors. It was while he headed for a clean set of clothes that he caught a look at himself in the mirror.

It was just as well that he had met no one on his walk -- they might have thought they were seeing a ghost.

His hair hung, lank and dirty, in rat's tails around his ears and his face was streaked in grey and red, as if a drunk man had tried to apply stage makeup. And, if you looked too closely at his eyes, you could still see the fear dancing deep down in there.

He cleaned himself up as quickly as he could, wincing as he plucked the small particles of gravel from his knees. After washing he noticed that the damage was not as bad as he had originally feared, and he covered the small cuts and bruises with light bandaging from his first aid kit.

His trousers were completely ruined and were consigned immediately to the bin, the rest of his clothes being hung up to dry on the makeshift clothes line above the stove. By the time he had put on the clean clothes and had another very welcome cigarette, the rigours of the day were almost forgotten, the only external evidence being slight bruising to the heels of his hands, several minor cuts, and a couple of small indentations from which he had dug out pieces of gravel.

These he could explain away as having happened when he tried to rescue the dinghy. If he played the story in the right way, he could come away looking good about the whole affair.

He would have to be careful when sitting down and he supposed that he would stiffen up overnight, but hopefully Meg would not notice anything wrong. Unless that is he ended up without his trousers. If it went as far as that, he didn't think Meg would mind the presence of a few bandages.

It was well after eight o'clock before he finally left for the pub. He carried a flashlight with him, although there was still enough light to see his way along the path. He knew from experience that the trip homewards could be treacherous if the mist or fog descended.

The night was deathly quiet, a silence broken only by the rustling of the grass in the soft breeze and the far off sound of waves coming ashore on the cliffs below. Far to the north the island was darker and he could not make out the outline of the Mansion House, nor the light from the north lighthouse which was usually visible at this time of the evening.

He supposed that the mist was still hanging over that end of the island and hurried his steps. Tom's warning about the mist had seemed silly and superstitious when considered in the daylight but now, with night falling and dead silence all around, Duncan didn't want to find himself proved wrong.

As he got closer to the pub he was puzzled to see no lights. The whole area, outhouses and all, was in complete darkness. Had they lost their generator supply?

It was not unknown. On two nights last year he had spent long evenings in the pub, the cavernous room lit only by candles and the few customers huddled around a huge log fire for warmth. At least Jim always had a plentiful supply of both good stories and whisky.

But Jim had installed a new generator just last spring, and had been proud of the fact that he had never had any trouble with it, even although he had done it all himself and was renowned for his lack of knowledge when it came to things mechanical.

Duncan was glad he had remembered the torch as he picked his way up the path.

As he reached the door of the pub, his worries increased. There was no sound -- no clinking of glasses, no convivial conversation. Surely the students would have reached here by now? They were usually hanging around waiting for Jim to open up at six. He pushed the door and it opened freely, swinging inwards with a loud creak.

He stared uncertainly at the black space behind the door. Did he really want to go in there? It was like those long ago games of hide and seek which they used to play in the forest. It was particularly hurtful if you were the seeker and the rest, not merely hiding, but gone home, had left you wandering in the dim semi-darkness, vainly searching for someone to touch.

The darkness still beckoned. Where could they all have gone? Maybe there had been an accident, one of the students caught at high tide under the cliffs?

It was not completely unknown. Last year two canoeists had got into trouble and had been forced onto the rocks. Duncan could well remember the thrumming of the helicopter as it passed over them. He supposed it could have happened again. But that time there had been noise and bustle, and a great deal of shouting. Surely he would have heard something?

He stood and listened to the silence. On a night like this he would have been able to hear a helicopter, or any other engine, at some distance. There was nothing.

Maybe the fog was deadening the sound. Or maybe they had left a note for him in the bar. Whatever the cause, he was getting nowhere just standing there. He moved into the darkness.

It was even quieter inside, all sounds from the waves stopped by the thick stone walls. He turned on his flashlight and played it across the room, an oval as it crossed the floor, thickening into a circle as it climbed the wall. All seemed normal.

On his left hand side his hand groped until it found a light switch which he clicked on, with no great hope of a result.

To his surprise the room was flooded in bright light from the neon strip overhead, momentarily dazzling him. When his eyes adjusted he could see that the shop was unchanged from usual, there was no evidence of anything out of the ordinary.

He walked through the small room, heading for the bar, trying to avoid making any loud noises. For some reason he was loath to break the silence, feeling that, if he did, something would know that he was there, something that would come screaming out of the darkness. He shook his head. Still frightened of the dark after all these years. Sometimes he was disgusted with his own cowardice.

The bar was still in darkness, only a small patch of floor illuminated by the light from the shop. He knew that the bar lights were controlled from a panel just to the left of the doorway and he found it without difficulty, switching on all available sources of light.

The bar also looked normal. The stools were stacked on the tables, all the glasses had been cleaned and all the ashtrays were empty. It was strange to stand in a completely empty pub -- it had the same feeling as an empty church, it felt almost religious.

It was obvious that no one had been here all evening. Whatever the problem was, it was taking up a lot of time.

There was no way he would find them -- not in the mist and the dark, not if they weren't making a lot of noise. He pulled up a barstool and sat down, lighting a cigarette as he pondered the situation. He felt self conscious sitting here alone smoking. What he needed was a drink.

He stepped behind the bar. The till lay open, a wad of notes visibly showing. John was a trusting soul. But not that trusting -- he would never have left the pub with his money lying there in plain view.

To Duncan it felt like the temperature had suddenly dropped several degrees, and he felt the hairs at the nape of his neck against his collar.

He started to whistle tunelessly, suddenly more afraid of the silence than of causing any disturbance. He poured himself a large whisky, several measures larger than he would normally drink, placing the right amount of money in the till.

Carrying the drink with him, he walked around the room, giving it a closer inspection, checking for anything out of place, anything that would give him a clue as to what was going on.

It was not until he was right at the end of his first circuit, facing the entrance to the shop, then he noticed the blood on the floor. It was one single smear, smaller in size than the nail on his little finger.

His first thought was that his bandages had somehow come undone, that he had inadvertently been bleeding, but when he checked, all was clean. It hadn't come from him.

'So what?' he thought. 'Someone gets a nosebleed and Jim misses a bit when he is cleaning up. No big problem.'

But it was a problem, and he knew it. Something was completely out of whack on this island, something which was making him more afraid by the minute. If something had happened, it had been fast. There was no sign of a struggle, no chairs knocked over, nothing broken.

He stood, noticing the floorboard creak as he did so. That was when he remembered the cellar. Turning, he approached the trapdoor. The door was lifted by a single large iron rung set next to an old rusting lock. He took the rung in both hands and heaved. The door rattled in its fittings, but otherwise didn't move -- it was obviously locked.

There was little more which he could do. He could phone for help but then he would look foolish when the rest of the islanders turned up.

He started to wonder if this was another of Jim's elaborate practical jokes. He had been set up before by the landlord -- on one famous occasion ending up locked out on the walkway at the top of the lighthouse, naked except for a pair of underpants. The pictures from that debacle came back to haunt him every couple of months. But for this to be a joke everyone on the island would have to be in on it -- including Meg. He didn't think this was her style.

Whatever had happened, he would feel safer if he carried some sort of a weapon. He headed for the kitchen.

Here he found more evidence that whatever had happened had been sudden. Someone had been preparing a meal. There were chopped vegetables on the counter by the sink and, on the large pine table, a partially chopped onion. Beside it sat what he was looking for, a ten inch kitchen knife, heavy bladed and with a strong, sculpted grip.

Whatever had happened, the person preparing the vegetables had either not thought to use the knife or, a more disturbing thought, had no time to reach it.

He took the knife, balancing it in his right hand. It was sharp and ugly and felt oddly reassuring. He gave it a few practice swishes in the air, then stopped when he realised how foolish it must look.

It was time to move on. Leaving the kitchen he returned to the bar. He finished off the whisky in one swallow, feeling its heat burn on the way down to his stomach.

He retrieved his flashlight from the bar and, switching off the lights behind him, headed into the shop.

Maybe he should use the radio? He wondered why he hadn't thought of it sooner. The worst that could happen would be that he was left looking like a fool. On the other hand he could possibly find out it anything was going on.

The radio was located in the small room at the rear of the shop which doubled as a Post Office. The door leading through was slightly ajar. His grip on the knife tightened, turning his knuckles white.

He pushed the door open, wincing as it creaked loudly. It swung open, letting a wash of light into the room. The first thing he saw was the radio on the floor, smashed into several large pieces. The receiver wire led off across the room, around the corner caused by the open door, and out of his sight.

Suddenly, a smell came to him, the heavy coppery odour of blood. He could taste it in the back of his throat.

He didn't want to find out what was behind the door.

What if it was Meg?

What if there was still somebody there, at this very moment, standing quietly behind the door, wielding an axe, ready to cut him down when he entered the room?

He pushed the door violently inwards and almost jumped into the room, knife brandished in front of him as if it were a gun. Immediately he felt foolish.

There would be no nature trips for the tourists for a while.

The body lay on its side, curled up like a foetus. The head had suffered terrible damage and was squashed and pulped into an almost unrecognisable bloody mass.

Unfortunately, not totally unrecognisable -- the shades lay slightly to one side, trampled flat to the floor and the T-shirt, although soaked in blood, still bore the unmistakable Deep Purple Logo. It could only belong to one person.

A pool of blood had spread in an amorphous blob around the body and had congealed to black in several places. Duncan bent down, ostensibly to check for life signs, although even his untrained eye could see that life had long since gone.

Duncan felt ill. He could taste the coppery blood, sticking to the back of his throat. He stood, and backed away, tears springing at the corners of his eyes.

Questions span in his head, but he couldn't catch hold of them for any length of time.

Where was Meg?

And what about her mother? Was there a maniac on the island, or was what he had just seen the result of a domestic dispute? Either way, he had to get help.

The telephone was on a desk above the body, but it too had been ripped from its socket. It wasn't one of the new types either -- there was no way of reconnecting the line.

Trying not to look down he left the room, closing the door behind him. The only other radio on the island was in the north lighthouse and he knew that there were no other telephones.

He had two choices: either he could set off on a four mile walk over the length of the island, chancing that he would meet a maniac on the way or he could go down to the harbour and take the pub's boat out.

He chose the walk. On the walk he didn't have to face the trip down the cliffs and besides, he would pass John Jeffries' farm house on the way. Maybe he could enlist some help.

On leaving the pub he closed the door behind him and was immediately enveloped in damp watery blackness. The mist had come down while he had been inside and even now clung softly to his clothes and nestled into his beard. He switched on the flashlight but it was nearly useless, barely illuminating the wall of the nearest outhouse less than ten feet away.

Picking out the beaten track with his light he walked northwards, trying to ignore the shadows which he imagined were tracking along beside him.

The mist enveloped him totally, cutting off all sound so that he walked in a vast, damp greyness, only the outline of the path to keep him on the straight and narrow. As he walked, his mind churned over what he had found in the pub.

He wouldn't believe that it had been a domestic incident. The couple had argued, of course they had -- what couple doesn't argue from time to time. But there had been genuine affection there. Even Duncan, with his limited viewpoint on relationships, had been able to see that. And it had been a domestic tiff, why had Jim been caught in the radio room?

It just didn't add up.

He found it far easier, if a lot more disturbing, to believe that a maniac was at large, one who had killed Jim and abducted the women.

But for what reason?

There he was stuck. And how would a maniac manage to abduct both women -- especially when they were both strong willed? Another thought struck him, one which made him stop in his tracks, the flashlight shaking in time with his trembling hands.

What if the woman were dead as well? What if the killer had hidden their bodies? Or what if there were two killers?

He sat off again at a faster pace...the fog was thickening.

Two minutes later he stood outside John Jeffries' farmhouse, listening for any noise, anything at all that would tell him that he was not alone.

The building was in darkness, no visible signs of life. With his first sweep of the flashlight he had seen that the front door was wide open and that one thing, more than anything else which may have seemed wrong, had made him stop.

John Jeffries was a distrustful man, always double locking all the doors before venturing out from his house, even if he was only going to the barn to milk the cow. For his door to be open was an ominous sign.

Duncan couldn't decide on the best course of action. Should he go in, and possibly find a body or should he make speed for the lighthouse and safety? He found that he couldn't abandon the farmer, no matter how objectionable he might be. Trying to keep his light steady, he headed for the door.

The door led straight into the main room, a large spacious room with a low, heavily timbered ceiling. He swung his light around, catching a glimpse of himself, wide eyed in the mirror, but there was no other movement. The heavy old fashioned furniture loomed darkly in the shadows -- shadows which seemed to creep along the walls, stalking him.

He was about to turn and check the kitchen when his left foot hit something heavy on the floor, something soft which moved several inches before resting against his shoe.

He turned the light downwards to the rug at his feet and retched as he saw what was lying there, almost bringing up the raw whisky, feeling it burn up his throat as his eyes took in the horror.

It was a forearm, a human forearm, roughly torn from the rest of the limb so that the loose flesh hung from the elbow in ragged edges. A small amount of blood, no more than a thimble full, puddled beneath it, velvety black in his flashlight.

The hand was wrinkled, grey hair in a forest

across its back, and Duncan had guessed the owner, even before he noticed the jewellery.

There was a ring on the third finger, a large heavy gold ring which John Jeffries always used to tap on his glass in the bar to signify when he needed another drink. The habit had always annoyed Duncan intensely, but it looked like he'd never have to worry about it again.

He bent down for a closer look, seeking to make sure, when the back door of the cottage slammed open with a crash that shook the whole house.

Duncan didn't believe that he could possibly move so fast.

Ten seconds later he was back on the path, heading northwards as fast as the mist would allow, his fingers tightened around the knife in his right hand, the flashlight swaying wildly in the mist, illuminating first the path, then shadows, then the path. The only sound was the constant rasp of his breath and the rhythmic thudding of his feet against the gravel.

He had to stop five minutes later, his lungs burning, his already bruised joints crying out for rest. He felt around his knees, noticing the dampness spreading there, blood having soaked through his bandages. It didn't feel too bad though -- there was only a small amount of blood and there was no pain.

He stood, bent over, hands on thighs, dropping the knife and flashlight on the ground at his feet. He continued taking in huge whoops of air, trying to tell his heart and lungs that they were still alive, that it was okay to breathe in and out, okay to pump the old blood around.

After a few minutes his breathing calmed and his heart stopped threatening to leap out of his ribcage.

What kind of maniac would chop off someone's

hand, then leave it lying around? Then another thought struck him. Where had the rest of the blood gone?

If someone had cut off John Jeffries' arm, there should have been blood everywhere, spattered over the walls, the floor, the ceiling. He wasn't an expert, not by any means, but he reckoned that your heart didn't stop pumping just because you've had your arm chopped off. There should have been pints of the stuff. So where had it been?

He decided that he didn't have enough information. His best bet was to get help. Get to the north lighthouse and call up the professionals on the mainland. They would know what to do.

When his breathing slowed to a reasonable level -- still not back to normal but slow enough that he could think of something else other than sucking air -- he noticed the depth of the fog around him.

It was like being wrapped in grey damp candy floss, hanging in soft tendrils in the air all around him. All was silent, a heavy deep silence.

There were no landmarks available to let him know how far he had come, only the gravel road and a glimpse of the heath on either side, but he guessed that he must be close to the site of the dig.

The students!

How could he have forgotten about them? If they weren't at the pub and he hadn't passed them, maybe they were still at the dig, working late. No, that wasn't feasible. They would find it difficult working in the fog and blackness without some strong lighting, and he couldn't see anything other than the thick grey wall.

Unless they were underground? If he kept moving he should come across them pretty soon and at least be able to hear if anyone was around The thought of meeting another human being gave him fresh impetus. He hadn't seen anybody since Dick and Tom, and that had been in the morning. Even on this island that was a hell of a long time to go without seeing another living person. He picked up the flashlight and knife and continued northwards.

Barely two minutes later his flashlight beam picked out the first of the student's tents, looming large and orange out of the fog. By sweeping the flashlight around he could make out the rest of the tents in their rough semicircle but there was no sign of movement, no lights and no sound. He called out, a bit louder than necessary.

'Hello? Anybody there?'

Immediately he regretted it. His voice was swallowed in the fog, dead before it had gone ten yards. The silence returned.

Nervous now, he struck the flashlight under his right arm, keeping the beam facing ahead of him as he lit a cigarette, fighting hard to keep his hands from shaking and taking three attempts to get the lighter and the cigarette in the same general area.

Now what? Did he search for the students or head for the lighthouse? He decided that the students could be anywhere. They could have gone out on the pub's boat, they could have gone for a walk or they could even be at the north lighthouse. Maybe a party had been announced while he was out in the boat?

He was rationalising, trying to fool himself into believing that there was nothing wrong, that he hadn't really seen Jim's body, that there wasn't a disembodied arm on the floor of John Jeffries' living room.

One thing he did know: he didn't want to spend any more time alone in this grey quietness. He finished his cigarette and, replacing the flashlight in his left hand, once more headed northwards.

He had barely started walking when he was stopped by a noise, a rasping coughing sound from straight in front of him. It immediately reminded him of the seals earlier.

As he stopped and stood still, the grass ahead of him rustled, the sound of something heavy moving around.

'Who's there?' he called out, swinging the flashlight upwards from the path, pointing it towards the noise. He could see nothing but the tufts of grass, swaying lightly in the wind.

He was answered by two distinct, simultaneous coughs, one from his left and one from his right. A darker patch of greyness began to take shape in the fog, a large lumbering greyness, bigger than a man, heading towards him, just outside the range of his light.

For the second time that evening he turned and ran, this time heading back southwards.

He had only one thought in his mind. Get to the boat. That was his last hope. Once on the boat he would be able to make quick time, even in the dark. He wasn't afraid of sailing at night. He had been out several times on fishing trips and knew that the north lighthouse illuminated a large area which, even in the fog, would be enough to guide him there. And when he was on the boat, he would be safe. Nothing could get to him out on the water.

He ran, trying vainly to listen for pursuit, keeping the flashlight as steady as possible on the path in front of him but unable to prevent it swinging wildly from left and right. His lungs started to burn and it became harder to draw breath as he kept trying to pump his aching knees, faster as his system dumped adrenaline, faster until he was in full flight.

At one point he ran off the road and had a terrifying couple of seconds before his flashlight picked out the gravel only two yards to his right. He had been lucky -- the path veered quite close to the cliff edge in this area, and he had a mental image of himself falling endlessly through the air before being broken on the rocks below. His legs almost betrayed him then, and he had to fight to keep upright, to keep himself moving.

He reached the pub before he had to stop, leaning with his back to the wall, keeping his flashlight facing back along the path as his heart thumped and his breath wheezed coldly in his throat.

The mist was thinner than it had been and he could make out the shapes of the outhouses around him, sitting squat and black against the dark sky. He decided against going back into the pub and locking himself in. He didn't think he could stand spending a night with the body of his friend, knowing that someone -- or something -- was lurking outside.

He finally allowed himself to think the unthinkable -- that whatever had committed the atrocities he had seen might not be human, but he was now thinking in terms of escaped animals, large animals, possibly bears. He still refused to consider any explanation involving the supernatural, it meant too big a change in his view of the way the world worked.

He was more prepared to believe that a cargo ship of rabid bears had escaped and, after climbing a two hundred foot cliff, had rampaged around the island, managing to kill one man, abduct two women and tear the hand off another man without leaving any blood behind and without anyone raising an alarm. He was straining his own credulity to the limit but, for the time being, it was holding.

Once he was back to the path, he turned a full circle, eyes straining to see further than the range of the flashlight, all senses alert for the slightest, movement, smell, or sight out of the ordinary, ready to flee at the slightest hint of movement.

Nothing moved, nothing but the thin wisps of fog drifting slowly from the north. He began to breathe a bit more easily as he set off for the harbour.

He walked slowly now, trying not to make a noise, walking on the edges of the path to prevent the scrunching of feet on gravel signalling his presence. As he turned at the fork, heading seaward, he noticed that the fog had thinned out considerably, turning into a fine drizzle of rain which pattered lightly against his forehead.

It was only now that he realised that he was heading for the harbour and that he would have to walk the path on the edge of the cliff. There was nothing else for it. Besides, it was dark. He wouldn't be able to see the extent of the drop. And after his experience on the stairs he was confident that his legs wouldn't fail him this time.

A short time later he was ready to test his theory. All was quiet apart from the gentle lapping of the waves beneath him as he stood, his light illuminating the corner in front of him.

He walked forward, confident at first, but two steps and a weight shifted in his stomach and his knees started to tremble. He managed one more step before he had to sit down, hard, as his legs gave way beneath him.

'Come on,' he told himself. 'You got up those stairs today, and that was a lot worse than this.' His brain knew it, but it had neglected to tell his body. His legs still refused to work.

Shaking, he sat for several minutes, his back to the rock wall, looking out over the blackness, emptying his mind, searching for calm, before he started shuffling sideways, bringing new pain to his rear and his already battered knees.

He moved along several feet, managing to get himself round the corner before he was stopped by a crunch of falling rock and a patter of pebbles, seeming to come from the path above him.

Straining, he listened, but there was no repeat. And then he heard it -- something was breathing -- a heavy liquid sound, in and out, in and out, a gurgling slow breathing, coming closer. Before he realised what he was doing, he stood and flung himself along the path away from the corner, almost blind in the dark, his flashlight pointing upwards into the sky, scrambling away from whatever was following him.

Too late, he found that he had forgotten about the slight turn in the path and fell, screaming, imagining the rocks waiting patiently below.

The fall was a short one, barely three feet before he was rolling and tumbling down the grassy bank of the shore, trying desperately to protect both the flashlight and the knife. He hit a large boulder, jarring his right hand and sending the knife spinning off into the darkness.

He heard it clank against a rock just before he stopped tumbling, and silence descended once more. Before he moved he did a quick mental check for broken bones, but he seemed to be whole, apart from a dull ache in the wrist which was no worse than the aftermath of a long game of tennis.

Sitting up, he shone the flashlight back up the slope but there was no sign of any pursuer, only the blank featureless rock wall and the flattened grass which marked his passage. He turned back to the sea and, standing up, picked out the dim outline of the small boat, bobbing only a few yards away.

He couldn't see the knife -- it could be anywhere. He decided to give it up as lost. There would probably be something on the boat he could use as a weapon. Anyway, once he got going, he didn't foresee needing one. Nothing was likely to attack him at sea.

He waded out to the boat, the water never getting above his knees, and pulled himself aboard. All the time he listened and watched, all the time wondering if something was going to snatch at him out of the darkness and drag him into pain and oblivion.

He wasted no time in casting the boat off and got the small outboard engine started at only the second attempt. As the boat got under way he switched on the small onboard light and switched off his flashlight, clipping it on his belt in case he needed it later. Suddenly he felt a lot calmer, the light rocking of the boat soothing him, and he began to relax.

The events of the preceding hours began to seem like a dream, and for the first time he wondered if he was going mad. Could the whole thing be a hallucination, brought about by the stress of the ascent up the stairs? He'd heard of people who had such experiences, but it had all seemed so real, so vivid. He put it to the back of his mind. The important thing now was to get to the north light and safety, somewhere he could put the nightmare behind him.

He let the boat head outwards as he lit a cigarette, finally able to relax as he left the shore behind.

The sea was dark and mildly choppy but the small boat seemed to cleave through the slight swell easily enough. He had a look back at the shore but was only able to see the outline of the island, a blacker patch against a black sky. The boat had just moved out of the confines of the small harbour when he heard the scratching.

It wasn't constant. First there was a mild scraping, as if the boat were running over a piece of wood, but then it turned into an insistent, rhythmic scratching, as if someone were pulling a nail across the boat's bottom. He was just about to stop the engine to investigate when the boat started rocking underneath him, first to the left and then to the right, then back again, the amplitude of the swings ever increasing.

Before he had time to react and steady himself he was dumped head first into the water, the boat falling over his head and trapping him under the keel. He was momentarily disoriented and could not decide which way was up, but he soon got himself under control.

He knew that he wasn't going to be able to right the boat -- it was far too heavy for that. Besides, he was going to be okay -- he could handle himself in the water with a confidence which he completely lacked on land.

He had no desire to hang around and see what had caused the problem. He took a deep breath and swam out from under the boat, surfacing several yards from the upturned keel. Turning, with the grace of an experienced swimmer, he kicked out for the shore, his crawl stroke only slightly impeded by the light anorak.

It only took him twenty strokes before his trailing arm hit the bottom. He pulled himself up and headed for the shore, wading strongly through the surf, the water barely reaching the top of his thighs. The undercurrent was strong, and small pebbles danced around his feet, but he was managing to fight against it and was making good progress when he felt his left foot catch something, something which felt like a lump of driftwood. He tugged, hard, but his foot was caught and he lost balance, tumbling flat onto his stomach, into the dark black sea.

He kicked out, trying to free his foot, but something tugged in the opposite direction, something which had him in a clamp round the left ankle, gripping tightly, trying to pull him back into the deeper water. He kicked out with his right foot, encountering something hard, and kicked again and again until his legs cried out in pain. Slowly he was pulled backwards and salt water ran into his mouth, causing him to cough and splutter.

Panic set in and he thrashed out, kicking even harder. His foot hit something soft and yielding and the pain flared, white heat in his ankle. But he was free. He scrambled through the small waves, pulling himself out of the surf and up the beach.

He was in the small bay beyond the harbour, with no way round except by wading through the sea. There was no sound apart from the surf and the gunshot crackle of the pebbles as they rushed into the sea. He looked out into the blackness. There was no way he was going back into the water.

The only way out was straight up the cliff.

Then he remembered the last conversation he had with Jim. Could he go through the smugglers cave? Surely whatever was after him would not know about the cave. He limped off towards the stand of rhododendron bushes, taking out his flashlight but not yet switching it on, trying to be quiet as the small pebbles settled around his feet.

When he got to the bushes he saw a greater patch

of blackness behind them. He hoped it was the cave --
he was rapidly losing his strength -- the events of the
day beginning to catch up with him. All he wanted to
do was to lie down and let the world go its own way for
a while.

He knew that he couldn't stop. If he did he
would never get started again.

The bushes proved tough going but he was finally
able to part them enough to slip through to the cave
beyond. At least the tangle of growth showed no-one
had come through this way for some time, and the
bushes had closed again behind him, hiding his
presence from view from the shore.

He had one final look around, but the scene had
once again changed to calm, no movement except the
tiny wavelets rushing up and down on the rocks and
sand. He listened, but heard nothing apart from the sea
and its gentle lapping.

Entering the cave by feel, he groped his way
along the damp wall until he passed round a corner.
From the sudden feeling of space and the texture of the
sounds around him he realised at once that he was in
the main chamber and that it was now safe to light the
flashlight -- the light would not be seen from the
outside.

He switched on the torch and slumped,
exhausted to the damp floor of the cave. As he passed
the light around he looked for another entrance, the
way up to the secret passage beneath the pub. By the
time he was calm again he had found two likely
options.

The first one came to a dead end after no more
than three yards, ending at a dank grey wall. It was as
he turned towards the second that he heard the noise,
the cold slapping of something wet and heavy on the

rock near the entrance, then the rustling as something big tried to make its way through the rhododendrons.

What the hell was after him?

His idea about the bears was beginning to seem more and more absurd. Whatever was after him seemed to have intelligence and guile far beyond what he would expect. He didn't have time to think -- the noise got closer, rhododendron branches cracking as a way was cleared by brute force.

That led urgency to his movements as he headed into the second passage. The noise behind him got louder, forcing him to move faster and he almost fell as he turned a corner and came upon a steep flight of steps.

'Shit. More bloody stairs,' he whispered, then immediately clamped his hand over his mouth as the echoes whispered around him. At least these stairs were enclosed by rock.

He climbed, his torchlight barely penetrating the blackness. The walls ran with moisture and his feet slid precariously among the thick green slimy growth on the steps. He couldn't hear anything above the noise of his laboured breathing but he wasn't about to stop to listen. He forced himself to move faster, trying to ignore the aches and pains in his body.

As he climbed he tried not to think of what might be up ahead. He remembered that the cellar door to the pub had been locked, but he would cross that hurdle when, and if, he ever reached it.

In the mean time he had no choice but to climb -- climb and pray.

The path narrowed and got appreciably steeper, taking him round a series of turns until he had no idea of direction, but as long as he was still climbing he wasn't worried. Surely he must be near the top by now?

Turning a corner he walked face first into a mass of spider's web, the white threads sticking to his eyelashes, his hair, and his hands as he tried to brush it away.

He was thinking about the Lord of the Rings, about Shelob's Lair and giant eight-legged predators when he heard the noise behind him, the padding of wet feet on the stairs.

He turned, swinging the torch beam down the stairs... and looked into two large silver eyes as Gollum came up the steps towards him. At least that was his first thought but then he saw the rest of it -- the fish-scaled body, the webbed hands and the silver pointed teeth which gleamed wetly in the torchlight.

He turned and fled up the stairs, almost stumbling over the first step, hitting his shin hard on the stone and bringing a new flare of pain to his already bruised ankle. He began to take the stairs two at a time as the torchlight swung widely around the walls.

His feet skidded in the slime underfoot and several times he nearly fell, but he managed to keep going. The path became even steeper and he was almost forced onto all fours but the sounds behind him were getting louder and he imagined he could smell the thing's foetid breath as it got closer, and closer still.

He was stopped short by a large oak door. He turned the huge iron handle but it refused to budge and he just had time to scream, one long wail of fear and disappointment before he had to turn and face his attacker.

It was on him fast. The smell hit him first -- the odour of rotting fish, then he was fighting for his life. One huge hand swung towards his face and the torchlight glinted on sharp edges as he ducked and brought his arm up to parry the blow.

He kicked out, hard, and had the satisfaction of hearing a grunt of pain before something hit him on the side of the head. He stumbled, falling to the ground, his head hitting the rock wall. It loomed over him, a black shape in the gloom and he heard a faint gurgling in its throat as it reached for him. He cried out, a scream which caused his assailant to step back before coming forward once more.

The door behind Duncan was flung open and there was a shot, deafening in the confines of the corridor. The creature fell away down the stairs, its screams falling with it until they faded into silence.

Duncan looked up and, just before blackness took him away for a while, stared into the barrel of a shotgun and, somewhere behind it, already falling out of focus, Meg's wild frightened features.

10
Sam

Sam couldn't find the master. He wasn't with the sheep -- Sam had been to look. The sheep had all been huddled in a group, and hadn't moved when Sam tried to herd them. Sam hadn't bothered to persevere. When he was a young dog he'd taken great delight in making the sheep go to the right places, but he was getting slow, and he knew it.

After visiting the sheep Sam went over to the lighthouse, looking for Duncan, needing a biscuit. Duncan always had biscuits -- he was a good man.

It was full dark by now and old Sam couldn't see very well in the dark, but his sense of smell was as strong as ever. There were many strange smells in the night -- the sour smell of the sheep, the faint taste of Duncan -- the man had been close to here today -- but most of all, the smell he found almost everywhere he went, the smell of blood.

Sam had made his way slowly to the farmhouse but the dark things were there, milling around, seemingly investigating the area. There were many of them, and he didn't like the smell they gave off. He circled round the farm, giving it a wide berth.

By this time his stomach was rumbling with hunger. The young people always had food and had fast become his new friends. They had biscuits and meat, but best of all, they had chocolate. His tail wagged in a Pavlovian frenzy as he thought of all the good things the young people had. And they played with him. Maybe they would be nice to him.

He headed across the island, taking care to avoid the areas which smelled too much of the bad things but when he got to the campsite he found that more of the black things were already there and the smell of blood was stronger than ever. Sam dragged himself into some rubble from the old Mansion house. He knew this place. It was a place where the master never came, a place where he could hide when the master was angry. He found a secluded spot, hid himself away and whimpered as he watched the black things move slowly around the mound.

It was getting colder, and there were even more of the black things than before, but Sam didn't move, even when the things lit a fire and began to dance around it.

Sam stayed cowering in the rocks and occasionally whimpered quietly to himself. There were too many bad things.

11
1,400 Years
Ago

Calent was dying.

Not quickly, and not for some time yet, but there was a weariness in his bones and a heaviness in his heart.

And the tribe decayed with him.

Over the long years they had adapted to their exile, their bodies slowly moulding themselves into new forms, forms better adapted to their dark existence. And deep in his mind Calent had also moulded himself anew -- his rage and his hate chewing away inside, its blackness eating and festering in the black corners.

In those early years, just after the entombment, he had hurled his rage against the spells which bound them, throwing himself mentally and physically against the barriers. But the Mother was too strong, and he could no longer feel the strength of the Father.

He carried some of it inside him -- he knew that. It was the Father who kept him alive, but he couldn't marshal that strength -- he would die if he used it.

For long days he stood in the mound, his mind reaching outwards, across the island, trying to make contact with the stone. But there was never any response.

At first, and for several hundred years, he touched with many minds, but they were all strong with the Mother, and he recoiled from contact. He fell back on the old ways -- a simple thing, but all he had power for. It was something he had learned in a time long past, something he'd learned from his father, a trick passed down from father to son in the name of the Sky Father.

He talked to them in the depths of night, in the quiet times when they were at their most vulnerable, while they were asleep. He sent them dreams. Red, fiery nightmares, dreams of being alone in the dark, dreams of dismemberment -- he knew what frightened people -- he had always been good at that. He drew a small degree of satisfaction from feeling the fear, but that soon passed. And so did the people. Not all at once -- they went in dribs and drabs over the years, until finally there was only the idiot minds of the birds.

For long years he waited, hoping against hope that the Father would return for him. But all that happened was that he grew weaker, and the tribe died and degenerated around him.

Many times he thought of ending it, of lying down and dying, but the hate wouldn't leave him alone, it kept burning and eating inside, driving him on through the years.

And finally, when both he and his tribe were at their lowest ebb, people came. There was one among them who reminded him strongly of Dron -- even through the weight of the stone and the spells he felt that this one was so strong in the power of the Mother -- the pictures were at the front of his mind. In the pictures the Mother carried a child, but she was still recognisable.

Calent trembled as he felt them approach the mound, a mixture of trepidation and excitement. The mound itself trembled as their hammers burst the stone, and Calent prepared to pounce, ready to rip and tear, but a strange lethargy came over him and he felt the binding spells of the Mother weave their web around him. Inside he fumed, but his body was betraying him, carrying him meekly out of the mound, out to face his tormentors.

They had built a fire, a great conflagration which blazed away in the centre of the island. Calent was shocked to see that the forest was gone, the island having been cleared completely, leaving it bleak and barren.

There were men around the fire -- heavy jawed, black haired men in long, dark robes. There was no fear in their eyes, even though Calent knew he must look monstrous to them. They were all watching a large man -- the one who held the power which held Calent bound.

This one was a huge bear of a man, his black beard cascading over his chest, his hair flying wild behind him and the power of the Mother burning fiercely in his eyes. He marched towards Calent, back-lit by the fire, his robe billowing out in a great fan.

He thrust a piece of wood at Calent, a long piece crossed with a shorter piece. It meant nothing to Calent, but the power of the Mother poured out of the man, enough to force Calent to his knees.

The bearded man shouted at Calent in an unfamiliar tongue, but Calent could see the pictures -- the man wanted him to bow to the power of the Mother.

He was forced to bend closer to the ground, then closer still until he was almost on all fours. The man stood over him, his voice raised until it was almost a rant, the piece of wood jabbing in the air above Calent's head.

Still he was being forced lower to the ground, his hair now brushing the grass. He looked up to the sky, searching in vain for the Father -- but it wasn't the Father's time. Calent gathered his power and managed to raise himself to a crouch. He opened his jaws wide and screamed his rage, causing the robed man to step back, a sudden wash of fear over his face.

Calent was rewarded by a sudden burst of energy -- not much, and certainly not enough for him to fight the Mother's man, but it brought a leap of joy to his heart -- the stone was still here, and the Father still remembered him.

He was careful not to let his feelings show as the bearded man stepped towards him once more.

Yet again the wooden cross was thrust at him, and this time he cowered before it -- he was quite pleased with the small cry of terror which he let slip from his lips.

He allowed himself to be driven backwards, back towards the mound, all the time keeping his eyes averted to one side, not looking the Mother's man in the face. The man shouted, one more word which Calent didn't understand, but he understood the intent -- he crawled back into the mound. He hated doing it, hated grovelling in front of this barbarian, but he couldn't give the Father away. So he crawled.

All the time the man followed him, almost screaming now, the other robed men shouting along with him, all of them dancing in front of the fire like some barbarian tribesmen. Calent despised them, and the old urge to rip and gouge flowed heavy in him, but he crawled into the mound on his hands and knees, and allowed them to shut him in once more.

He heard them cavorting above him, but a small smile played across his lips. The Father was still there, the stone was still there.

He would learn patience, and he would live, and one day he would reclaim his birthright.

12

Dick

Even the short trip across the island proved too much for Angus, and Dick was alarmed to see him lying slumped against the door of the car. He pulled to a halt at the top of the cliff and turned towards the policeman.

'Can you make it down the steps?' Dick asked, but there was no reply. Angus stared sightlessly ahead, lost in his own world of pain, his eyes sunk deep in the features of his screwed up face, a face which was white as ivory.

'Shit,' Dick said to no one in particular. 'I'd better go and get Tom. Stay here and don't move.'

He needn't have bothered -- it didn't look like Angus was going anywhere for a while. Dick was no expert, but it sure looked like a heart attack from where he was sitting.

The fog was thick and clammy and felt cold against his skin when he left the car. It was nearly nightfall and there was a red glow visible through the mist to the west where the sun would be going down into the sea.

When he got to the cliff-top he could only just make out the shape of the building at the foot of the steps. Tom hadn't put the light on, and that in itself was a minor miracle. Even though weeks could pass before a ship crossed through the channel, Tom had always made sure the light kept to schedule. He hoped the old man was all right -- he was going to need help to get the policeman down the stairs.

The door was locked when he reached it, and he remembered the sound of the bolt being drawn as they were leaving. He pounded on the door with his fists, then again, harder, when there was no answer. It was only after he shouted Tom's name that he got a reply.

The door opened, but only by a few inches, and Tom peered round its edge, his face pale and drawn. The old man didn't say a word, just stared at Dick as if he were a stranger. By this time Dick was cold and wet and angry.

'What the hell is the matter with you? Didn't you hear the car?'

Tom didn't answer, peering past Dick into the fog.

'Angus?' Tom said, and Dick was surprised to hear a tremor in his voice.

'He's in the car. And I'm going to need your help getting him down the stairs -- it looks like he's had a heart attack.'

The old man's face went paler still, mirroring that of the man back in the car, and he shook his head slowly from side to side, as he backed further away from Dick.

He tried to speak, and nothing came out for a while, his mouth working furiously to no avail and in the end he merely clamped his jaws tight shut and just stared at Dick.

'Well. Are you coming or not?' Dick asked, and finally got a reply.

'I'm sorry Dick -- I cannae do it. I cannae go out into the fog.'

The old man didn't look sorry -- he looked

frightened out of his wits.

'Listen old man,' Dick said, his anger clearly showing in his voice. 'There's a friend of yours out there who needs your help. Now I know you're scared - - but so am I, and I've been through a damn sight more than you have today. So are you going to give me a hand?'

By this time Dick was past caring. He was going to get the policeman down, put him into a bed, and head for the whisky bottle. And if Tom didn't like it, he could shove it.

He turned his back, not waiting for a response, and made for the step, listening for Tom's footsteps behind him. Old Tom didn't even have a chance to move before the sound of a shotgun blast boomed across the small harbour, its echoes swallowed quickly by the thickening fog. Dick started running, taking the stairs two at a time and he was more than half-way up the flight before he wondered what he was going to do when he reached the car.

He was too late anyway. The passenger door of the land-rover was lying on the ground, torn off its hinges and bent into a twisted, buckled piece of scrap.

He had one look in the car, just long enough to see the spray of blood across the seat and spattered flecks of red on the windscreen. Again he tasted the coppery tang at the back of his throat and he had to swallow, hard, to keep down the rising bile. Apart from the blood there was no sign that Angus had ever been there.

He had to take a closer look anyway, and soon wished he hadn't. The policeman had been wearing the seat belt -- Dick could remember clicking it into place, but whatever had taken the man, it had managed to tear the belt from its housing.

Dick found the shotgun, or the remains of it anyway, on the ground by the door. Its barrel had been bent to almost a right angle, like a prop from a circus strongman's act, and he tried not to think about the brute strength that would be required for the action. He bent to pick it up, and heard a sound behind him, the crunch of feet on gravel.

In one movement he turned, swinging the gun like a club, and almost didn't have time to turn the blow aside as a startled Tom jumped away from him. In the darkness the old man looked like a ghost -- only the deep pools of his eyes showing any semblance of life.

Dick found that he was shaking, trembling from his shoulders all the way down to his fingertips.

'You daft old fool -- I damned nearly killed you,' he shouted, then went quiet as his shout was answered by a harsh cough from deep in the fog.

He looked at Tom, and Tom just stared blankly back at him. He was about to speak when the sound came again -- a coarse rasping hacking.

And a second later Dick heard something else, something that caused his legs to go weak and nearly made him fall to the ground.

Something out there was breathing.

Neither of them stopped to think.

Thirty seconds later Dick was back in the kitchen, breathing heavily and wondering how an old man like Tom had managed to beat him down the stairs.

They stared at each other and he could see his fear reflected in the old man's eyes. Tom locked the door once more, making sure that the bolt was held securely.

'Angus?' the old man asked again.

'They got him,' was all Dick would say. 'Christ, I

need a drink.'

Tom put the whisky bottle on the table and sat down opposite him. Dick was shocked to see that the old man looked at least ten years older than he had that morning. There were deep lines at the corners of his eyes which Dick had never noticed before, and his skin had taken on a sickly grey pallor. As he reached for the bottle his hands shook so much that Dick had to take over the pouring.

The whisky went down in one smooth gulp, burning its way to his stomach, and he was about to pour another when he realised that he had forgotten something.

'The radio,' he said. 'We've got to tell someone what's happened.' He was out of his chair and on his way when Tom spoke, his voice almost a whisper.

'Maybe that's not such a good idea.'

Dick turned back, not sure if he'd heard rightly.

'What do you mean -- not such a good idea?'

Tom looked thoughtful, and at first Dick thought he wasn't going to reply, but after he'd had another long gulp of whisky he spoke.

'Maybe we should sit it out -- see if it passes over.' Tom said, never raising his eyes from the drink in front of him. Dick heard the tremor in his voice as the old man continued.

'Angus died because we called him. Do you want more deaths on your conscience?'

Dick didn't have to think about it.

'Come on Tom -- there's more people involved than Angus. There are the students for starters -- then there's the folk from the pub, and Duncan.'

Another thought suddenly came to him.

'And there's a boat load of tourists due tomorrow

-- God it would be a massacre. No Tom -- I've got to call somebody.'

'Go on then,' the old man said, sitting down hard on the chair and immediately reaching for the bottle,

Dick left Tom with the whisky and headed for the radio. He got through to the coast-guard at the second attempt.

'Stoney Light here. We've got an emergency.'

He recognised the voice which replied. John Phillips was one of his drinking partners on his bouts of shore leave and the pair of them had shared many hangovers together over the summer.

'What kind of emergency would that be Dick -- run out of women again?'

Dick wasn't in the mood for flippancy.

'Just listen will you,' he said, and heard the sharp intake of breath at the other end of the line. 'We've got at least ten dead here, and Angus is one of them. We need help -- preferably armed help.'

He could tell that John was having trouble taking it all in -- this was a bit different from the usual requests the coast-guard had to handle. It was long seconds before he heard a coherent question, and even then it only confirmed his suspicions.

'What is this Dick -- some sort of sick joke?' Dick heard the disbelief in the man's voice. He wasn't really surprised -- he wasn't sure if he believed it all himself yet.

He laughed, a cold hard thing, and again he heard the sharp of breath at the other end of the line.

'Having you been drinking Dick?' the coast-guard asked, and Dick had to laugh again.

'Aye John. I've been drinking. But not enough. Not yet anyway.'

He heard the confusion in the coast-guard's

voice.

'Honestly Dick. If you're having me on, I'll swing for you.'

'No joke John. Just get some help out here fast.' He was about to sign off when he remembered the important thing. 'And cancel the ferry for tomorrow. I don't think it would be a good idea to have tourists on the island. Not for a while yet.'

He cut the line before the coast-guard could ask any more questions, Further conversation would have been useless -- he would only have to explain things, and nobody would believe his story -- not in the cold light of day.

This way they would at least send someone to investigate, and he knew John well enough to know that he wouldn't take any chances.

When he got back to the kitchen he noticed that the level of the whisky bottle had dropped considerably. He took the bottle away from Tom, who only put up a token resistance.

'I don't think we should have any more of that,' Dick said, putting the bottle back on its shelf. 'One of us is going to have to keep awake. I've got no intention of letting those things creep up on us.'

Tom was shook his head again, a forlorn hand reaching out towards him, pleading for the return of the bottle, a chance of oblivion.

'Come on son. Give it back. They're going to come for us, and I don't want to die sober.'

'For God's sake man,' Dick said, taking the old man by the shoulders and shaking him. 'Pull out of it. Help's on its way.'

Tom laughed, and Dick was shocked by the lack of humour in it -- it was the sound of a man who is already dead.

'More men with guns will no' make much difference -- it's a minister we need. You cannae kill these things with guns -- they're devils, pure and simple. You just mark my words they're coming -- and there's damn little we can dae about it. So why don't you just give me the bottle back?'

Dick knew that the bit about the guns wasn't completely true -- he'd blown most of the head off the one who'd attacked him -- he didn't think it would still be walking around. And if it was still walking -- well maybe then he'd believe in devils.

'What do you mean?' he asked the old man, more to distract his attention from the whisky bottle than for any genuine desire to know. 'They seemed like flesh and blood to me.'

Tom looked up at him, his eyes sad.

'Aye, maybe. But they're got power -- an evil power, and only a man of the cloth will be able to put them back down into the pit where they belong. Let me tell you a story.'

Dick groaned. 'Not another one of your stories, please. I've had enough for one day.'

The old man shrugged and sunk his head onto his chest. After a few minutes he began to snore quietly.

Dick got out of his chair, slowly, trying to avoid scraping the legs across the stone floor. He headed for the inner staircase, and as he passed the radio room the set squawked at him. It was probably John, trying to get in touch with someone, anyone, to verify Dick's crazy story. He closed the door and ignored it. 'Let them worry,' he thought. 'It'll make them come all the faster.'

He climbed the stairs, checking all the shutters on the way, but Tom had already battened down the hatches all the way up. He was left with only the light itself to check.

The stairs opened out into the light-room, and it felt strange being in the room with the darkness and the fog outside and the light inactive. He thought about starting it up, but Tom was the boss, and besides, he thought that this time the old man was probably right. There was no sense in attracting attention to themselves.

He circled the light keeping to the walkway until he reached the outside door. It too was locked. Old Tom was certainly worried, but Dick couldn't see anything managing to scale the sheer walls of the lighthouse. He got the correct key from the large number he kept in his pocket and went outside.

He came up here a lot, usually to sit on the cast-iron balcony and watch the sun going down, but tonight there was only the fog and the silent dark,

Previously he had always enjoyed the solitude of this spot, but tonight he was on edge, feeling as if he was being watched. The fact that he could only make out soft shadows on the cliff edge made him nervous. He knew that that they were probably only bushes and shrubs, but his mind was furnishing him with pictures -- lurid, three dimensional fantasies of eight foot monsters with rows of razor sharp teeth, saucer eyes staring and watching him as he stood, unprotected on the walkway.

He made a quick circuit of the tower, not caring to stop. It was only when he got back to the door that he chanced a look over the side.

The fog was too thick to let him see the sea, but there was no sign of movement on the walls of the tower, and Dick was pleased to note that it looked as smooth and insurmountable as he remembered. He went back inside, being careful to lock the door behind him.

He switched off the single-bulb overhead light as he left, and was startled by a quick movement to his left. He turned sharply, and came face to face with his reflection in the smooth glass of the window. He looked nothing like the person he had been that morning. His eyes were wide and bloodshot and his hair seemed to be growing out of his scalp in clumps. He looked tired and old -- a man ten years older than he actually was, and when he looked closely he saw the flecks of blood which still peppered his face.

'Devil's blood,' he thought to himself, and again he saw that great head come apart as his shotgun blast blew it back to hell.

Suddenly he was crying -- deep racking sobs that brought hot pain to his chest. His eyes stung as heavy tears suddenly sprung at the corners. His image wavered as the tears obscured his sight, and he had to sit down on the floor as his legs buckled beneath him.

Images from the day played out in his mind, and they came in no particular order -- the pain on the policeman's face, the sight of the swaying girl on the cliff-top, the blood on the grass, the bodies in the chamber, but most of all, the explosion of blood as he fired the shotgun.

He curled himself into a foetal crouch as the sobs came louder, and his hands covered his ears as it to cut out the noise.

He stayed on the floor for a long time.

When he finally got moving his legs were unsteady and he had to push himself up, feeling the rough stone scrape against his hands. He had to lean against the wall as he made his way down the stairs where he headed for the bathroom and scrubbed his face until his skin tingled and he looked red and raw. When he finally looked in the mirror there was no trace of blood. He used some water to smooth his hair down, but there was still no disguising the redness in his eyes.

He hoped that the old man was still asleep -- he didn't want to be seen in this condition.

He needn't have worried.

Tom had slumped in his chair while Dick was away, and he now had his head and shoulders laid on the table, Dick had a sudden panic when he couldn't see any movement, but just as he moved forward Tom let out a loud, grumbling snore, so loud that he woke himself up.

If Dick hadn't felt so tired himself it would almost have been comical.

'What time is it?' the old man muttered. Dick looked at his watch and was surprised to find that it was nearly nine o'clock -- he'd spent nearly two hours at the top of the tower.

Tom excused himself and went to the toilet. When he came back he went straight to the fridge and produced two cans of beer.

'I know you think we should stay sober, but we're going to have a wee drink for Angus,' he said, laying a can in front of Dick. 'We're the only ones that know he's dead -- so we're the only one's that can give him a send off.'

Dick wasn't about to argue -- a cold beer was just about at the top of his priority list at the moment.

'To Angus,' he said, opening the can and raising it to his lips. The beer tasted so good that he had to stop himself draining it in one motion. He made himself put it down, if only for a few seconds.

They drank in silence for several minutes before Tom started talking.

'He was a fine man. A bit pig-headed maybe, but he always did the right thing. We grew up together you know?'

Dick hadn't known that, but he wasn't about to interrupt an old man who had tears running down his cheeks.

'There were three of us -- me, Angus and big Jock -- the three caballeros. We were together when he had our first drink in a pub, together when we first starting going out with the lassies, and together when we did oor National Service. Now there's only me left.'

His voice broke and the tears ran faster.

'He was a good friend and I'm going tae miss him.' He raised his glass again. 'To Angus.'

Dick replied in kind. Neither of them spoke again until they had finished the beers.

'So what do we do now?' Tom said, his voice back under control, and Dick realised that there had been a shifting in their relationship -- Tom was looking to him for guidance. He was so amazed that it took him several seconds to reply.

'I think we should just wait,' he said, and he saw the relief in Tom's eyes. 'I hope that John Phillips will have sent someone out by now -- I don't think they'll be too long, even in this fog.'

Tom seemed to think for a second.

'Do you mind if I use the radio?' he asked.

'I'm not going to stop you, if that's what you mean,' Dick replied. 'Who do you want to call anyway?'

Tom looked sheepish. 'Just a few old friends -- and Angus's wife.' He held up his hand before Dick could protest.

'Dinnae worry. I'm no' going to tell her what's

going on. I'll just tell her there's been an accident and that John Phillips is coming out. I don't want her sitting up all night not knowing what's going on. And you never know -- Angus might still turn up alive.'

But Dick did know. There had been too much blood in the car -- Angus wasn't coming back.

The old man left the door of the radio room open but Dick was none the wiser -- the conversations all took place in Gaelic, and he didn't understand a word of it. He did know that Tom called two different people, and that one of them sounded like an old man and the other was a woman, but that was the sum total of his knowledge.

Tom looked more at peace with himself when he came back.

'So -- what's it to be? More beer? Or the radio. Or how about I beat you at chess again?' the old man asked.

Dick secretly pined for a television. Before he'd come to the island he'd been addicted to several soap operas, especially the Australian ones, and it was only through his mother's letters that he could keep track of the convoluted plots.

The radio had become his main lifeline to the outside world, but there was a problem -- they could never agree on what to listen to. Tom was very much the staid older man when it came to listening habits, and his choice of programmes often made Dick feel like climbing the walls with boredom. There were only so many shipping forecasts you could listen to before you started going crazy. Sometimes he wished for a gale, a hurricane, anything to liven up the solid seriousness of the reports.

'Chess,' he said, 'It'll occupy the mind until

someone gets here.'

Dick felt cut off from reality. Several hours ago he had been a room filled with dead people, and now he was sitting down to play a game of chess. A part of him wanted to throw open the door and run -- anywhere, just to get away. Then again he was beginning to wonder if there was anywhere safe to run to.

He sat quietly in his chair while Tom set up the pieces. He supposed it was part of getting older, accepting the inevitable. And at the moment he felt very old.

Tom taught him to play chess when he first arrived. His early games had been quick and disastrous, but lately he had surprised Tom, and himself, by starting to win.

Not often, but often enough to worry the older man. And he'd had his mother send a couple of books on the subject. He was beginning to understand the reasons for some of Tom's opening moves and could even anticipate some of his traps.

The fact that he was now able to play the complex game continually amazed him. When he was a schoolboy, chess was the provenance of the mathematicians and the "swots". No one who had failed the eleven-plus need apply. He'd shunned it then, in favour of football and snooker. But now he was finding it easy. He supposed that was another part of getting older -- you got to notice that the things you thought were difficult were only difficult because you had been excluded from doing them.

Tonight was certainly turning into a night for insights.

He came back to the present when Tom tapped him on the hand.

'Left or right?' Tom asked.

He chose left and got the black pieces. Tom made his first move and they were both soon lost in the intricacies of the game.

It went slowly, neither of them going for the attack, and the game got bogged down in a mid-board tangle. Soon they were spending more time thinking between moves, and Dick found his mind wandering back to the day's events. He had to force himself to concentrate on the game.

It was during one of Tom's thinking periods that he heard the noise, the distinctive sound of an outward motor.

Both men looked up at the same time, their gazes meeting across the table. The noise got closer, and Dick was sure that a boat had entered the harbour.

'I'd better go and have a look,' he said, getting out of his chair and picking up a torch from a hook behind the door. He saw the fear creep in at the back of Tom's eyes. 'Lock the door behind me if you want -- I'll make sure I shout when I get back.'

Tom wasted no time in closing the door behind Dick, and he heard again the rasp of iron as the bolt was drawn across. The fog had got thicker if anything and he couldn't see down into the small harbour. There was definitely a boat there though -- he heard its engine as it switched to a lower gear. He wondered how the pilot was getting on, navigating in the fog.

He was afraid to call out, not wishing to draw any attention to himself, so he walked slowly down to the harbour. Suddenly the engine noise stopped and the night fell silent until a voice rang out.

'Hello. Is anybody there?'

He recognised the voice of the coast-guard, John

Phillips. He moved closer. He saw the glow of his torch first, then the slight figure of his friend came out of the fog and into his torchlight. He swung the beam around, but there was no one else.

'So where's the cavalry?' Dick asked. John smiled back at him, but the grin died when he saw Dick's face.

'Come on Dick -- you can't expect me to call out the army on the basis of one phone call. I had to come out and see what's going on for myself. If need be I can use your radio and have somebody here within the hour.

Dick felt betrayed -- he'd expected more trust from John, but then again, the story had been outlandish. There was only one way to make him understand.

'Oh aye, I'll show you what's going on all right. But you're not going to like it. I just hope you didn't eat a big meal tonight. Come on.'

He walked off towards the cliff, with John following on behind.

'Maybe we should go inside first?' John asked as they passed the door to the lighthouse, but Dick wasn't having any of that.

'No. We've wasted enough time already. If you'd brought help as I asked we wouldn't have to do this.'

Now it was John's turn to be angry.

'What do you expect. I spoke to the Doc, and he said that the girl was in deep shock and not making any sense.'

The coast-guard was beginning to breathe heavily as they climbed the stairs, and his voice was strained as he continued.

'Neither the Doc or the copter pilot saw anything out of the ordinary when they were here -- and Angus isn't available for comment. Think how stupid I'd look it I called out the army only to find two stir-crazy lighthouse keepers.'

'Aye,' Dick thought, and didn't say 'And how stupid you're going to look when you finally have to make that call anyway.'

Then he had another thought.

'Did you radio Jim and Anne at the pub? Was there any reply?'

He turned round to find the coast-guard looking sheepish.

'Sorry Dick,' was all he said. Dick gave a snort of disgust and headed for the land-rover.

He shone his torch on the ground, saying nothing, forcing the coast-guard to look at the blood, at the bent shotgun. Finally he showed him the door and the bent hinges. John moved to look inside the car and Dick stood off to one side -- he'd seen enough blood for one day.

He realised that he was straining to hear, listening for any noises out in the fog, waiting for that barking cough so that he could justifiably run for the protection of the tower. It was quiet, and he felt the need to talk.

'Hurry up John -- I don't think we should stay out here too long.'

John backed out of the car and turned to face him. He could see that the coast-guard was confused -- confused and suddenly wary.

'Okay Dick -- fun time's over. What did you do with Angus?'

He continued before Dick had time to reply.

'Oh, I don't think for a minute that you and Old Tom killed him. But something has happened -- hasn't it?'

This was going to be the hardest bit, explaining

what had happened during that day. It made it all the more difficult when you had to explain it to a complete sceptic like John.

Besides, he didn't intend to do any explaining out here in the fog and the dark.

'Let's go back to the tower -- we'll be safer there,' Dick said. He was already heading for the steps when John's call stopped him.

'No. I think we should go out to the mound. I heard some of the girl's story from the Doc -- I think I'd better have a look round.'

Dick's heart sank and he felt the hairs at the back of his neck rise as John waved him towards the car.

He made one last try as dissuading the coast-guard.

'Why don't we wait till daylight. We might miss something important in the dark.'

But the coast-guard refused to be swayed.

'No. I think it'll be best to do it now.'

'You drive,' he said, still waving Dick towards the car. 'And tell me what happened to Angus on the way.'

The coast-guard sat in the back seat, and they both tried to ignore the red smears on the seats as they got into the car. They couldn't ignore the smell though, and Dick was glad that the passenger door had gone, letting in just enough fresh air to keep the nausea down.

The headlights of the land-rover barely made an impression on the fog as he turned the car round and the engine sounded unnaturally loud after the previous stillness.

'Third time lucky,' he muttered under his breath.

He was aware that John had turned against him, believing him to be guilty of some imagined violence against the policeman. The only way to convince him was to take him to the mound -- but that didn't mean he had to like it.

As he drove he recounted what had happened to Angus and himself earlier in the day, but he did little to dent the coast-guard's scepticism -- in fact it seemed only to make John more wary.

'You think I've gone loopy, don't you?' he asked.

The coast-guard didn't reply, and Dick was about to complain when he saw the orange glow in the fog ahead.

He slowed down and killed the engine. John leaned forward towards him and was about to speak when Dick stopped him with a wave of his hand.

A harsh chanting reached them through the fog, and Dick thought that there were at least twenty voices in the chorus. The orange glow flickered wildly and he soon realised that he was looking at the glow of a fire -- a large fire.

The men looked at each other, and Dick was sure that he looked as puzzled as the other man.

'Leave the car here,' John said. 'We'll try and get a bit closer.'

Dick didn't complain, but he was thinking about Tom's story, about Columba and the opening of the mound.

The fog clung to his face and felt cold in his lungs as he left the car. He noticed that John was about to switch on his torch and just managed to stop him in time by putting a hand on his arm. In the dark, they crept closer to the fire.

Dick reckoned they were getting close, and put out his arm to stop the other man, He pointed off to his right, to where a path led off to the ruins of the Mansion House.

The fog was clearing, being blown on a slight breeze. They speeded up, neither wishing to be caught in the open. By the time they reached the ruins they could see clear sky above them. They climbed a broken down wall, taking care not to dislodge any stones. At first Dick couldn't see how they could watch the scene and still remain hidden, but then they found a vantage point which they could settle behind and look down on the scene around the mound.

The fire was huge, blazing angrily into the night, sending sparks spiralling towards the sky. Pieces of the archaeologist's scaffolding, tents and sleeping bags, all burned merrily.

The creatures stood around it in a circle, chanting in coarse bass voices. They seemed to be holding hands, staring at the sky and Dick stopped counting when he reached thirty. The last wisps of mist cleared completely and he got his first close look at the creatures around the fire.

They were huge -- the tallest of them over eight feet. They were broad shouldered and thin waisted, with builds like Olympic swimmers, and their eyes were like two saucers fixed into their heads, eyes which shone golden in the firelight.

Their hair gleamed jet black, hanging in huge swathes down their backs, seemingly growing, not just from their heads, but down their spines as well. Their hands looked big enough to crush a man's head.

Their arms looked all wrong, and it took Dick several seconds to figure out what it was… they had an extra joint between elbow and hand. From this joint a long curved talon stretched out behind the arms, a talon which looked capable of gutting a man from groin to chest with very little effort.

From this distance it was impossible to guess at

any differences between the sexes. They were all naked, but there were no obvious genitalia -- their torsos stretched in smooth unbroken flesh between their legs.

A portion of the circle suddenly broke, and six more of the creatures appeared from the mound, carrying something above their heads. Their pace was slow and Dick was reminded of pall bearers at a funeral. As they got closer to the fire he could see that his analogy was apt -- they were carrying the body of one of the creatures.

Dick let out a gasp as he realised that it was almost headless -- it was the one he had blasted with the shotgun.

The group reached the edge of the fire and all the creatures suddenly fell quiet as the body was lifted to arms length then thrown on the fire. As one the creatures threw their heads back and howled to the sky, a high keening which raised goose pimples on Dick's arms and sent a shiver along his spine.

But even that wasn't the worst thing. The thing which kept drawing his gaze was the bodies lined up in front of the fire. There were three of them, two of the students behind the professor -- he knew it was the professor -- he recognised the mop of silver grey hair.

They were tied firmly to stakes and were only six feet from the fire -- Dick could see smoke beginning to rise from their clothes. They were all dead -- that was obvious from the empty blackness of their eye sockets and the gaping holes in their chests, but they had been stood up against the stakes in a semblance of life, and bonds around their foreheads ensured that they stared straight forwards.

Suddenly the howling stopped.

The tallest creature moved out of the circle and

strode towards the staked bodies. There was fluidity to its movements, reminding him of the grace and power of one of the big cats. Its hair bounced behind it, and Dick saw that it was streaked in silver. He judged that the creature must be nearly nine feet tall. Dick suddenly felt cold, and was aware of the grey condensation from his mouth as he breathed.

Something bad was about to happen -- he felt it in the air, but he was unable to draw his gaze away.

The creature leaned towards the body of the professor. It spoke -- a guttural, barking sound which echoed across the night, like no language Dick had ever heard. Its hands made some passes in the direction of the fire, and a new flare shot sparks into the sky. The creature pointed one long finger straight at the professor's head and gave out a loud shout.

The fire flared spectacularly and Dick automatically shrank further down in his hiding place, but the creatures' attention was all on the dead body of the professor.

Dick stopped breathing as the dead body jerked, just once. The crowd let out a moan which was silenced by a gesture from the tall creature.

It spoke several words, again followed again by the pointing finger, and the professor -- the dead professor, began to move, pulling against the bonds.

The dead man's mouth opened in a gaping yawn and a cry of pain emerged, the sound of a man in torment, the dark, empty eye sockets staring straight at the creature. His arms thrashed against the stake and the body jerked like a marionette driven by a mad puppeteer.

The tall creature left him standing there and moved in front of the bodies of the students.

The night fell silent once more, broken only by

the crackling from the fire as something collapsed inwards in a sudden shower of sparks.

The tall creature spoke again, his voice carrying clearly across the distance. Dick felt power in the air, his hair standing on end -- the same sensation he remembered from some long ago school day when the teacher invited them to touch a Van Der Graaf generator.

The same pointing was done and soon all three of the bodies jerked and thrashed on their ropes. And all the time the circle of creatures stood silent, staring into the fire.

Dick heard a moan from his right and turned to find John with his head in his hands, mumbling quietly to himself. Just the one word, but repeated over and over.

'No, no..'

He patted the man on the shoulder, but got no response before turning back to the scene around the fire.

The tall figure moved back in front of the professor. It raised its arms in the air and there was the sudden crackle of electricity, again bringing memories of the Van Der Graaf. Blue sparks ran between its fingers, crackling loudly above the sounds of the fire and causing the creature's hair to rise in a black halo swirling around its head. The sparks increased in intensity as it brought its hands slowly together, slowly forming a rolling ball of electric flame.

The circle of onlookers began to murmur softly and Dick felt the hairs on his forearms stand on end as the static increased.

The creature raised itself up on its toes, hands stretched above its head, hair flying wildly around its face. It cried, a shout which sent the fire flaring brightly then flung its hands forward, sending a silver ball of sparkling energy into the heart of the fire where it exploded in a shower of rainbow sparks.

The crowd sighed -- a great falling moan, and the creature fell to its knees as if exhausted. The only movement was the jerking of the three staked bodies and the red flames from the fire.

Dick thought that the show might be over, but then the fire began to seethe and boil as if someone had poured gasoline into its heart.

Three distinct balls of flame rolled out of the inferno, targeting themselves on the staked bodies. He watched, astonished, as the balls rolled over the bodies, first hitting their feet then crawling up their legs before engulfing them in a searing, roaring ball.

The circle of creatures began to dance as the bodies burned and the sweet smell of burning meat wafted across the island accompanied by the screaming of already dead flesh.

Dick had to cover his ears -- the pain in the voices was more than he could bear. How could dead flesh be reanimated in this way? What the hell was going on here?

He remembered to breathe and felt the coldness of the air as it cut into his lungs. He was distracted by a noise beside him and turned to find John, doubled over and retching. There was a sudden silence from around the fire, and at first Dick thought that they had been discovered, but all attention was now on the tall creature.

The fires around the three staked bodies had died, leaving them black, smoking ruins. Dick was glad to see that all movement had stopped.

The creature moved forward once more his

finger pointed at the professor. Once more the air was filled with power and the gathered crowd let out another low moan. There was a load crack from the burnt out body and a tremor ran through its length. Dick gasped as the charred head lifted from its chest, slowly and as if with great effort. The black mouth opened in a gaping yawn and the black eyes stared back at its tormentor. Even from this distance he could see the thick oily smoke pouring from the eye sockets.

The tall creature spoke, a sing-song chant which was echoed by the others in the circle. Small blood-red fires sprung up in the depths of the dead man's skull and there was a sudden red flare as the hole in the chest blazed.

The chanting got louder, and the circle became more frenzied before being stopped by a gesture from their leader. All went quiet and still, again only the crackling from the fire disturbing the silence. There was a sense of anticipation as if the creatures were waiting for some sign. The fire suddenly burst into life again. And then a voice spoke from the dead man's mouth.

The voice boomed, a deep melodious ringing, but there was no warmth in it and Dick's skin crawled. He was aware that John was trembling beside him and he heard the coast-guard's teeth rattle.

The language seemed to be the same as that spoken by the creatures, but it was difficult to be sure. John had buried his face in his hands again and seemed to be crying, but Dick was unable to draw his gaze away from the fire and the scene around it.

The creatures fell to the ground and prostrated themselves in front of the burnt body, hands all pointing at the blackened, charred creature. Dick heard the soft murmuring of their chants -- it sounded much like prayer.

More flames appeared around the body, and the remains of the ropes binding it fell away. It walked, stiff legged at first, then more steady, moving towards the tall creature and as it opened its arms small flames appeared on the palms of his hands.

It spoke, only one word, but its meaning was clear even to Dick.

Give it to me.

There was a movement near the mound and a figure appeared. A high pitched cry echoed around the circle, and as the figure got closer to the fire he cold see that it was a smaller version of the creatures, one that was most definitely female, and it was carrying a child which lay still and quiet in her arms. It took Dick several seconds to realise that the child was also one of the creatures.

The leader took the child from its bearer and the crowd fell silent once more as he held it out to the charred body. Dick couldn't bring himself to look away as the child was taken and the flames sprouted once more.

This time it all took place in complete silence. Flames engulfed the child and it flared in a glowing white ball. There was an explosion of colour, like a giant firework, and when his eyes recovered there was only the smouldering remains of a fire and the creatures.

A song began, quiet at first, then building to a crescendo of cacophonous noise. To Dick it sounded very much like a song of joy. Two minutes later the creatures began to filter back into the mound.

Soon there were only the stars and the fire and the burnt out bodies of the three captives.

Dick turned to John and saw that he still had his

face buried in his hands. He touched one of the coast-guard's arms and the man jumped as if prodded by a stick. When he took his hands away from his face he had gone white, his lips showing deep red against a pale ivory skin.

'Are they finished?' he asked, his voice barely a whisper.

Dick nodded, and helped John off the ground. In sign language he indicated that they should leave, and they climbed down from the ruins, taking great care not to dislodge any stones. They waited until they were well away from the mound before they dared to speak.

'What did we just see?' John whispered. 'Did it really happen?'

Dick wasn't sure. It could have been an imaginative piece of trickery -- but that meant ascribing a high degree of intelligence to the creatures. He wasn't sure what he feared most -- the fact that they might be intelligent or the fact that they might have a degree of magical power. Most of all he didn't want to think about the thing which had animated the professor's dead body.

'I don't know,' he finally replied. 'It seemed to be some sort of ceremony. Something almost religious.' And thinking back on it, that's what it had felt like -- the almost sepulchral silence, the chanting, and the final, awful sacrifice. It reminded him of some things he'd read about pagan rituals -- the sort of thing performed by bored stockbrokers in their pseudo-witchcraft ceremonies.

But this had been real. Real and much more sinister. He didn't really want to analyse it too much -- he was afraid he might go mad if he had to consider all the implications.

'Let's just get back to the tower,' he said, keeping his voice low. 'Old Tom seems to know something about these things -- we'll ask him.'

John seemed happy with that prospect, but refused to go back to the car, in fact, he was terrified at the prospect.

'No way. The noise would bring them out. I think we should walk. It's not far anyway.'

The look he gave Dick was pleading, almost pitiful, but if truth be told Dick wasn't too keen in going anywhere near that fire again. He led them off to the cliff top where they soon met a small path. It was only then that they chanced using a torch, and even then they only used one of them. The moon appeared from behind a cloud and the fog had dispersed completely.

Dick looked at his watch and was surprised to find that it was two o'clock in the morning -- the ritual had taken over two hours. It was time they got back.

He suddenly thought of Tom. The last thing the old man knew was that Dick had gone outside to check on a boat. That had been about three hours ago.

He hoped Tom had done the sensible thing and stayed put. The thought led urgency to his actions and he started to walk faster.

They had got halfway along the cliff when they started to hear the rustling in the rhododendrons to their right. John stopped suddenly and Dick nearly walked into him.

'Did you hear that,' John said, and his voice brought another rustle. Dick peered into the bushes but could see nothing but blackness and shadow. He shone his torch into the gloom and there was a sudden rustle as something moved away from them, only for the noise to reappear several yards further down the path.

Something was trailing them.

'Keep moving,' Dick hissed. 'Maybe it's afraid to take on two of us.'

He started walking again, even faster this time, and soon they were close to running. And all the time the thing in the bushes kept pace with them.

'We'll be out of the rhododendrons soon,' Dick said, his breathing beginning to become laboured. 'Maybe it will give up.'

John didn't reply, only upped his pace again. Dick was more than a little worried about running along a cliff-top in the dark, but the thought of being caught by the creatures forced him to speed up, his torch frantically trying to pierce the darkness, to show any possible obstacles in their path.

The rhododendrons gathered closer to the path just ahead. Dick was almost at full pelt now, and John had trouble keeping up. The coast-guard put on a sudden burst of speed, panting furiously as he passed Dick. He got five yards ahead... and that's when it came out of the bushes.

Something black and low and fast leapt out in front of the coast-guard, bringing him crashing to the ground in a screaming bundle of flailing arms and legs. The black shape was on him fast and Dick was moving forward when John began to scream even louder.

As Dick got closer he began to laugh, and by the time he reached the prone figure of the coast-guard he was guffawing loudly.

John was still screaming, his eyes squeezed closed, hands flailing wildly at the thing which was now sitting on his chest. If he'd opened his eyes he would have seen the sad brown eyes of Sam the sheep-dog.

The dog's tail wagged freely from side to side as it leant forward and licked at John's face. This brought another scream of terror.

Dick had to forcibly control himself -- the laughter was in danger of flipping over into hysteria -- he felt it building in him, the need to just keep on laughing, cackling maniacally until the men in the white coats came to take him away to a place where he would always be comfortable and there was nothing to frighten him.

He couldn't completely get rid of the grin though. Old Sam was probably the least frightening inhabitant of the island at the moment.

'Here Sam,' Dick said, 'Heel'.

Reluctantly the dog left its "catch", waddling over to Dick and allowing him to tickle it behind the ears. Dick had to fight off a sudden attack on his groin, pushing the dog away. It immediately keeled over, playing dead, legs waggling ineffectually in the air, teeth bared in a wide grin. A more submissive creature it would be difficult to find.

John groaned loudly and Dick looked up to see him getting sheepishly to his feet.

'Bloody dog. I think I've pissed myself,' he said.

That set Dick off again -- he couldn't help the laughter, a combination of humour and a release from the tension he had been under all day. At first John scowled at him, but soon he too was doubled over with laughter. Sam sat between them, his tail still wagging excitedly, confused at the strange antics of the men, getting more excited by the second, and when Dick let out a particularly loud laugh, he began to bark in unison, the sound carrying loud and clear through the still night air.

Dick was quickly brought back to earth.

'Quiet Sam' he ordered, his voice now no more than a whisper, and the dog slumped to the ground, ears flat against his head. The dog whimpered quietly and looked so sad that Dick immediately felt guilty. He gave the dog a quick pat on the head, which elicited the tail wagging again.

The trio were silent for long seconds, but there was no sound other than the gentle lapping of the waves on the rocks two hundred feet below them. Dick realised he had stopped breathing, and when he looked across at John he could see the fear in his eyes. He signalled for John to follow and they set off again at a fast walk.

The moon showed them the way to the tower. Dick made John stop on the cliff-top as they stood at the top of the steps, surveying the scene below.

There was no sign of violence, and he could just catch a chink of light escaping from the shuttered kitchen window.

He prayed that Tom was all right.

Sam bounded ahead of them down the steps. It knew the path well - it was a regular visitor to old Tom who always had a biscuit to spare for the friendly dog. It jumped up to the big wooden door and began to scratch against the wood.

Dick was just close enough to hear the yell of terror from inside the tower.

'I've got a gun, and I'm not afraid to use it,' he heard Tom shout.

He almost laughed again as he had a mental image of the old man behind the door, terrified of the sheepdog.

'There's no need for that Tom,' he called. 'It's Dick and John.'

This time the old man didn't dither, he let the men and the dog in, quickly slamming the door behind them. Dick turned towards the old man and was surprised to be grabbed in a hug.

'My God laddie, I thought I'd lost you as well.' Tom hugged him harder, then harder still until Dick was getting worried for his ribs. He patted the old man on the shoulder, looking over at John who grinned like a Cheshire cat.

He was shocked by the show of affection, but as he hugged the old man he felt tears spring in his eyes. He realised that he loved the old man, loved him like a father, and that he hadn't been admitting to himself how much he was worried about the old man's safety.

He motioned with his head towards the radio room, and John got the message.

Dick pushed Tom out to arm's length.

'And it's good to see you again, you old bugger. I'm sorry it took so long -- but just wait till you hear the story we've got to tell.'

The old man wiped tears from his eyes.

'A story is it? Aye, I suppose there will be tales to tell after this. I just hope I'm around to tell them.'

'Of course you will,' Dick said. 'There'll be plenty of free drams for you out of this in years to come. Get us a whisky and I'll tell you a story that'll make your hair stand on end.'

It was only then that he noticed the guilt in the old man's eyes.

'Can it no' wait till the morning -- I'm expecting a visitor who will understand it better than me -- somebody who knows the ways o' the devil.'

Dick was about to ask him what he meant when John came back from the radio room. He cradled the remains of the radio set in his arms.

Tom didn't give them time to ask any questions.

'I thought you were both dead. I could nae take the chance of anybody else coming here... there's too many dead already. I could nae stand anybody else going the same way as Angus.'

Dick moved forward, and for a second he considered striking out at the old man, but Tom sat down hard in his chair and buried his head in his hands.

'I was scared -- can you not understand that. I thought this was going to be my last night on the planet, that they were going to come for me. Then that radio started squawking at me. So I tore it off the wall and smashed it. I'm sorry. I'm so sorry.'

He buried his head in his arms again and began to cry. Dick and John stood over him, unsure as to what to do. Only Sam understood instinctively what was needed. The dog nuzzled Tom's legs until he couldn't be ignored, then jumped into the man's lap, forcing Tom to pay attention and begin to pet the dog.

'Can it be fixed?' Dick asked John, nodding towards the mass of wires and bent metal, knowing already that the lump of junk would never work again.

John confirmed it by shaking his head.

'I don't think so. Even if I knew anything about the electronics, it would be a long job -- and I don't think we're going to be allowed to sit around and fix it - - do you?'

Dick thought about it. The creatures had been doing a good job of getting rid of anyone who happened to be around. He just hoped that the people from the pub were okay.

'That's it then -- we take the boat,' Dick said. 'We have to stop the ferry from coming in the morning.' He looked to John for support, but the other man backed away.

'Not tonight Dick. Let's leave it till the morning, eh? My wee boat can get over to the mainland in two hours -- that's plenty of time. I think we all need to try to get some sleep.'

Dick got a surprise when Tom supported the coast-guard.

'John's right. It'll be best if we wait till morning. I don't want to be out on the water in the dark, in a small boat.'

Thinking about it, Dick realised that he wasn't keen on the idea either.

'All right then -- first thing in the morning. But we sleep in shifts -- I wouldn't feel completely safe otherwise -- we never know what those things will do.'

The others agreed and they worked out a rota. John was to take the first shift, until four o'clock, Tom would do four till six and Dick got the early shift. He realised that it meant he probably wouldn't get back to bed afterwards, but he wasn't too sure he was going to sleep much anyway.

He was wrong about that. Two minutes after his head hit the pillow he was fast asleep. Some time later he began to dream.

He was in his old bed, back in his flat in Glasgow. In his dream he didn't see anything wrong with that. He was just coming up out of sleep, having been woken by some repeated noise. The room was dimly lit from outside by an orange street light which cast red shadows across the carpet. He was in that state between awake and asleep which causes the imagination to run riot and the heart to lurch at the slightest unexplainable noise.

And then the noise came again. Something was climbing the stairs -- no, not climbing as much as slumping, the noise like a wet fish being slapped on a fishmongers slab. He didn't know how he knew, but it was coming for him, and it was more than halfway up the stairs.

The shocks caused by its movements were jolting the room, the red shadows quivering in the mirror, making the reflected room shake.

The air in the room became damp and then damper still, he had the impression of water glistening on the carpet, droplets running down the walls, covering the ceiling and dripping, red and bloody from the light fitting. There was a salt tang of sea water in the air. He tried to cower under the blankets, reverting to childhood, tucking his legs in under the covers to make sure that his ankles didn't get grabbed by a clammy frozen hand.

Whatever the thing outside was it had finished climbing the stairs and was dragging itself heavily across the landing towards his door. He was not really worried, he knew that it was a dream, vivid maybe but still just a dream and that he would almost certainly wake up before it got too frightening. It always had happened when he was a kid.

His radio alarm switched itself on, some unremarkable dance song spinning its bass run around the room, sending further tremors through the walls, dislodging a small shower of droplets from the ceiling and causing the light bulb to sway alarmingly. The whole room began to throb as the music got louder, then louder still. Whatever was outside was now so close that he heard its heavy breathing, even over and above the now deafening music.

The door, behind his back and out of sight, opened slowly and it came into the room, bringing with it a stronger tang of sea and the thick decaying odour of rooting weed.

He felt something take hold of the duvet and pull it away from him. He resisted as hard as he could, pulling back and holding tightly but the pull was too much, dragging his body sideways across the bed and onto the floor which squelched wetly as his shoulder hit it and turned his head to face his attacker.

The Creature From The Black Lagoon stared back at

him, a large blue-green scaled body topped by a big-maned head, green saucer-like eyes unblinkingly scrutinising him. The mouth seemed to be full of teeth, a razor sharp forest of them, and somewhere down there a thick black tongue slithered wetly.

The creature reached down, grabbing his shoulders tight, sinking small sharp claws into the flesh beneath shoulder blades, lifting him up to face the rows of teeth and breathing one word which woke him up.

Dick blinked twice, the act of wakening clearing his memory of the dream, leaving only a vague remembrance of the horrors. He rubbed his eyes, and groaned loudly as he lifted his head from the pillow. He looked up into Tom's tired eyes.

He held his head and groaned again, twice for effect, but he didn't raise a smile on Tom's face.

'Six o'clock and all's well,' Tom said with no trace of humour. 'Now get yourself out of bed -- I need it, John's out cold in mine.'

'Anything happening?' Dick asked, and this time he almost got a smile.

'You mean apart from being struck on a remote island surrounded by hordes of raving devils, and, probably the worst thing, an empty whisky bottle?'

'Oh Tom. You didn't drink it all did you?'

There was a definitely a smile there now.

'No me laddie. It was yon coast-guard pal o' yours. I think we might have trouble wakening him up later. Now, are you getting out o' that bed, or am I coming in there with you?'

Dick had scarcely got his feet on the floor when Tom flopped, full length and fully clothed, onto the mattress. There was a creak and Dick turned to see Sam come in the door, warily, as if expecting at any moment to be chased away. Before Dick could say anything the dog jumped onto the bed and nestled beside the old man.

'Down,' Dick said. 'Off the bed Sam,' but the dog stayed where it was, staring up at him with those big brown eyes. It was as if he knew there was no conviction in the man's voice.

Dick didn't think there was anything wrong in it. If the old man and the dog could give some comfort to each other then so much the better.

'Okay. Stay there. But I warn you -- he snores.' The dog let out a large yawn and snuggled its head deep into Tom's armpit. It crept closer to the old man and stared up at Dick with one eye, as if daring him to scold it.

He left them to it.

Tom had left a pot of coffee on the stove -- one of his early morning specials, as thick as low-grade oil and just about as tasty. This morning he wasn't about to be choosy -- he needed all the help he could get if he was to stay awake. He poured himself a cup and headed slowly for the stairs.

This had become another daily ritual -- the early morning coffee at the top of the tower. It wasn't the coffee -- most days he ended up pouring half the cup over the edge, watching the stream of black liquid fall away to the rocks below. No, it was the solitude. It was like prayer, a charm to ensure a good day ahead. Today he had another reason for his ascent -- he needed to make sure that the tower was still secure. He could imagine the black bodies of the creatures swarming up the rock, and he needed to banish that image from his mind.

There was no sign of activity from the main room where the light was housed and there was a clear blue sky outside. Mentally he relaxed -- only a fraction, but enough to feel the tension seeping from his shoulders as he opened the door and went out onto the walkway around the tower.

His peace of mind didn't last long. He circled the tower slowly, admiring the clarity of the view, but when he turned to face the cliffs he almost wished the fog had returned.

Four bodies were lined up along the top of the cliff, sitting in an upright, cross-legged position, and even from his position he could see the deep empty blackness of their stares.

He wasn't so far away that he couldn't recognise the burly frame of the policeman at the end of the line. But that wasn't what caused his heart to race and his blood to pound hotly in his ears.

Beside the policeman he recognised John Jeffries but it was the smaller figure to the right that drew his eyes.

He wasn't going to be having any more tête-à-tête discussions in the pub, and there would be no more time to get to know her -- Sandra stared blindly back at him from empty eye sockets as he screamed, just once before clamping a hand tight over his mouth. Tears sprung unnoticed to his eyes.

In his shock he dropped the cup, and distantly heard the crash as it smashed against the rocks. And then he heard it -- the distant hum of an engine.

He managed to pull his gaze away from the cliff top and saw, still far out to sea, the approaching motor boat.

13

Sam

Sam was happy to be with good people again. He hoped the master wouldn't be too angry with him for being away so long, but he was on the bed, and he intended to stay there. He hadn't been allowed on the bed since he was a puppy.

The soft sheets felt good and comforting. He snuggled up closer to the old man, trying to ignore the smell of fear.

He'd smelled a lot of that smell -- all of the people had it. It made him frightened as well, but the old man had fed him and he felt tired, even though the food had stank of cat.

The old dog nuzzled its nose into the old man's armpit and slept.

At some point he dreamed.

A black thing was stalking him through the farmhouse, a black thing which stank of dead fish and seaweed. Sam was running, faster and faster, but he couldn't get away and the black thing was getting closer.

In his dreams Sam's legs twitched and he whimpered, but he didn't wake up and he was still being chased, around and around the dark cold shadows of the farmhouse.

14
130 Years Ago

Calent had learned patience, but it had been hard.

The island had been quiet for many centuries, with only the occasional visitor to break the monotony. And none of them had come anywhere near the mound. Calent could sense the fear in them, and he wondered if the Father was exerting some influence -- but surely if the Father had his power back he would have helped Calent.

Many times he tried to spread his mind, to seek the stone, but the spells of the Mother were still strong, and he couldn't feel it.

His tribe degenerated further over the long years, but they were still able to multiply. The death toll was high, and the children died young more often than not, but enough were born to ensure continuation.

And Calent himself stayed strong. It was something of a mystery how he managed to stay alive, but he assumed that the Father had work left for him to do. The years grew long, then longer yet, and still Calent waited.

Finally he was rewarded.

He had been sleeping for a long time. Days had turned into weeks, weeks into months, and months into years. He dreamed, reliving past glories, but always there was a portion of his mind which stayed alert and watchful.

Then one day he came, the weak man, the one who could be moulded. Calent sensed him as soon as he landed -- the quick mind flitting this way and that like a small bird pecking at a too large piece of bread, the endless quest for new things, the desire for power. This man could be used.

He had to take it slowly at first -- soft dreams, glimpses of riches, only enough to hold the man's interest. In those early days there were many people on the island, and the ground rumbled and groaned with their workings, but soon they left, leaving the weak man and two others. These two had no imagination, no dreams, and Calent wasn't able to reach them.

He still had the man though, and as the days went on Calent forced his influence on him, his dreams promising great power and untold riches. He showed the man the mound, its stones burst open to reveal a pile of precious stones and jewels, spilling in a flood out into the sunlight.

But the man's dreams didn't stay with him through the day -- he seemed to forget in the sunlight. Calent began to use more and more power, aware that he was draining something fundamental out of himself, but it was the only way to concentrate the man's mind.

He began to draw the man to the mound during the day, and soon he found it easy to see the pictures in the man's mind. He searched through the man's memories, and soon found the Mother there, but she was weak. There was another picture in the mind, a man impaled on a cross of wood. It held great power for the man, but it had no sway over Calent -- he had nothing to fear there.

The man's mind was easy to control, and Calent felt a rising anticipation as preparations were made to open the mound. He reached out and grabbed the man's mind, hard, at the same time feeling another part of his strength leave him, but it was enough for the man to start digging. Calent rejoiced as the fetters and spells fell away.

He stood, just under the earth, and waited for the first signs of entry. He heard the scraping as the man came closer and felt the old anticipation rising. He hoped the Father would be waiting. He reached out to the man, urging him to dig faster, again feeling more strength leaving him. That didn't matter -- the Father would sustain him once he was free.

Small flakes of earth began to fall from the sides of the mound, then larger pieces, until finally the wall fell in with a crash and a stream of fresh, salt-tanged air swept through the chamber, causing Calent to tremble and shake with the almost orgasmic pleasure of it.

He stepped towards the hole, at the same time as the pale, frightened face of the man showed on the other side.

The man shrieked at the sight of Calent, a high pitched, almost feminine sound before turning on his heels and running. Calent let him go -- he didn't need him any more, and he didn't have the strength to force his will on him any further. He widened the hole before pushing himself out into the cold night.

He raised his head to the sky, and howled his pleasure -- the Father beamed down on him, and already he felt the old glory beginning to sing in his blood. He turned back to the mound and called for his tribe.

They came out slowly, tentative. Of the whole tribe Calent was the only one who had ever seen the sky, the only one who knew the Father.

There, on the grass before the mound, he

introduced his people to the Father, and once again pledged his allegiance to the old ways. His people danced in their ecstasy, but inwardly Calent was worried. He had searched for the stone, needing its power, but he couldn't feel it.

He ordered his people into a circle as he called the old plea to the Father. When the chant finished the night fell quiet as Calent waited for a sign.

When it came it wasn't what he'd expected.

A noise cleaved the air, like a thunderclap, and the female beside Calent fell to the ground, blood pouring from a massive wound in her chest. Calent turned towards the source of the sound.

The first thing he noticed was the house -- a massive stone edifice that reminded him somewhat of the glories of Atlantii. The figure of the man was dwarfed by its magnificence, but Calent's attention was once more drawn to him as he raised something to his shoulder, something that Calent guessed was a weapon.

There was a flash, then another thunderous roar, and something hot and fiery sped past Calent's face. He heard a groan and turned to find another of his tribe writhing on the ground, a fist-sized wound in his shoulder.

When he turned back the man was doing something with his weapon. Calent had never encountered anything that could kill at a distance so effectively, but he couldn't let the man pick off his tribe. With a howl he launched himself forward, into the face of the weapon.

The man didn't have the nerve to stand against such an onslaught. He turned and fled before Calent could get within twenty yards of him, heading for the open door of the house.

Calent followed -- slower than he would have liked. He was getting steadily weaker -- the task of controlling the man's mind had taken too much out of him. He was afraid that he might be finally dying. He vowed that if he had to die he would take this man with him.

The man reached the house a mere five yards in front of Calent, and slammed a heavy oak door shut behind him, but even in his weakened state Calent drove it off its hinges, pushing it out of his way as if it were weightless.

The man was already off across a large hallway, heading for a staircase, and had reached the bottom of the stairs when Calent stepped across the threshold.

And stopped, riveted by a sudden surge of power which drove through his body like a thunderbolt.

The stone was here, under the floor. Calent sent out a mental probe, and was answered, but from some way below him. This man had built his massive house on top of the stone.

Once more Calent howled, this time in rage and frustration, and another burst of power ran through him, buckling his legs and forcing him to his knees, but when he was finally able to stand he felt strong, young again. He looked at the man, seeing him for what he really was, a small, insignificant animal against the power which Calent now held.

Calent drew himself up, his bulk filling the doorway, and smiled, showing the man his row of fangs. The man squealed once more and began to run up the stairs.

Calent followed, slowly, savouring the chase. He was halfway up the stairs when another figure appeared at the top -- one of the man's servants, an old, bent man, with wispy white hair and black funereal dress.

He threw something at Calent, something which blazed redly as it tumbled down the stairs, and Calent stepped back as the oil lamp burst at his feet, splashing fire across the cloth hangings on the walls.

The fire spread quickly, eating away at the walls in frenzy, but Calent paid no attention to it. He calmly stepped over the blaze, feeling no more than a mild heat on his legs, and was on the old man before he had time to lose his shock. He lifted the servant above his head and, with one long scream sent him into the fire, offering him to the Father.

Somewhere above him he heard the scurrying of feet as the master of the house tried to escape, fleeing ever further into the house. Calent followed, a new joy in his heart, the thrill of the chase and the power of the Father flowing through him.

He finally caught the old man on the roof, stalking him amongst the buttresses and turrets as the fire raged redly below him. At the last the man tried to use his weapon as a club. Calent took it from him as easily as taking a doll from a baby, and, showing the man his teeth, bent the steel end of the gun into a right angle before sending it sailing into the night.

The man cried and pleaded for his life, speaking in a language completely foreign to Calent. The impaled man on the wooden cross was at the front of the man's mind as Calent lifted him, then sent him over the edge to follow his weapon to the ground.

He stood on the roof of the house and cried his allegiance to the father as the flames sprouted from the windows beneath him.

Calent had to jump from the roof to escape, but even that was easy -- the power of the Father sustained him and he did himself no harm.

Later he stood with his tribe and watched the house burn. It blazed readily, and Calent began to hope, began to believe that the stone would be retrievable once the heat had subsided.

The tribe were so intent on the fire that they didn't notice the small group that appeared from the direction of the cliffs to the north -- and that was nearly their undoing.

Thunderous sounds rent the air, and three of Calent's people fell before he finally managed to marshal the tribe and send them back into the mound, taking their dead with them.

Calent alone stayed to face the attackers -- he was not yet ready to give up his freedom.

Many of the attackers held weapons like the one he had recently taken from the man from the house but the Father was blazing overhead, and at least some of the old power was back. Calent felt confident.

Right up until the point where the man in black strode out of the small crowd.

Calent's heart sank. This one was strong in the Mother, and, although the wooden cross was among the pictures in his mind, it was the Mother who was the foremost -- the hated Mother, suckling her damned child at her breast.

Involuntarily Calent shrank before him.

The man spoke, and again Calent didn't know the words.

'Get back into your pit, spawn of Satan. I abjure and command you in the name of Jesus and his holy mother Mary.'

The image of the Mother seemed almost alive in the air between them, and Calent was forced to back off. He tried to reach the stone, but it was too far away, and the Mother's power was too strong.

Calent hissed at his attackers, just once, before once more crawling into the mound.

He cursed the men loudly as the earth was drawn over his prison, and screamed his rage as the spells of the Mother spun their web over him, but a small part of him rejoiced.

The spells were weaker than before, and he knew that the Father and the stone were still there, still strong. His time would come again, and this time he was sure he wouldn't have long to wait.

And he had been right. The years had seemed to fly past, and more people came. And this time he didn't have to force their minds to do his bidding -- this time they wanted to come into the mound.

This time he was waiting, and he was careful.

15

Duncan

Duncan woke in the bar's cellar, pulling himself out of a dream which had ended with the Creature from the Black Lagoon bending over him. He shivered, a chill spreading through his body, before he carefully opened his eyes.

Meg was wiping his brow with a damp cloth that smelled suspiciously of beer and he was sitting up, leaning against a beer barrel.

He looked around the room, seeing the crates of spirits, the kegs of beer and the boxes of snacks. He looked up into her eyes and tried a smile.

'Don't tell me. I've died and gone to heaven,' he said, before memory came back in a rush.

He remembered the flight up the stairs, the wide eyed creature which pursued him. Meg looked down at him, her eyes showing signs of tears -- tears and tiredness.

'I don't think I hit it,' she said. 'The gun is a bit heavy for me.'

'What the hell was it?' he said, struggling to get to his feet. Meg forced him backwards with a firm push.

'Shush. You've had a bad knock. I don't think you should move for a while. Besides -- I think this might be the safest place to be.'

Her voice held a tremulous note, as if at any minute she might burst into tears, and her hands shook as she brushed her hair away from her face. She looked so lost, so alone, that all he wanted to do was take her in his arms and crush her to him. But before he could move she backed away, out of arms reach. He didn't have the strength to move after her.

He glanced at the door and was relieved that it was shut and locked with a huge iron bolt.

'OK' he said. 'I'll stay put for a while. But what the hell was that thing -- I thought that Gollum had come to get me.'

Meg laughed, but even that sounded more like a sob. 'Oh no. it's real enough. A bogeyman. A story from when I was just a baby.' Her voice was low and there were tears in her eyes as she turned away from him. Once again he moved to hug her but she pulled even further away from him and sat down on a crate in the corner.

'They're dead aren't they?'

She never gave him a chance to reply. With her head down, her hair hanging over her face, she began to speak, her voice a dull drone, devoid of emotion.

'I was changing the barrels when it happened. Mum had called me a little bit earlier, telling me that dinner would be ready soon. I moved towards the steps, and was just about to go up when Dad appeared at the cellar door.' She lifted her head and pointed at the hatchway in the roof.

'He was frightened and he had a shotgun in his hands. He helped me up then something came out of nowhere and knocked him away. The trapdoor shut on me and for a second I thought that Dad had done it trying to save me, but then I heard the struggle overhead. I couldn't just sit and listen to it -- I had to do something. I got myself up the steps -- and when I got to the top the thing already had Dad around the throat.'

She had begun to cry harder, but Duncan didn't think she noticed -- she was lost in the moment.'

'I couldn't see Mum -- I think she was in the kitchen, but I saw one of the things go in there. I think I was in shock -- Dad started to scream and I saw the thing drag him away.'

'I'm not really sure what happened. I picked up the shotgun and tried to fire it, but nothing happened the first time, and the creature dropped Dad and headed for me. I only just managed to get the trapdoor over my head before the thing reached me. I think it must have jumped on the trapdoor -- I was forced to the ground as the door hit me heavily on the head.'

She showed him the bruise on her head.

'While I was lying there the trapdoor began to open and one of the things pushed its head through the gap. I managed to get to the gun and this time it fired one shot. I don't think I hit it though -- the trapdoor fell closed at just the wrong time. I managed to lock the door, and I've been down here ever since.'

There was a second of silence before she spoke again, and Duncan had to strain to hear the whisper.

'They're dead -- aren't they?'

There was nothing he could say. He lifted her to her feet and held her close, felling the hot wetness of her tears on his shoulder. They stayed that way for a while.

He was surprised when she started nuzzling his neck, and even more surprised when she lifted her face to kiss him.

The kiss started out as something hard -- hard and desperate, a frightened person looking for comfort and reassurance, but it soon grew into something more, something warm. Her body pressed against him and he was acutely aware of the warmth and heaviness of her breasts against his chest as she pressed even closer.

'I want you' she whispered in his ear, and he felt her hands at the buttons of his shirt. He held her out at arms length, looking deep into her eyes. She didn't stop working on his buttons, and he had to lift her face to his before she stopped.

'Are you sure?' he asked, but he didn't really have to -- he could see the need in her eyes. He wondered which answer would frighten him more.'

'Yes,' she said. 'I need you. And I need you now.'

She pulled him to the floor, neither of them noticing its cold dampness as they quickly divested each other of their clothes.

Their lovemaking was over quickly, but while it lasted it was furious and wild, two people reaffirming the fact that they were alive. Meg made most of the action, surprising Duncan with her ferocity, and moved in a rhythm which soon became too much for him to bear.

He tried to slow her down, to prolong the moment, but she was insistent, her thighs gripping him tight, her teeth nibbling his neck. When she cupped his testicles in her hand he could stand it no longer and came, long and hard.

They screamed in unison as they came together.

When it was over they lay in each others arms until a growing awareness of the cold forced them to dress.

Sometime later he told her his story and she gasped loudly when he told her that he had been in the bar earlier that night.

'I heard you,' she said. 'I thought that they had

come back so I kept quiet. You tried the trapdoor --
didn't you? God you gave me a hell of a fright.'

When he told her about finding her father's body
she went pale, but she didn't cry, merely asked him to
keep going.

When he'd finished they broke open a bottle of
whisky each and raided the cigarette cartons for a brand
they could smoke.

They sat, each with their own thoughts, watching
the locked door, waiting, neither able to allow
themselves to sleep.

After a while she began to talk. Duncan was
afraid to break the flow and contented himself with
sipping whisky and smoking cigarettes as she tried to
explain what had happened.

'It's all got to do with the old house. We should
have listened to old Tom -- he was against the dig in
the first place. He tired to get the dig stopped you
know? Even wrote a letter to the Secretary of State. At
the time we all laughed at him and his superstitions.
Mum and Dad were even looking forward to the extra
custom that the students would bring.'

There was a hitch in her voice and she took a
long sip of whisky before continuing.

'But what are they?' he asked, almost afraid of
what the answer might be. She thought for a long time
over her answer.

'I don't really know. Old Tom tells a story of a
tribe of evil men from a barbarian country who
worshipped a long forgotten god and who practised
cannibalism, and I've heard another story of a group of
heathens who were cursed by Columba, but I don't
think anyone knows for sure. But I know one thing --
those students should have left well alone.'

She lapsed back into silence as they drank yet

more whisky. But neither of them got drunk and neither of them slept much. The night passed slowly.

At some point Duncan thought he heard a noise in the bar above them. He tensed, all of his muscles bunching up, and he gripped the whisky bottle so tight that his knuckles went white. Meg sat upright and they both looked at the ceiling, as if willing themselves to see through to the bar beyond.

The sound wasn't repeated but it was a long time before his muscles relaxed enough to let him raise the bottle to his lips.

'Probably mice,' Meg said. 'Dad's been trying to get rid of them for years.'

She started to cry again. Duncan crawled over to her and held her tight, but the tears didn't subside for a long time.

At eight in the morning Meg decided it was time to move.

'We can't stay here forever. I think we should head for the North Light -- they're got a radio over there, and that's the only other way to get a message out -- Old John Jeffries never held with telephones or radios. We need to get over there and find out who, if anyone, is still alive.'

Duncan wasn't sure and began to protest, but Meg wasn't to be denied.

'And there's a boatload of tourists due at three o'clock this afternoon. If we don't do something they might be the next victims. Do you want that on your conscience? We can't let them get ashore -- you never know what might happen.'

She managed a small, tight grin.

'Besides -- it's breakfast time and I'm hungry.'

Duncan realised that he was famished -- despite

the whisky and the stiffness in his joints he felt capable of eating a large breakfast. Just then his stomach led out a huge, empty sounding rumble, causing them both to grin.

'OK' he said. 'Let's do it.' He moved to the trapdoor, noticing the scarring caused by the shotgun blast.

He pulled the bolt free and pushed the trapdoor open, carefully so as to avoid creaks. Slowly he poked his head above floor level, half expecting to have something big and ugly stomp on him.

Morning sunlight streamed into the bar, dancing motes of dust drifting in the still air. He looked around, slowly, making no sudden movements, but the bar was an empty as it had been the night before. He motioned for Meg to follow and pulled himself up into the bar.

His footsteps echoed in the barn-like room but there was no other sound. Meg joined him and gave him the shotgun before clinging tightly to his left arm as they peered into all the corners and behind the counters. It seemed they were alone. The only place they didn't look was in the radio room -- neither of them felt up to that yet.

They looked into the kitchen, and Duncan made a move towards the fridge but Meg pulled him away, back into the bar.

'I can't,' she said. 'Not here. Not where she was when...'

Her voice tailed away and she started to cry -- deep heaving sobs which seemed to come from the pit of her stomach. Duncan led her outside, out into the sunlight.

'Stay here. And if you see anything, don't waste time calling for me -- shoot first.' He handed her the shotgun and went back in. He didn't want to, but the need for food had forced itself to the front of his mind.

He found a carrier bag and loaded it with fruit and chocolate, eating a bar while he packed. In the fridge he found some cans of soft drink. While looking for more food in a cupboard in the kitchen he found six shotgun cartridges, their weight feeling comforting in his palm. He stuffed them in his trouser pockets along with some more chocolate.

Before leaving he covered Jim's body with a tablecloth -- it was the only thing he could think of doing.

When he got back to her Meg had her back to the wall, facing out over the lawn towards the sea. Her face was pale and he could see from her eyes that she had been crying again.

'Anything?' he asked, but she shook her head as she handed him the shotgun.

'Nothing. It's so quiet, so peaceful. How can things be this beautiful -- it's not fair.'

His mouth ran away with itself before he had time to think.

'Nature is never fair,' Duncan said. A phrase he'd used on several occasions when his hippy friends began to extol the virtues of "The Earth Mother". He realised as soon as he'd said it that he'd said the wrong thing.

She screamed at him.

'Nature. Who said anything about bloody nature. Those…those animals killed my family and you just stand there blithering on about nature.'

She turned her back on him and headed for the road.

Duncan was crestfallen. He was definitely out of practice at this sort of thing.

'Hey. Wait up', he called after her, but she was

walking faster now and as he started to follow she broke into a run.

'Meg' he shouted again, but she was getting ever further away from him. He followed her as fast as he could manage but she was fast, and unencumbered by a shotgun and by the time he reached the road she was already a hundred yards ahead.

It looked like she was running full pelt, her heels kicking up behind her. He thought of shouting again but decided to save his energy for the chase.

Again he felt as if he were in a dream. He'd spent the last day running up and down this damned island, first being chased, now chasing. He had a feeling that it might not be too long before he was being chased again. He tried to up his pace, but the exertions of the last day were getting to him and he was finding difficulty in managing anything more than a trot.

When he reached John Jeffries' farm he stopped. A fine mist hung over the north end of the island, close to the ground in a long curtain. Meg was running straight for it.

This time he did shout -- long and hard until he was hoarse, but she kept running. His breath came in great whoops and he felt blood on his legs from his wounds. He stopped, bent almost double and waited till his heart stopped pounding against his ribs.

He broke open the gun... it had been empty the whole time. He rammed two shells into place and started after her again, leaving the bag of food on the ground behind him.

The path dipped down into a small hollow, temporarily blocking her from sight, and Duncan forced himself to hurry. But when he got back to level ground there was no sign of her.

There was the smell of burning in the air -- the

charcoal after-taste of a barbecue. Duncan slowed, stopped running and began to walk slowly, listening for a clue as to where Meg might have gone.

There was a sudden revving of an engine, and Duncan turned, just in time to see the island's land-rover heading northwards. He hoped that Meg was aboard it.

There was a noise to his left, a crackling as of a wood-pile settling. He turned towards it, and that was when he noticed the remains of the fire.

There were three burnt out stakes straight ahead of him, and at the foot of each stake there was a black, smoking mess. Duncan stepped closer, trying to make out what had been burnt, getting close to the middle stake. Then he saw the fingers -- the brown smoking bones and the burnt flesh of a human hand.

He stepped backwards, left hand covering his mouth, then stepped back further as the smoking fist clenched, then unclenched. It turned, palm downward, and pushed against the ground. Another hand appeared from the amorphous mass, and a head pushed up out of the smoking rib cage.

Duncan blinked once, and there was only the black charred mass on the ground once more.

'I must stop eating those mushrooms,' he muttered to himself, then forced himself to pay attention as he caught a movement from the corner of his eye, over towards the mound. He had to force himself to take a step as two of the creatures emerged from the opening and came towards him.

He raised the shotgun and let off both barrels but he wasn't used to firearms and his shots went high and wide, the recoil almost knocking him off his feet. He moved backwards, torn between keeping his eyes on the creatures and making sure that he didn't lose his balance again. Already he was deep into the rubble of the ruined house and the going underfoot was getting treacherous.

He risked a glance behind him as he fumbled with the gun, trying to reload, watch his pursuers and figure out where he was headed all at the same time.

They herded him into a cul-de-sac, the decaying remains of a room, three walls of which still stood. Hunger flared in their eyes as they pushed him backwards. By the time he got the shotgun loaded he had his back to a wall and they were only ten feet from him.

He was only going to have time for the two shots. Considering that today was the first time in his life that he'd ever used a gun he figured that his chances were slim.

They were still coming. He took out the one of his right, his one shot blowing its head apart. He turned into the embrace of the second creature and just managed to bring the gun up between them. Long clawed fingers reached for his eyes and he watched, transfixed, as they closed in. Praying, he pulled the trigger. This time the explosion from the gun nearly deafened him and he was blown off his feet to land in a pile among the rocks. He scrambled away as fast as he could over the rubble.

It wasn't until he was out of the cul-de-sac that he turned to look. The two bodies lay side by side, pumping out hot red blood onto the grass. Suddenly they didn't look so strong.

Duncan pulled himself out of the rubble, making sure to keep the ruins between him and the mound, and limped northwards until he felt safely out of the ruins of the Mansion.

It was only when he tried to stand that he realised that he no longer had the shotgun -- he had dropped it sometime after the final shot.

He knew that he needed it, that it might be his only chance, but there was no way he was going back to look for it.

And then he remembered why he was here. He wondered what had happened to Meg. She could be anywhere on the island by now but Duncan hoped that she was headed for the lighthouse. That was the only place he might have a chance of finding her in the fog.

Besides, if she hadn't reached the safety of the lighthouse before he got there, he could always enlist Dick's help.

And then another, terrible, thought struck him. What if the lighthouse turned out to be like the pub, just another silent, empty tomb, another mystery?

He hoped he would be able to have more fire-side drinks with Dick, hoped against hope that Dick was still alive. Despite the bright sun overhead he felt a cold shiver in his spine as he headed for the cliff path, heading for the mist.

He was distracted by a noise behind him, a rumbling as of the tumble of rocks.

He turned around...the mist was beginning to creep in around him. Back in the ruins of the Mansion figures moved in the mist -- tall grey figures, taller than any man.

Duncan dropped to the ground, flattening himself into the earth, trying to make himself as inconspicuous as possible as he crawled closer. Not too close -- just close enough to get a better view of what the creatures were doing.

Looking at the creatures he was reminded once

more of Gollum, and shivered as he remembered how close they had come to getting him the night before.

They were shifting rubble, moving large boulders as if they were pebbles, throwing them yards through the air, working with a purpose, single-mindedly digging their way into the ruins.

Duncan crept closer as the mist drew in and his view became impaired. He was amazed at the strength of the creatures, and wondered what they were searching for. He didn't have to wait long to find out.

In less than two minutes the creatures had excavated a five foot hole in the ground beneath the rubble when suddenly they stopped digging and stood straight, raising their eyes to the sky and letting out a howl, a noise so loud that Duncan had to cover his ears with his hands, wincing at the pain the movement brought.

For long seconds the creatures didn't move, and Duncan wondered if the show was over, but his gaze was diverted by a movement in the fog.

The biggest creature he had seen so far emerged from the fog. And this one was different. It wasn't just its age or its height -- this one carried an air of power, an air of something which Duncan immediately identified as evil.

It barked an order -- just one word, but the force of it made even Duncan want to obey. As one the rest of the creatures went down into the hole where another bout of activity started, dark brown earth flying upwards in great clouds. Ten seconds later another howl went up, even louder this time, and the old creature joined with them.

A stone was brought out of the hole, a boulder some two feet across, a boulder which, even in the dim daylight, seemed to glow in phosphorescent blue despite the badly charred contours of the rock.

Duncan had seen something like it before, in a museum, and he recognised if for what it was -- a meteorite, something flung out of the deep space. He wondered what the creatures wanted with it, and then he sensed the power in it and a cold chill ran through him.

The old creature put its hand out to touch the stone and blue sparks flew amongst its fingers. Duncan felt the hair at the back of his neck stand on end and there was suddenly a tension in the air. The stone seemed to suck in mist in great strings, like dry ice at a rock concert, but only in reverse, as if being watched in rewind.

The creatures howled their joy once more before the stone was carried off towards the mound, carried slowly and with great reverence.

The old creature walked behind the stone and the last thing Duncan noticed before they faded into the fog was the joy in his eyes, joy and expectation.

Duncan waited until he was sure that the creatures had gone before crawling over to the hole they had made. There was nothing to see, only a hole in the ground. It looked like they had got what they came for.

He didn't know why, but Duncan felt cold, cold and afraid. He was sure that the creatures now had a new weapon -- something which would greatly increase their power for mayhem. He had to get to the North Light -- it was their only hope of warning the world outside as to what was going on here.

He turned back northwards, listening for any noises in the fog, but there was only deep silence, not even the sound of a seagull.

Duncan felt tiredness threatening to drag him down to the ground, and lifting his feet seemed too much of a trial -- the events of the last day were catching up with him, and he was aware that his mind was blocking out thoughts, giving him busy work to keep him occupied.

He was daydreaming about his laboratory back at university when a noise brought him out of his reverie, a human, recognisable noise, the sound of a land-rover engine being gunned.

Again he remembered Meg, and he found the energy to get moving again, heading for the sound. As he got closer he heard screams and that forced him to move faster. He didn't know how he was going to deal with it if any of the creatures were menacing Meg, but she was in trouble, and he had to try.

Limping, bloody and exhausted, he headed towards the screams.

16
Dick

Dick stood at the top of the lighthouse watching the small boat come closer, trying to make out who was piloting it. It was still too far away for that, and the glinting light from the dancing waves threatened to blind him, causing him to squint, but he kept watching anyway -- anything rather than think about those blank, eyeless stares which were even now boring into his back. It was almost as if they were daring him to turn, daring him to confront them.

He was still looking out to sea when he heard a groan behind him.

'Christ, my head hurts,' John said, but still Dick didn't turn round -- he wasn't ready for that yet.

The coast-guard was talking, more to himself than for any need of conversation.

'I should know better at my age -- trying to hide in the bottle never works -- it just leaves you feeling like shit -- and nothing has improved by the time the morning comes.'

Dick continued to ignore him -- he knew that the coast-guard was still trying to come to terms with the previous nights' events.

'Who's in the boat?' John asked, but still Dick didn't reply. He was just about to warn the coast-guard not to turn round when he heard the gasp.

'Jesus Christ!' he heard the man say, before the

dry, stomach turning retching began. Still Dick couldn't make himself turn round.

The boat was much closer now and Dick couldn't make out who it was, only that he seemed to be dressed all in black. He hoped to hell it was another policeman -- a younger, fitter policeman than Angus had proved to be. John was still retching behind him. He turned towards the man, trying, but not quite succeeding, to keep his eyes from straying to the bodies on the cliff-top.

'Come on John. Let's go and see who our visitor is. Maybe he'll have an answer to what's going on.'

He led his friend down the stairs, and met Tom coming out of the bedroom. The old man looked like death warmed up -- big black bags under his eyes, his hair awry.

'Get yourself back to bed -- you need to get some sleep.' Dick told him. 'We've got a visitor, but John and I will deal with it.'

The old man shook his head.

'No -- I think I ken who it is. And if I ken him, he'll want to get going right away.'

Dick realised that this must be the owner of the one of the voices he'd heard on the radio the night before, and his suspicions were proved right a couple of minutes later when they helped the pilot dock the boat and the tall impressive figure of the Rev. McCallum stepped onto the jetty.

Dick's heart fell. The old man must be at least seventy, and Dick had always felt he was a bit loopy -- a bit too keen on fire and brimstone. He didn't think he was going to get much help from this quarter.

He did have to admit that the old man exuded confidence, but Dick suspected it was born more of his holier-than-thou self righteousness than of any great inner strength. He hoped he wasn't going to get a sermon -- he might just tell the old man exactly what he could do with his religion.

Tom and the old Minister shook hands, strangely formal, and Dick was suddenly aware that the old man held the Minister in awe, and had that old-fashioned sense of reverence to the Ministry.

'Hello Tom,' the Minister said, and Dick could imagine the voice booming out from the pulpit, preaching on the sins of the flesh. Dick could remember another old red-faced man from his youth, one who used to lecture the boys on the sins of masturbation, while at the same time touching them up between the pews.

He almost smiled as the old man turned to him.

'Dick,' he said, a welcome of a sort, but in that one word Dick heard a lot -- the admonishment for not joining old Tom in his trips to church, the voice which said, "everything's all right -- I'm here now". Dick had never been happy with the Ministry's sense of absolute righteousness, and was even more sure that this old man was not going to be able to help them. He merely nodded back, not trusting himself to speak.

'Old Tom called me last night,' the old man said. 'He tells me the devils have come back. I've come to send them back into the ground where they belong. They will fall before the power of the Lord.'

Dick had to stop him -- he had a feeling that a speech was on the way, and it was definitely too early in the morning for that kind of thing.

He was saved having to talk by the man John.

'I think you've had a wasted journey. We're just leaving -- I'm not staying here a minute longer than I have to.'

John looked around for confirmation, but old Tom was suddenly looking at his feet, a sheepish expression crossing his face as he shrugged his shoulders. John turned instead to Dick.

'Come on Dick. It was a group decision. We're leaving on my boat. We decided, didn't we?'

The coast-guard looked so terrified at the prospect of staying that Dick wanted to help him, but now it was his turn to look sheepish.

'I've been doing some thinking. I don't think I can leave without checking up on the people in the pub. I would never forgive myself if I left without making sure they were OK.'

John was crestfallen, and the wild, frightened look was back in his eyes. He was close to tears as he backed away from them, back towards the boat.

'I can't do it Dick. I can't go back across the island. Don't ask me to do it.'

Tom was the first to speak, and there was gentleness in his voice as he walked over to the coast-guard and clasped an arm around John's shoulders.

'You go on John. Get back to the mainland and call out the troops -- the more the merrier. We need some help anyway, if only to pick up the bodies. Me and the Minister are going to put those devils back where they belong.'

There was a resolve in the old man, a hardness which hadn't been evident for a couple of days, but his eyes still betrayed his fear.

John looked torn between two loyalties -- needing to get off the island, but not wanting to leave anyone behind, until Dick pushed him towards his boat.

'Tom's right you know. Someone needs to get back and inform the authorities. God knows what I would tell them, and they're more likely to trust a coast-guard than a stir-crazy lighthouse keeper. Get yourself back to base -- and quick. I'll make sure these two don't get up to too much mischief.'

He pushed John onto his boat, clapping him hard on the shoulder one last time.

'Are you sure you won't come with me?' John said, addressing all of them, but looking straight at Dick, as if he was looking at him for the last time.

Dick could tell that John didn't think he would see any of them again -- not alive anyway, but he had to stay. If nothing else it was his duty.

Just as John was starting up the boat old Sam bounded out of the lighthouse and jumped off the jetty to land at John's feet. He looked up at Dick and barked, just once, as if wondering why anyone with any sense would want to stay on the island.

Dick felt an almost overwhelming urge to go with them, but he couldn't leave the old man, couldn't go without checking out the pub. He watched the boat going, and the further away it got, the more he wished he had gone with it. John only looked round once, just long enough to give a single wave, before the boat rounded the cliffs and was lost from their sight.

The three men hadn't spoken since the dog jumped on the boat. Dick didn't know about the others, but he suddenly felt very much alone, very much exposed. The sooner they got on the move, the better he would feel.

The old Minister broke the silence first.

'It's a terrible thing Tom -- terrible times to have to live through. I never expected the old times to come back. You and I are getting far too old to be fighting with devils -- that's a young man's game.'

He put an arm around Tom's shoulders.

'But we'll just have to show them all that there's life in the old dogs yet.'

The old Minister was so sure of himself, so confident, that Dick almost felt that he would succeed.

Then he remembered the ritual around the fire, the show of power he had witnessed, and a cold chill settled in his bones.

Tom's demeanour had visibly improved -- his back was straight and his eyes were clear -- it was almost possible to see strength in the old man -- an echo of the younger man, the one who had fought for his country, not the one who had cowered, terrified in the tower the previous night. Dick couldn't find it in himself to share Tom's new found sense of purpose.

'I don't think you realise what you're dealing with here,' he said, trying to fill the others with the dread he felt. 'These things are savages -- mindless killers -- I don't think they'll be afraid of two old men.'

The Minister turned towards him, staring into Dick's eyes for a long second before applying.

'Oh, I know well enough what we have to deal with. The parish records are clear enough on the matter. The devil has many forms, but he cannot hide from the Light of Jesus.'

There was an almost missionary gleam in the old man's eyes, and a dangerous certainty in his power to defeat "the devils". Dick decided to stick near old Tom and get ready to run when things turned hairy -- he didn't share the same faith as the old men, and he wasn't sure that the "devils" would take any notice either.

'Were the old stories right? Are they coming from the mound again?' the Minister asked.

'Aye,' Tom said. 'Same as the old days. Christ knows how many they've killed this time.'

Dick noticed the scowl on the Minister's face.

'Blasphemy will only serve to help our enemy,' he said, his voice harsh, but there was a softness in his eyes as he looked at Tom.

'I'm sorry,' Tom said, and Dick was amazed at the deference in his voice -- it was almost as if the Minister was a headmaster and Tom a contrite schoolboy. The view was strengthened by the Minister's next words.

'That's all right Tom. Just don't let me catch you doing it again. And remember -- the good Lord sees all our deeds.'

Dick was getting increasingly angry with the Minister, angry with his certainty and his condescending manner. But most of all angry with himself for being overawed by the old man.

Before he could speak up, the old man started talking again, this time in a whisper, but a whisper which carried the force to make them obey.

'I think we should pray.'

Dick wanted to tell him what he could do with his prayers, but just as he was about to speak he felt a hand on his arm and turned to see Old Tom looking up at him. The old man didn't have to speak -- Dick could see the pleading in his eyes. He kept his mouth shut, deciding he would do anything to help the old man get through what was coming, and bent his head as the Minister began to pray.

The Minister's voice echoes around the harbour, the only sound on that still morning.

'Dear Lord, we are your humble servants and we have need of succour. Help us to face what is to come and give us strength that we may bring the glory of your presence back to this island.'

Dick sensed a movement, and looked up to see the Minister looking at the row of bodies on the cliff-top before continuing.

'Take these brave souls into your bosom. They are innocents and have come through the valley of pain and suffering so that they may come to you. Let them sit by your side and give them peace.'

Dick found tears in his eyes and quickly wiped them away. That was the trouble with religion -- you thought you could ignore it, get by without it, then, when you were least expecting it, it hit you with a dose of love and compassion that completely overwhelmed you.

He had missed a bit -- the Minister was still speaking.

'Lend us the strength of your strong right arm, lend us the force of your love, let us walk in death's shadow without fear, sure in your power, strong in your love, Jesus Christ our Lord.'

'Amen.'

Almost as one Dick and Tom echoed the last word before lifting their heads.

The Minister was smiling, his eyes glistening.

'We walk with the strength of Jesus,' he said, and Dick was once more sure that the old man was mad, a feeling that got stronger as they headed for the stairs up to the cliff and the old man started singing at the top of his voice.

Tom joined in and Dick watched as they marched upwards, the strains of "Onward Christian Soldiers" echoing around the cliffs.

Dick would feel more comfortable with a more tangible power, and hurried to the kitchen.

He picked their biggest knife from the rack and immediately felt more secure with the heavy steel in his hand. It was only as he was on his way out that he remembered that they were on their way to the mound. It would be suicidal to go without some form of light. He took the black rubber flashlight from its hook and attached it to his belt, then stuffed two heavy duty emergency flares in his pocket. Someone had to look after the practicalities, and it looked like he had drawn the short straw.

The two men were nearly at the top of the cliff, and he had to hurry to catch them, trying all the time not to look at the sightless bodies which watched as he climbed.

The old men had temporarily stopped singing as they reached the cliff-top, the sight of the ranked bodies seeming to sober them. It was Dick who spoke first.

'We can't just leave them like this. It's not right.'

He couldn't look at the bodies -- every time he glanced in that direction he was reminded of the girl's soft lips, her kind voice and, worst of all, her sparkling, dancing eyes as she flirted with him. He kept having to fight back tears, but moved away when Tom tried to comfort him. It wasn't comfort he wanted.

Although he was afraid, there was a cold place in his heart, a place that wanted revenge -- revenge for Angus, revenge for the students, but most of all, revenge for his lost future.

The Minister's voice was full of pity.

'We don't have the time to bury them properly. Be sure -- they will all get Christian burials. First we must banish the devils and remove the taint of the devil from this place -- but I think we should pray again for them.

This time Dick didn't bow his head, and he didn't

pay attention to the prayer -- he'd had enough homilies for one day. Besides, something else was attracting his attention.

The fog bank crept up the island towards them and, not for the first time, Dick felt that it was alive -- a sentient cloud created by the creatures to mask their movements. And, in the fog, something moved, something large. He was about to pull Tom away, getting ready to run, when he heard the noise of a car engine and recognised the shape of the land-rover as it emerged form the fog.

Someone else was still alive -- that was his first joyous thought as he started to run towards the car.

He was still a hundred yards from it when he recognised Meg's alarmed features behind the wheel, her eyes wide with fear, her hair a tousled mat bouncing in time with the car as it tried to negotiate the rutted track.

He was still fifty yards from it when he saw the creatures emerge from the fog behind her -- five of them, running in a pack like jackals after a weak kill, converging on the car. She must have seen them in the rear-view mirror, for at the same moment, Meg started to scream.

Dick was dimly aware that the old men were following him, but he was leaving them behind as he sprinted on, unaware that he was muttering to himself, 'Come on, come on,' -- urging Meg to speed up.

For a second it was as though she had heard him -- he heard her gun the engine, putting her foot down hard -- he could imagine her stamping the pedal to the floor -- but the old car didn't respond; there was a crunch as the old gears failed to mesh, and a sudden, almost stunned silence as the car ground to a halt.

The creatures were on it in a matter of seconds,

crawling over the roof as Meg's screams got louder. None of them seemed to have noticed Dick yet, and he had no idea what he was going to do when he finally reached the land-rover, but he kept going, Meg's screams ringing in his ears.

Three of the creatures concentrated on the driver's side door, trying to force their way through. Great dents were punched in the body work of the car, each blow bringing a fresh scream from Meg.

A fourth creature sprawled on the roof of the car and seemed bemused by the windscreen.

It was the fifth one which really worried Dick though. While he was still ten yards from the car it had found the space where the passenger door had been and pushed its way into the seat, oblivious to Meg's flailing legs. He was close enough to see the talons gleam as they reached for Meg's ankles.

He let out a howl, a great scream of defiance, an instinctual thing with no thought for the consequences, hoping only to distract the creature.

The creature on the roof of the car reacted first, raising its head and staring straight at Dick. He was close enough to see its pupils contract, just before it launched itself off the roof, too fast to allow Dick time to think.

The picture froze itself into his mind, like the freeze frame of a video.

Long black hair streamed behind the creature like a cape, making it seem almost bat-like, an impression strengthened by the glint of the thin, needle sharp teeth. Long taloned arms reached out in front of it, and the fists clenched and unclenched as if in anticipation of closing round Dick's throat. Worst of all, it smiled as it came for him.

He just had time to raise the knife in front of him before he was knocked heavily to the ground. It felt almost as if a wall had fallen on him.

A moment later he was struggling beneath twenty stone of flesh, looking into the face of an angel of death. Saliva dripped from the creature's wide mouth, grey ropy streams of it, and Dick gagged and almost choked as some of the vile stuff dripped into his own open mouth.

His right arm was pinned to his side, held down by the weight of the creature, and his left was only partially free. He managed to raise his left hand, and almost cried with relief that the knife was still there.

The creature brought its teeth closer to his face, then closer still, and he had a vision of his face being ripped clean off, muscles and tissue and skin all torn away in one hot flare of pain.

Meg screamed -- a higher sound, somehow more full of terror than before, and Dick found enough strength to free his left arm.

The knife came up and went in, and Dick had the satisfaction of seeing pain in the creatures' eyes, a pain which brought a howl as he plunged the knife in again, and again.

The creature was struggling on top of him, trying to reach the source of the pain as Dick kept plunging the knife into it, feeling hot blood gush down his forearm, feeling the knife slide wetly into the tissue, over and over.

Suddenly he felt a jolt as the knife hit something hard, and a terrible rasping as it grated against bone.

The creature's movements became ever more frenzied as it forgot about the knife and tried to reach Dick's face again. He squirmed his head to one side as the great jaws came down, and he felt something tear at the side of his head, followed quickly by a hot rush of blood on his neck. He guessed that a piece of his ear had gone, but he didn't have time to think about it -- the creature's head came up for another attack.

He thrust his knife into the creature's side.

'Die you bastard. Die. Die. Die.'

The weight on him lifted, suddenly, as if the creature had been dragged off him and he could sit up. Old Tom had grabbed the creature by the hair, taking huge clumps of it in both hands, and had forcibly pulled the creature off Dick. Unfortunately he had also become the object of its attention.

Dick stood, shaky on his legs, and saw beyond Tom that Meg was being pulled from the land-rover and that the other three creatures were now between him and her. He had a sudden, sinking feeling that they were all going to die -- and very soon.

He did the only thing he could think of -- he thrust the knife deep into the nearest creature's left eye, forcing it deep. The eyeball popped and the knife slid through soft tissue until it came up hard against bone. The creature squealed, just once, before the knife was torn out of Dick's hand and the creature jerked as if in the throes of a fit. It fell to the ground, dropping in a faint and, with one final twitch, was dead.

The remaining creatures howled in unison and, as one, headed for him. At least they had left Meg and Tom alone.

'Run,' he shouted at them, as the creatures moved in on him and he prepared to take at least one of them with him.

Then the air was filled with the resonating peal of the Minister's voice, a sound which stopped all movement and caused the creatures to turn and watch the old man.

'Begone foul demons. I abjure you in the name of Jesus Christ our Lord.'

The Minister walked towards Dick -- his old black bible held out before him like a shield. He was straight and upright and Dick was reminded of one of the ancient prophets of Israel, striding forth to smite the heathen. The Minister stopped in front of the creatures and spoke again.

'Leave this place and go back into the pits of hell which spawned you. You have no place here. Go -- in the name of Jesus -- Go.'

For a long second there was no movement, then one of the creatures seemed to laugh, a strange, barking sound, as it moved towards the Minister. Dick shouted again, hoping to distract the creature, but this time he had no effect.

The old man raised his arms to the sky.

'Dear God, let these creatures feel your power.'

And the miraculous happened.

A cloud moved and warm, strong sunlight suddenly bathed the scene, so strong that Dick had to turn his head away. The creatures moaned, a deep tortured sound. They crouched closer to the ground and shrank from the light, cowering beneath its brightness. The old Minister walked towards them, thrusting his bible ahead of him.

The creatures backed off, loping quickly towards the fog. They didn't look back and were soon swallowed in its gloom. The last to go was the one which Dick had wounded and thick blood caked its side.

It seemed to be slowed by its wounds and Dick got a certain small satisfaction as it dragged itself away, hunched into a crouch with its pain. Soon it too was lost in the fog.

The Minister fell to his knees in prayer.

'Thank you Lord, thank you.'

Tom stood beside the Minister, looking bemused, staring at the sky and shaking his head as if he didn't believe what had just happened.

Tears streamed down the Minister's face.

Personally Dick wasn't convinced of any great miracle, and he certainly wasn't ready to acknowledge the power of Jesus -- they had just been lucky that the sun came out at the right time. Even he was smart enough to realise that creatures which normally dwelt in caves would be wary of strong sunlight.

But anything which got them out of danger was welcome -- he just hoped it didn't give the others a false sense of security -- he had a feeling that there was worse still to come.

The Minister was still on his knees, muttering to himself in prayer. Tom had already moved to help Meg. She sobbed uncontrollably as she pressed herself against the old man, and she had her eyes squeezed tightly shut, as if trying to block out some unwelcome sight.

Dick turned his attention to the creature on the ground. Studying it, he was forcibly reminded of his dream the night before -- the creature crawling up his stairs to accost him in his bedroom. The thing that lay at his feet had many similarities -- the wide eyes, the talons and, most of all, the stink of rotting fish.

He didn't want to look at it, didn't want to have anything to do with it, but he had to get the knife back -- it was their only weapon and he had a feeling he was going to need it before too long.

The knife seemed to be stuck against the bone in

the creature's skull and he had to tug hard before it slid wetly out of the hole, trailing behind it a slimly mass, a trail which Dick realised sickeningly must be the remains of its eyeball.

He couldn't help noticing that the other eye had become cloudy -- a grey-green milkiness, and that the creatures' skin seemed to have stretched, taking on a red colour.

'Sunburn' he muttered to himself, forcing down a manic laugh. 'The bloody thing is getting a tan.'

He was trying to wipe the knife clean on the grass when Tom shouted -- more of a loud whisper than a shout, but enough to make Dick take notice.

'Dick -- look. Over there.'

He followed the old man's gaze and saw something moving in the fog, something that moved slowly, something that was bent over and hunched. At first he thought it must be the creature he had wounded, but then he looked closer and realised that this was someone smaller, someone he thought he recognised.

Before Tom could stop her Meg had broken away from him and was running towards the fog. Dick stood up and began to follow her, then grinned as he recognised the battered figure of Duncan as the scientist came out of the fog and was almost knocked over when Meg ran into his arms.

17

Anne

Anne had no idea how long she had been sitting on the throne. She had slept once, but didn't know for how long, and there was no way to tell if it was day or night.

She only knew that the throne was her place -- as long as she was there the creatures wouldn't harm her.

Earlier she had tried to move, tried to leave, but the creatures had herded her back to her place, gently but firmly, as if scolding a naughty schoolgirl. And so she had stayed there, uncomfortable on the rough throne, but unable to leave.

At least there was one thing to be grateful for -- the old creature -- Calent, had been gone from the chamber for a long time. She found that she feared his return -- especially if the activities of the others gave any clues as to their plans for her.

They fornicated at every available opportunity -- Anne couldn't bring herself to call it love -- and in every part of the chamber. And they did it with glee, with singing, and dancing -- it was like a perpetual orgy, so much so that Anne had to close her eyes against the scenes. That didn't keep out the moist, wet noises though. She tried to imagine being taken by one of the monsters, finding that it didn't take much effort to imagine those rough hands on her body, that foul breath on her face. She vowed to herself that she would die first.

She had been sitting with her eyes closed for a long time when the room went quiet -- only the roaring of the water in the pool to be heard, and then the chant went up again.

'Calent.'

'Calent.'

The noise was almost deafening, rising to a crescendo, echoing around her in maddening whispers. She didn't want to open her eyes, but her curiosity got the better of her sense.

Calent walked into the chamber, carrying above its head a huge rock -- a rock which blazed in blue brilliance.

Electricity ran over the creature's body, causing its hair to stand in a writhing halo, causing its eyes to gleam blue in the dim light of the cavern.

It carried the stone around the chamber, and as it passed all the creatures stretched to touch it. At first Anne didn't recognise the expressions on their faces, and then she saw it for what it was -- awe. Awe and reverence.

Although the rock must weigh at least six stone the creature carried it as if it was papier-mâché -- no sign of strain in his muscles as the rock was pumped over his head, like a weight lifter showing off in the gym.

Calent did a full circle of the chamber, and as he passed the creatures fell to the ground in supplication until he was the only one left standing, facing her. He grinned, a wide smile which exposed all his teeth, but there was no joy in it, only the crazy flickering madness and the expectations of victories to come.

He turned back to the throng, and began a song as he carried the rock over towards the pool. There he finally put it down on a stone outcrop, laying it into a hollow which looked like it had been made for the purpose. The throng sighed as the blue aura dimmed, leaving only a dull grey stone.

Calent still had the blue glow in his eyes.

He raised his arms, and began to chant, and once more pictures were forced into Anne's mind.

She saw the creatures fornicating in front of the stone, fornicating with her as yet unborn son. She saw the females giving birth to healthy, strong creatures -- all teeth and muscle and power, and, finally, she saw them pour out of the mound in an endless horde, their eyes shining with the blue power of the stone.

Calent dropped his arms and the throng roared its appreciation while he just stood there and smiled that evil smile of his while Anne got the now familiar cold shiver down her spine.

The old creature beckoned in her direction and she felt something grip in her mind, something which brooked no refusal. She tried to resist, but her legs betrayed her, taking her down off the throne, down towards the creature. Her mind was shouting at her, telling her to flee, but her body refused its orders, marching to the beat of a different drum. Calent's smile got broader as she came to his side.

She felt the creature run a smooth hand over her stomach, heard the throng cry out in an awesome roar, but she was still unable to pull away, unable even to cry the tears she felt inside.

Calent raised a hand and the crowd was silent once more. He beckoned into the crowd and one of the creatures raised itself to its feet.

Anne saw that it was a female, and in its arms was a small, struggling creature -- a baby. As they came closer she saw that the child was badly deformed, its arms withered and bent, like twigs on an old, gnarled oak tree. The female smiled in joy as she put the child in Anne's arms.

The child looked up at Anne and, although it wasn't human, although it was deformed, she felt the heat of it, the blustering, burgeoning joy of new life. Before she could react the vice took a stronger hold of her mind and turned her towards the sky stone.

The stone began to blaze as she approached it, a cold, blue flame which sent flickering shadows around the chamber, but strangely, the closer Anne got to the stone, the less she felt the vice in her mind.

Calent was ordering her to place the child in the flame, but she felt no compulsion to complete the act. She clasped the child closer to her chest as the throng of creatures began to mutter.

She was dragged away from the stone, Calent's strength nearly tearing her left shoulder out of its socket, and once more the vice took its grip in her head.

The child was dragged, screaming, from her grasp and she was left, unable to move, as Calent himself took the child to the stone.

It was becoming difficult to see the creature, so intense had the blue flame become as he approached the stone. She saw him lift the child into the blue blaze, then had to look away as the stone seemed to explode in a rainbow flash of dazzling, searing colour.

When she turned back there was only the grey stone, something black and charred and misshapen draped across it. Calent seemed to have grown, his great age fallen away from him, and blue light danced across his whole body

The crowd exploded in a riot of noise, dancing around Calent as if possessed, and some of them fell on the ground, copulating in a mad animal frenzy. And through it all Anne had to watch, immobile and unable to even close her eyes, as the creatures celebrated and Calent looked on, the madness blazing in his eyes.

Calent raised his arms and the crowd fell quiet once more. He had just started to speak when he was interrupted by a commotion at the chamber's entrance. A group of creatures entered, three of them carrying a fourth between them. Even in the dim light Anne saw that the one being carried was severely wounded.

Her heart missed a beat, and she wanted to cry out in joy -- someone out there was fighting back, but she was still held in Calent's mind grip.

The wounded creature was brought before Calent and laid on the ground at his feet where it whimpered like a whipped dog.

It looked up at Calent, and Anne saw the raw, unashamed pleading in its eyes. The mind grip which Calent had placed in her suddenly fell away, and at the same moment the creature stiffened, a tremor running through it, forcing it to its feet. The effort seemed to cause the creature great pain, but still it was pushed upwards by the power of Calent's will until it stood, almost to attention, in front of its leader.

Anne found she had control over actions again, and her mind told her to run. But where was there to go? There were at least fifty creatures between her and the cavern's entrance -- she didn't think she'd get very far.

Calent's eyes blazed in blue fire and the creature in front of him began to dance. Anne saw the black blood ooze from its wounds as it spun, arms extended like some grotesque spinning top, faster and faster as it danced away among the throng.

As it passed each creature it was slapped, hard, bringing fresh gouts of blood, blood which the throng began to smear over their faces. And still the creature spun, silent and awful.

Anne saw Calent's eyes blaze once more, and the creature began to jump as it spun, sending blood spraying over the crowd which swayed and moaned. As it reached the farthest corner of the chamber the creature stumbled, almost falling, before turning back into the throng. As it turned towards her Anne saw that there was no life left in its eyes -- it was surely dead. The blood had stopped flowing from its wounds and its dead eyes stared blindly at her.

But still it spun, and still the crowd moaned, their swaying becoming more frenzied, until the room was a mass of writhing bodies once more. And still the dead creature danced among them, on and on. And above them all Calent grinned.

18

Duncan

'I still think we should get the hell out of here,' Duncan said.

There hadn't been much time for explanations, but he got the gist from Dick. He couldn't believe they intended to go into the lair of those creatures -- especially after he'd told them about the dead he had seen around the remains of the fire.

It was Meg who convinced him.

'I'm just as keen as you are to get off this place -- but we haven't found Mum yet, and I can't leave until I know for sure what happened to her. I'm sorry.'

She clung on to his arm, bringing a dull ache to his bruised muscles, but he managed to find a smile for her.'

'OK. I suppose someone had to look out for you.'

He bent down to lightly brush her cheek with a kiss, but was stopped by a shout from Tom.

'Hey. Come and see this.'

The creature which Dick had killed was still lying near the car, but there wasn't much of it left.

It was burning up in the sun, its skin withering, already the texture of old leather, and as they watched the lone eyeball bubbled and blistered, as if boiling from beneath.

'It doesn't look so much like the bugger I dreamt

about,' Tom said. Dick and Duncan both gasped at the same

Duncan got it out first.

'What do you mean -- the one you dreamt about?'

The old man looked sheepish.

'Och, it was just a nightmare, like being a kid again. One of these things,' he said, nudging it with his foot, 'It attacked me in my bedroom. Bloody thing nearly made me wet the bed.'

It would almost have been funny if it wasn't so true. They soon ascertained that they had all had the same dream. All except the Minister.

'The good Lord protects me from the sendings of the Devil,' he said, but there was a look in his eyes that made Duncan sure that the old man was lying. He didn't press the fact.

'Somehow we've all been getting the same dreams. I don't know about you,' Duncan said, looking around the small group, 'But that make me even more afraid of these things. They can get inside our minds -- that makes them scary.'

The Minister was the only one who spoke.

'You mustn't let the Devil in. He is devious -- he knows when we are weakest, in our beds. Put it away -- we have work to do.'

Duncan thought that was the sanest thing he'd heard the old man say.

'So what now?' he asked, looking at the rest of them. It looked like young Dick had been appointed the leader and he seemed to be handling it well. The young man was in control, but Duncan didn't want to point it out to him -- he might notice that he had achieved the poise that he'd been searching for.

It wasn't Dick that spoke -- it was Meg.

'We've got to go down into the mound -- there's nothing else for it. But there's no way I'm getting back in that land-rover.'

Dick agreed. 'I don't think it's capable of taking us all anyway. And it would only draw attention to us. We should walk -- it's not far.'

Duncan fell in at the back of the group. Strangely he didn't feel as bad as he had only ten minutes ago -- his wounds still occasionally flared in pain, and his bruises provided a counterpoint of dull aches -- but he wasn't alone any more. He was in a group of people who were united in a single purpose -- that was infinitely preferable to being alone and on the run.

It wasn't long before the fog thickened around them and they had to close ranks to avoid getting separated. Duncan brushed against Meg and was rewarded with a tight little smile, but her mind was clearly elsewhere and he didn't push it -- it was enough for the moment that she was still alive.

He kept imagining figures in the fog, tall loping figures that moved like predators stalking their prey, smooth, silent and deadly, but every time he tried to look more closely they evaporated into the grey blanket, and when he stopped to listen, there was nothing to hear.

He was so intent on peering into the fog that he walked into Meg as she stopped suddenly in front of him.

Dick pulled them close in a huddle.

'We're very near now. I warn you -- it's gruesome in there. I'll try and keep the light off the worst bits.'

Duncan didn't think that anything could be worse than what he'd seen already that day, but judging by the anguish in the other man's eyes, he knew it was going to be bad. He forced himself to pay attention as Dick continued.

'I don't think we need to be heroes. We go in quietly, try to find Anne, and get out quick. I don't think we should draw attention to ourselves -- John will be here with the cavalry soon. I think we should leave it to the professionals.'

Duncan nodded in agreement, but the Minister wasn't going to be quelled so easily.

'I will not go skulking into the lair of the Devil. We will walk in the path of righteousness, strong in our faith and they shall fall before us like ears of corn under the scythe.'

Dick gave out a loud sigh of exasperation.

'I'm afraid that the rest of us don't share in your blind faith.'

But his words fell on deaf ears -- the old man was already striding from them.

'Shit,' Dick said. 'The crazy old fucker doesn't even have a torch. Well, we can always hope that he falls and knocks himself unconscious before he does any real damage.'

They set off through the fog after the old man, but when they got to the mound there was no sight of him -- it was obvious that he had gone on ahead alone.

Dick and Tom entered the mound, but Duncan didn't want to go in. His brain told him yes, but his mind told him no. Thirty years, and more, separated him from the terror of the cave, but his hind-brain hadn't grown any older in all that time -- the fear was still there, as strong as ever.

Meg was looking at him, puzzled, but Duncan was too busy struggling with his own particular demons to reply. Beads of sweat burst on his forehead and his teeth ground together, but still his legs refused to work.

Dick reappeared from the mound.

'All clear so far. Come on you two -- we've got to

get moving. God knows what the old fella has got himself into by now.'

Meg pushed past Duncan.

'Maybe you should stay here,' she said. 'Keep watch and make sure we don't get it in the back.'

It was the pity in her voice that finally got him moving -- that and the anger that flared inside him. He followed the others into the mound.

And immediately wished he hadn't -- the stench was almost unbearable. He kept his hand over his mouth as he followed the light from Dick's torch.

The second chamber was even worse, and he didn't think he'd ever forget the blank stares which greeted them. But by the time they reached the tunnel which led down into the earth, the nightmare was taking hold completely.

It was more cramped than the cave in his childhood memories, the grey slimy walls barely a foot away on either side. And it smelled -- damp and musty with more than a hint of rotting vegetation. He kept banging his head on the roof as he struggled to keep up with the bobbing light ahead of him and soon he was banging the walls as the grey rock closed in and the faint rays of light from outside faded.

The walls themselves were grey and faintly damp, the rock folded and convoluted, reminding him of the surface of a naked brain.

What with the memories and the pain they brought back he felt he was on a journey which was taking him down through his own mind, backwards, ever backwards, uncovering the layers like peeling an onion.

He followed Meg down the corridor, watching the light alternately illuminate then shade the wall as they went deeper.

At first all he heard was the padding of their feet, but after a while he began to hear something else, something which sounded like singing. It wasn't the creatures though -- this was a human voice, and Duncan shivered as the mournful strains of the twenty-third psalm wafted through the darkness.

They kept going down, deeper and deeper, and Duncan felt the weight of the stone pressing down on him, until he wasn't sure whether he was crouching to avoid the low ceiling, or to avoid being buried under tons of rubble. A cold weight had settled in his stomach and he was having difficulty breathing, but Meg was in front of him, and he had no choice but to keep going.

He became aware that he didn't have to crouch, that the ceiling was now some way above him, and at the same time Dick stopped them, pulling them once more into a huddle.

'This is as far as Angus and I got. It opens out here, so be careful.'

His voice echoed and whispered around them, and somewhere above a bat stirred into flight, bringing a squeal of terror from Tom.

Dick's torch lit their faces from beneath throwing them into skull-like shadow, their eye sockets flickering blackly.

Duncan had a sudden premonition that they were all going to die here in the depths of the cave. He began to tremble, a shiver which ran over his body, and he tried to pull away from the rest, but Meg stopped him with a hand on his shoulder.

'You'll be all right,' she said, but Duncan didn't think he'd ever he quite all right again. He wanted to be back in his lab, pottering around amongst the test-tubes and retorts, complaining about the boredom. 'Please God let me have the opportunity to be bored,' he prayed, silently. When the others began to move forward again he joined on at the end of the procession. He realised that he could no longer hear the Minister's voice, but there was a distant rumble, like a river in spate. He felt Meg reach out and take his hand in the darkness.

As they got closer the noise began to swell, and it was joined by hideous, raucous squealing.

They passed several entrances, caverns off to the side of their path. Dick shone his torch into one of them, but it wasn't enough to penetrate the blackness. They didn't need the torch to know that the creatures had been there -- the smell was enough to do that.

Duncan noticed that old Tom was getting increasingly more afraid and, more than that, looking more and more tired. He hoped they weren't going to have to carry the old man out, then immediately cursed himself for his selfishness. Besides, he was getting surer by the minute that they were never going to leave this place.

They kept moving forward, each of them silently hoping that the caverns were empty, that nothing was going to leap out and attack them from behind. Duncan could see better, and at first he thought that his eyes were finally getting accustomed to the darkness, and then he noticed the pale green luminescence which seemed to drip from the walls.

He didn't have time to study it -- they rounded a corner and walked right into the Minister.

The old man was crouched against the wall. He didn't look confident any more -- he looked absolutely terrified. He was muttering to himself, and they had to lean close to find out what he was saying.

'I'm sorry -- so sorry. There are too many of them.'

He was cradling his bible to his chest, rocking from side to side as if holding a baby. It was Tom who moved to comfort the old man. Dick crept gingerly along the corridor and peered around the corner. He stood still for long seconds before turning back.

His eyes were wide as he motioned for Duncan to come to him, his finger pressed to his lips for silence. Duncan was only just aware that Meg was following behind him.

Duncan peered round the cave wall, and looked into a vision of hell.

A large group of the creatures, too large to count easily, danced maniacally in the cavern beyond. Luckily they were all facing away from him, all except one, and it didn't look like they had much to worry about on that score. It was clearly dead -- its eyes dull and blind, and, although it still danced and capered amongst the rest, it was with the jerky, uneven movement of a puppet.

Duncan reckoned the puppeteer was the big creature at the far end of the chamber -- the one with the blue flame in its eyes, the one who was even at that moment bent over the slight figure of Meg's mother.

He was about to turn to Meg, to warn her of what she was about to see, when the black-clad figure of the Minister barrelled past him, almost knocking him to the ground. The Minister ran screaming into the middle of the chamber and all hell broke loose.

The Minister shouted, as if trying to make himself heard above the throng.

'I abjure you, Satan's spawn. Go back to the pit. Go back in the name of Jesus Christ our Lord.'

A sudden quiet fell over the chamber, and for a second it seemed as if even the vast waterfall had stopped its tumble into the depths.

And then the old creature -- the one which Duncan now remembered seeing when the stone was dug out of the ground -- laughed -- a great booming thing. It left Anne standing beside the waterfall and moved through the crowd towards the Minister.

At the same time Meg shouted in Duncan's ear.

'Mum!'

Duncan didn't have time to react before Meg had pushed past him and soon she too was in the middle of the creatures. He didn't stop to think. He launched himself into the throng after her. He was dimly aware of Dick shouting after him, but Meg was what was important -- he had to help her.

He had only gone two yards when he saw the Minister draw himself up to his full height in front of the creatures' leader, holding his bible out in front of his body.

'Begone, foul beast. Back to the slime which spawned you.'

The creature laughed again, an evil thing this time, and drove the bible out of the Minister's hands with one backward sweep -- an action which opened up the backs of the Minister's hands as if they had been hit by an open razor.

Tom screamed, a sound which echoed around the chamber but the creature paid no notice. It reached out and grasped the Minister round the throat, its talons puncturing the thin flesh and bringing great gouts of blood. The old man gurgled, trying to speak, but unable to form any words as the blood bubbled in his throat.

Duncan saw all of this, all in the seconds it took

him to cross the chamber. He was too late to help the old man, but his goal was still to get to Meg. He saw that she had almost reached her mother -- the throng of creatures seemingly hypnotised by the clash between their leader and the Minister.

He passed by within three yards of that clash, and saw that the Minister was already dead, but he had no time to stop -- Meg had reached her mother and was beginning to drag her by the arm. Anne wasn't moving, standing straight as a soldier to attention, eyes staring blankly ahead. He heard Meg shouting, almost screaming.

'Come on mum. Come on.'

She certainly couldn't see the creature which had suddenly started paying attention to her, the obscene, one eyed creature which drooled as it reached out for her.

Duncan was closing in fast, but not fast enough. His heart leapt as he saw the creature take Meg by the shoulder, saw the talons pierce her skin, heard her shriek as she realised her predicament. The creature turned her round so that she was staring into that great unblinking eye, and its jaws were heading for her face when Duncan barrelled into them, knocking all three of them to the ground.

He was momentarily stunned, and had to shake his head hard to bring things into focus, but he could drag Meg upright, away from the clutches of the creature. His big mistake was in looking down. He was standing on the brink of the pool -- his left foot only millimetres from the edge, with nothing beneath him but the roaring empty blackness.

His knees gave way almost immediately and he tried to fight to keep himself upright but he was given no time to retain his balance -- the creature brushed past him, heading for Meg again, and although it barely touched him, that was enough to send him falling to the ground, almost over the edge, knocking him onto his hands and knees

Duncan was aware of little except the roaring in his head, and, dimly, as if from a great distance, a shout of pain from Dick.

He managed to roll over, looking up to see Meg struggling with the creature. Anne was standing only two feet away, but she was still impassive, still staring straight ahead. Duncan couldn't be sure, but it looked like there was a single tear rolling down her left cheek.

'Anne. Help her,' he shouted, but got no response. Meg and the creature were locked in a grotesque waltz, dancing over him, and his mind flashed him back to his childhood, the other two boys fighting over him. He had a vivid mental picture of the creature falling, dragging Meg screaming into the depths. He could never let that happen -- he would never forgive himself.

He grabbed at the creatures' leg and heaved, making sure that it would overbalance outwards, away from the pool. The creature had other ideas -- it swayed backwards, releasing Meg, but pulling Duncan with it as he fell over the rim. It suddenly felt like his arm had been torn out of its socket as he was dragged across the floor and, before he had time to react, over the rim of the pit. It was only at the last second that he managed to throw out his other hand and grab onto the rim.

He felt a weight shift and then the agony hit his leg. He forced himself to look down and saw that the creature was hanging on his left leg, its talons embedded in his flesh just below his knee.

His arm was going to give way at any second. He

kicked out hard, and had the satisfaction of hearing the creature squeal in pain, then kicked out again, feeling the give as he hit the creature in the eye. His pleasure was short lived. His grip slipped, and for a heart stopping instant he thought it was the end, but then he managed to grab hold again, steadying himself. He didn't think he would last long.

There was another pain in his leg, higher up, and his weight shifted again -- the creature was climbing his body, using him like a ladder.

He struggled, as much as he was able without losing his grip, but the creature was pulling itself higher, now at his thighs, now his buttocks. He felt his scrotum crawl and contract as he realised just how close those fangs were to his privates, and he tensed himself for one, last struggle, just as the weight suddenly fell away from him and he almost lost his grip in the shock.

He looked down to see the creature fall away from him, screaming into the blackness, then looked up to see Meg, her arm raised, holding a large rock, ready to strike again if the first hadn't been enough.

'Are you going to hang around there all day?' she said, then laughed, a laugh which turned quickly into a sob. She bent down and helped him as he hauled himself out of the pit.

He looked down once, but there was no sign of the creature and, strangely, he didn't feel dizzy, his legs didn't betray him as he pulled himself up to stand beside Meg.

He had just turned towards her when the room blazed in a wash of brilliant blue light.

19

Dick

Dick had suddenly lost what little control he had of the situation. The Minister had rushed headlong into the throng before any of them could stop him, now Duncan and Meg were out there, right in the middle of the creatures.

It was the old Minister who held Dick's attention. He watched, stunned, as the old man was confronted by the leader of the creatures, and he was unable to bring himself to move as the old man was killed. All he heard was old Tom's voice, saying the same thing over and over again.

'No, No.'

Dick turned to face Tom and tried to comfort him -- soft, meaningless mumbling, as if talking to a child, his voice no more than a muted whisper.

Tom's head was shaking from side to side, his eyes wide with pain and fear. Suddenly Dick was left alone as the old man pushed past him, heading for the Minister.

Dick was only two yards behind him when he reached the creature, but even that was too far -- much too far. The creature didn't even drop the Minister. It held him at arm's length in its left hand, and backhanded Tom with his right, an almost contemptuous gesture, but enough to cave in the side of the old man's head.

Dick saw and heard it all in slow motion -- the gleam of light on the talons as they flashed in the air, and the sickening thud as the great hand made contact with Tom's head. Tom slumped to the ground, dropping with as much life as a sack of potatoes.

He was at Tom's side in less than a second, but even that was too late. He lifted the old grey head, and almost vomited as his hand sunk into the back of the head. He felt small pieces of bone slide and grate under his fingers. He looked down, tears almost blinding him, and saw Tom's clear blue eyes staring up at him.

The old man only managed a few words, blood gurgling in his throat.

'Keep the light burning,' was all he said, before the life left his eyes, slowly, like a stage curtain coming down.

Dick screamed, a long howl of anguish, and cradled the old man in his arms, oblivious to the blood which was soaking into his clothes.

He wasn't given any time to mourn. The creature dropped the Minister to the ground and began to dance on his body, all the time whooping with delight, sending the rest of the creatures into a frenzied ecstasy as it mashed the old man's body into a flat, shapeless pulp.

Dick could stand it no longer. With one defiant scream of rage he launched himself at the creature, catching it momentarily off guard, his knife slicing in between its ribs, bringing a smooth line of blood welling to the surface.

Dick yelled his joy and drew the knife back for another thrust, but he wasn't given the time to finish the action. The creature grabbed him by the arm, pulling him off balance, in one fluid movement bringing Dick's neck in range of its strong jaws. It had just began to lower its head when Dick saw the blue light fade in its eyes, just a second before a stronger, bluer brilliance filled the room.

20

Anne

Anne had been amazed to see the Minister run into the room, but that was nothing to her astonishment when Meg came through the throng towards her.

She wanted to grab her daughter, hug her close, just to make sure she was real. But she still couldn't move. She was still held tight in Calent's mind grip, forced to watch as he took the old Minister by the throat and took his life, as easy as wringing a chicken's neck.

Somehow she felt the old creature's joy, his ecstasy at defeating the emissary of the once-feared God, but there was something else there, an undercurrent of fear that Anne felt directed at her, something she couldn't quite identify.

By this time Meg was tugging hard at her arm, tryin to reach through to her. Anne saw, from the corner of her eye, the creature that was stalking behind her daughter, but she still couldn't move. Her mind strained, fighting to break the bond, but she couldn't even turn her head towards her daughter. At that moment Duncan came screeching out of the crowd, knocking Meg and the creature backwards, out of her sight.

She was still forced to look at Calent, holding the Minister in front of him, displaying the dead man like a trophy. Anne could only watch in horror as Tom was knocked to the ground, could only share Dick's pain as he screamed and knelt beside the old man. She felt a small tear roll down her cheek but was unable to brush it away. She heard Duncan shout out to her, but Calent still held her in his strong grip.

His fear was potent now -- she felt it like a strange doubling in her mind, the fear of the Earth Mother even as he stomped the old Minister into the ground -- it was the fear which now drove him.

And it was the Minister who provided the key. Him and the pictures which Calent now put fresh in her mind, the pictures of Columba.

She knew why the Minister had failed -- his religion had strayed too far from its pagan roots, too far from the Mother. Columba had been strong with the Mother, back then when Christianity was still in its infancy, when the influence of the old religion was still being assimilated into the young church. But over the centuries the Mother's role had faded, pushed to the sidelines. And with her fading had gone her power.

She knew why the Minister had failed. What she didn't know was how her new knowledge was going to help her.

Dick provided assistance on that score. She saw the knife enter Calent's body, and at the same instant the grip of her mind eased -- only slightly, but enough to let her move. She remembered the power she'd felt in the sky stone and, almost instinctively, moved towards it.

She felt a jolt in her mind, like a sudden surge of electricity, as Calent tried to regain control, but this time he was foiled. Anne felt warmth spread in her lower abdomen, a strange peace settling over her, and a new picture washed into her mind, a picture of her holding the sky stone, the creatures prostrate on the ground before her.

And this time the picture hadn't been forced into her brain -- it had come from inside her, from the new life she nurtured within.

She glanced over at Calent and saw him pull Dick towards him, at the same instant as she put her hands on the stone.

It began to hum, like a generator powering up, and blue dancing lights flowed around her hands. The heat in her abdomen flared, as if her very womb was on fire, and she lifted the stone above her head as if it were weightless.

The stone flared in dancing, perfectly cold brilliance, stunning everything in the chamber into sudden silence, like the unexpected flash of a camera.

Calent dropped Dick to the ground, and she saw Dick's pain as he gripped his left hand in his right. Then Calent started to come for her, striding purposefully across the chamber. As he approached her, as he got closer to the stone, his eyes began to blaze strongly, and the stone began to feel heavy in her arms.

She felt the probe in her head again -- the commanding hectoring voice, demanding that she put down the stone, trying to force its will on her.

She almost faltered, the stone threatening to drag her to the ground, but a movement behind Calent caught her attention. Calent must have noticed it too, for he turned, just in time to see Dick bearing down on him. The man had a knife in one hand, and something else in the other, something stubby which Anne didn't recognise.

Calent raised a hand to grab Dick's knife arm, but it had been a feint, and it was unable to stop the other hand coming round towards its face. There was a flash, almost blinding, forcing Anne to look away, a yellow after-image flaring behind her eyes.

She found she could lift the stone again, and when she could look back, Calent was yelling, a frenzied squeal, full of pain and anger. Something was burning furiously in its left eye socket, something that outshone even the blue light from the stone -- a deep, orange burning. It was only then that she realised what Dick had done.

He had punched a flare into Calent's eyes, a heavy duty rescue flare. Anne knew the damage it must be doing -- she had once seen a fisherman who had been burnt when some high-jinks went wrong, but she couldn't find any compassion for the creature beneath her.

Calent pawed at its face, but the flare kept burning, thick oily smoke wafting up to hang in a pall above their heads. Dick danced around the creature, trying to find an opening for a thrust of the knife, but unable to get too close to the flare.

Anne chanced a quick look round the chamber. The rest of the creatures seemed to have been struck into statues, all staring, unbelieving, at the thrashing, screaming figure of their leader.

Calent gave one more scream, this time more pain than rage or defiance, and managed to grab the stub of the flare, pulling it wetly out of the ravaged eye socket and sending it arcing into the waterfall where it hissed and spluttered before finally disappearing from view.

Dick took his chance and struck, his knife heading for Calent's heart, but he seemed to hit a rib, the knife sliding sideways, taking Dick off balance, bringing him to his knees where one kick from Calent knocked him sideways to the ground, gasping and scratching for breath.

Calent raised himself up to his full height, hands raised to the sky, screaming his pain. The left side of his face was one huge burn, black and red and suppurating. But there was still plenty of life left in his right eye, an eye which blazed in blue flashes as it turned to Anne.

She felt the mind grip again, but it wasn't compelling, it didn't reach the part of her which allowed her to lift the stone. And that part of her was growing -- she felt the heat of it inside her, strengthening her as she lifted the stone high above her head.

Blue lances of light stabbed towards Calent, but the creature raised its arm, seemingly catching the light in its hands. He began to chant, a harsh guttural thing, a sound Anne had only previously heard in her head.

'C'thulhu ryleh f'thang'
'Ia C'thulhu'
'Ia Ryleh'

The floor moved under Anne, a slight tremor at first, then a crash as a six foot stalactite fell to the floor, almost spearing Dick.

The rest of the creatures joined in the chant, and Anne felt herself weakening despite the growing heat inside her. She sensed a movement beside her and Meg placed a hand on her left shoulder.

Things happened fast after that.

Calent stepped forward, victory gleaming in his good eye, at the same time as the heat inside Anne flared like a sun. It was as if an electric circuit had been completed, as the power grew, and grew again.

Calent's hands reached for the stone, at the same

time as Anne's family brought the stone down, and down, hitting the creature's head, cutting off the chant like a needle lifted from a record, and driving through the beast, through its skull, through its shoulders, caving it in and battering it to the ground. Its eye blazed once in blue fury, and the mind grip hit her. She shrugged it off like water off a duck's back and drove the stone down one last time, and Calent's eye dimmed as its great head was squashed into a bloody, spreading pulp.

21
Duncan

Duncan couldn't believe what had just happened. For a second Meg and Anne had seemed to merge and grow, taller, then taller still, an impossible, eight-foot personification of woman, like a Neolithic sculpture, legs like tree trunks, hanging pendulous breasts and a massive, stretched belly, a belly in which an unborn child writhed with life.

It had raised itself high over Calent, and he saw the fear in the old creature's eyes, just as the stone came down.

He watched as Calent was killed, then he blinked, and when he looked back there was only Anne and Meg again, but there was something different about them, something in their eyes.

Anne lifted the stone again, and Duncan wondered how she was managing it -- there was no strain in her arms, no change in her expression. The remaining creatures fell back from her, cowering in the blue aura from the stone.

He finally found an urge to move, mainly driven by the sight of Dick, on all fours, making his way to the pathetic, still body of old Tom.

Meg and Anne started to walk across the chamber, the creatures falling back before them, and Duncan followed them to Dick's side.

The young man's face was streaked in tears as he

stroked Tom's head. Duncan bent down and gripped his shoulder.

'Come on Dick. We've got to get out of here,' he said, then stepped back, stung by the vehemence in Dick's eyes.

'I'm not going without him. I'm not leaving him here.'

Fresh tears flowed down his cheeks.

'I'll give you a hand,' Duncan said, but was pushed away.

'Just leave it to me. This is my job.'

Dick pushed himself to his feet, moaning and holding his chest.

'I think the bloody thing stoved in some of my ribs,' he groaned, then belied his injures by slinging the dead body of the lighthouse keeper over his shoulder in a fireman's lift.

Anne and Meg were quiet, an almost eerie silence as they showed the stone to the cowering creatures.

It was only a shifting of Anne's eyes, a quick flicker towards the exit followed by a small movement of her head, which told Duncan that it was time to go.

Afterwards he couldn't remember much of the journey out of the caverns -- only the dim blue radiance of the stone and the glint in the eyes of the creatures which padded along in the darkness behind them. Twice he had to catch Dick as he stumbled, but the younger man wouldn't let him near Tom's body. And once he looked into Meg's eyes and saw only an empty stare which gleamed blue in the darkness.

There was one question which kept pushing itself forward. 'What do we do when we get to the top?' he whispered to Dick, dismayed at the loud echoes which his remark sent dancing around them.

They were on one of the steeper parts of the climb, and Dick was almost unable to answer. Duncan saw with dismay that there were bubbles of blood frothing on the younger man's lips as he gasped his reply.

'Christ knows. I hope Anne knows what she's doing.'

Duncan said a similar silent prayer. From the look in their eyes it looked like the women were hypnotised. He didn't know what would happen if the spell wore off.

It seemed like an eternity before they reached daylight, an eternity of waiting for a creature to grab at him out of the darkness, an eternity of waiting for Anne or Meg to lose their composure.

They staggered out into the daylight, having to shade their eyes against the sudden, dazzling sunlight. Dick only managed to go ten yards before his legs gave way and he tumbled to the ground on top of Tom's dead body. Duncan ran forward, calling to the women for help. There was no answer, and when he turned, he was struck dumb by the sight.

They stood at the entrance to the mound, and Anne held the stone high above her head, its blue brilliance not dimmed by the sun. Meg clasped her mother around the waist, a strangely touching pose. Blue light flared in their eyes, a light that grew and expanded until they were surrounded by an ever expanding aura.

Their bodies seemed to grow and merge, four legs becoming two, two heads becoming one, until the archetypal woman stood once more before him. Long blonde hair flowed down its back, almost reaching its knees as it threw its head back and laughed, a joyful, gleeful thing, full of life.

The stone blazed, almost blinding even in the sunlight, as it was brought down hard onto the lintel stone of the mound.

The ground shook, just once, a tremor which knocked Duncan off his feet. The stone shattered, an explosion of dazzling blue fragments, and the mound collapsed it on itself with a deafening rumble.

Somewhere deep in the ground a cry of terror was abruptly cut short as another tremor shook the ground, then all was silent.

When Duncan looked round he saw that Meg and Anne stood over the fallen ruin of the mound, still clasping each other, but now their eyes were clear and bright as they hugged each other hard. He went over to join them, and was soon joined by Dick.

All four stood in the sunlight, feeling its heat warm them as tears rolled down their cheeks.

'What happened?' Duncan asked, but Meg and Anne only shook their heads, as if neither really understood.

Much later Duncan thought that Anne's last remark was the key, the remark that had come completely out of the blue and had almost been drowned out by the noise from the approaching helicopter.

'I think I'm going to have a baby.'

The End

About the Author

William Meikle is a Scottish genre writer now living in Newfoundland. His catalog includes over thirty five professional short story sales and twenty novels. His work encompasses a variety of genres, including Creature Features, Occult Detectives, Lovecraftian stories, Vampires, Sword and Sorcery, Scottish Fiction, and Science Fiction. Visit him on the web at www.williammeikle.com.